Coming Darkness

Coming Darkness

Susan-Alia Terry

Acknowledgements

Keith Abbott and everyone in his classes at the Jack Kerouac School in Naropa University for helping me develop this work from a loose collection of notes and ideas to a full-fledged narrative. Susan Livingston for your role as editor, even if life asked you to step aside. Rachel Johnson and Mindy DeBaise for your friendship, encouragement and enthusiasm. Joe Cook for the invaluable notes and feedback that helped me figure out what to keep, what to rewrite, and what to save for later. And to Rev. Treneater-Nur C. Horton for always being there to talk me down from the ledge and to help me remember who I truly am.

Dedication

To my Dad, who always believed in me, even when I didn't.

With a special thank you to CK for igniting the creative spark that inspired me to find my Voice.

One

"You're not wearing that."

Suppressing a sigh, Kai looked down and watched his clothes change. Instead of black slacks, shirt, and boots, he was now attired in tailored tan and cream—with loafers. He hated loafers. He turned, waiting for his lover to enter the foyer.

Lucifer, white hair unbound and loose around his shoulders, with a recently acquired black cat in his arms, entered the foyer and fixed critical silver eyes on him. For someone who always wore shades of white—and who knew there were so many?—Lucifer had a lot to say about what Kai wore. In fact, Lucifer dressed him with such dedicated fervor that anyone less sympathetic would call him obsessed. It was why Kai had been trying to sneak out of the house before Lucifer caught sight of him.

"Come on, Luc, that's not practical, and you know it," said Te, joining them in the foyer and changing Kai back into his original clothes. "How you expect him to do reconnaissance and retrieval in loafers and kakis, I'll never understand."

"Thank you," Kai said to him, smiling.

"I live with Philistines," Lucifer said with a mock sneer. "The least you could do is wear silk." Kai was now wearing a black, raw silk shirt, and he refused to admit he liked the way it felt.

"Are you both done?" he asked, trying for exasperation but only succeeding at fond acceptance.

Te laughed. Brown-skinned and gleaming from his bald head and single, gold earring to his white teeth, Kai was hard-pressed to remember a time when Te's silver eyes weren't sparkling with good humor. Always nattily dressed, he shared Lucifer's penchant for sharp, expensive clothes. Unlike Lucifer, however, Te had never met a color he didn't like or look good in. His current suit was red pin-stripe, complete with matching bowler hat, bow tie, and spats.

Lucifer gave them his patented put-upon look and, with his nose in the air, sauntered into the adjacent sitting room. Taking a seat on a couch, he stretched out, positioning his long, lean body to the greatest visual effect. The cat mirrored his posture and stretched out atop him. Even after more than seven hundred years together, Kai never grew tired of watching the one he considered his mate. Lucifer held endless fascination for him, as well as his love and devotion.

Te entered the sitting room behind Lucifer, took a seat in an antique wing chair, and put his feet up on the matching footstool. It was always a surprise that the old and delicate furniture in the house didn't protest when Te sat on it. But then, his size was deceptive. True, he was at least six-foot-five and powerfully built, but his personality, much like Lucifer's, made it seem like he was so much larger.

"What's on tonight?" Te asked when the sixty-inch smart television came on.

Lucifer made no secret about how much he hated humans. In fact, he'd go out of his way to expound on that hatred to anyone who'd listen. That didn't mean, however, that he didn't enjoy the food, clothing, and endless gadgets created by them. The house was filled with anything that caught his fancy, including the latest technology.

"*Housewives*," Lucifer answered as the channels flipped.

"Is that the one with Kendra?" Te asked, a bowl of popcorn appearing in his lap. Four more cats appeared, as if out of nowhere, and positioned themselves around the two seated figures.

"Not the Kendra you're thinking of, no."

The big demon made a face and shoveled a handful of popcorn into his mouth.

Kai leaned against the doorjamb, taking a moment to enjoy his little family.

"Wait, wait, go back," Te said.

"Is this *Rosemary's Baby*?" Lucifer asked, having flipped back to the channel requested. "Oh, it is. I almost missed it. Good catch." He looked up at Kai and crooked his finger. "Come on, you know you want to stay."

He was right. *Rosemary's Baby* was one of their favorite movies, and the pull to join them was very strong, but he had a job to do. Kai retreated to the coat rack by the door and removed his leather trench from it.

"I need to get going," he said apologetically, donning the coat. "Te, would you mind giving me a lift?"

Te looked over and smiled. "You sure? Gregory's not going anywhere."

"I'm sure."

"Then of course. Happy hunting."

With a last wave, Kai was gone.

Two

Starr Roberta Maxwell sat at her desk and contemplated killing her boss with the letter opener or, better yet, the stapler. It would take longer. Nothing was too good for William Ford Gregory III.

"Starr, did you fax those numbers to Geneva yet? What's taking you so long? And get me another cup of coffee. This one's cold," Gregory, a.k.a. the Asshole, bellowed through the open office door.

As she walked to the door to answer him—she felt yelling in the workplace was unprofessional—she cursed her mother's naming choice and aspirations for her daughter for the umpteenth time since coming to work here. Introducing herself as Roberta had been a wasted exercise. The man had known her full name and, upon seeing her for the first time, had refused to call her that, instead choosing to inflect "Starr" in such a way as to remind her that she was not and never would be.

Telling herself again that this was just a temp job, and that once the week was over, she could burn the son-of-a-bitch in effigy, she answered politely, "I faxed it twenty minutes ago. It's after two in the morning in Geneva, so I doubt anyone's there to receive it." She moved over to the desk and picked up his coffee cup.

"Of course they're there. That's what I pay them for. Where's my coffee? Slow *and* stupid. Makes me wonder what I'm paying *you* for."

Roberta sighed and tried to keep it together. "I'll get Mr. Prideaux on the line and get you your coffee now, sir."

She tried to make the "sir" sound like "fuck you" but failed. Her strict upbringing kicked in, refusing to let her be rude to her boss, no matter how rude he was to her. She hurried into the outer office, wondering which she should do first, the coffee or the phone call. She was screwed either way, so she refilled the mug, not bothering to brew fresh, but emptying the dregs that remained in the carafe. If she couldn't tell him to go fuck himself, she could at least fuck with his coffee. Wearing a small smile, she brought the cup back to his office and placed it carefully on the desk.

Returning to the outer office, she placed the call to Switzerland, preparing herself mentally to tell the Asshole there was no answer.

The line picked up on the third ring. "'Allo?"

Roberta inwardly collapsed in relief. "Yes, I have Mr. William Ford Gregory III calling for Mr. Pierre Prideaux."

"This is Pierre."

"Hold the line, please."

"Mr. Gregory, I have Mr. Prideaux on the line; transferring now."

"Pierre, you son of a bitch, how are ya? How's that beautiful wife? Excellent. Did your little girl get the birthday present I sent? Loved it, did she? Good, good. I know it's late, and I appreciate this; I really do. Listen, my girl said she sent you the fax. Well, did you get it? You did? Okay, this is what we need to do..."

Roberta quietly closed the door to Gregory's office, effectively muting his voice. She could feel her eyes prickling, and she closed them and held her breath, refusing to let herself cry. Hearing the concern and sincere apology in his voice just seconds after yelling at her made her want to break down. How could he be so nice to everyone but her?

Just three more days, she told herself. *Three more days, and I am so outta here.*

* * *

Cloaked in shadow, Kai sat on the high wall surrounding the Gregory compound. He'd been there two days now, watching the comings and goings, and was eager to get this job done. The complex where Gregory lived and worked was a huge, sprawling thing that covered at least forty acres of land in upstate New York, about an hour's drive from the city. The driveway was long and wound through the property until it reached the main buildings, which were hidden by foliage at the end of the serpentine path. Obligatory surveillance cameras dotted the landscape, providing more than adequate coverage of the property. There were guards posted at the gate and, Kai knew, at a checkpoint closer to the buildings. All in all, the security was surprisingly light and would not pose a problem.

What did pose a problem, however, were the cats. They were everywhere—prowling among the trees, hunting, playing with each other, and lounging in the grass. He could see no spot that was clear of the little beasts. There was no way to approach the building without causing a ruckus. No doubt, Gregory had anticipated an attack from Te and prepared accordingly.

A strong scent of ozone with an undertone of cinnamon filled his nostrils, and his lips tilted in a smile. "Uriel. Here I was, thinking you'd abandoned me."

"Careful, vampire, lest you grow too familiar," Uriel responded.

"As if you'd ever let that happen."

Kai turned to look up at the archangel, checking to see if his retort had gone too far. Even though Uriel had taken to accompanying him on these jobs, Kai had only just begun to relax in his presence and still felt uncomfortable with their banter. As usual, Uriel gave no signs of displeasure, although Kai had no idea what that would look like if he did.

Dressed in a black tunic with red accents, black breeches, and black leather boots, Uriel's shoulder-length, vibrant red hair framed attractive features that might as well have been carved in stone for all the expression they held. Kai wondered if Uriel's skin would crack if he dared to smile.

Uriel didn't look at him, but instead let his copper eyes roam the grounds. It was just as well. Having that heavy gaze on him always made Kai uncomfortable, as if Uriel was judging him and finding him lacking—which, given his general air of disdain, was probably true. Before these visits, Kai had known the archangel only by his reputation, through stories. Uriel was known as an assassin and a zealot. Grand-scale destruction à la Sodom and Gomorrah was in keeping with his reputation. This helpful version standing next to him was not. Of all of his lover's family, he found Uriel's presence the most unsettling.

"It appears you have a problem," Uriel said.

"Merely a nuisance," Kai bluffed, pretending he hadn't been on that wall for two days because of the cats. Leave it to Uriel to not only point out the obvious but also make him feel inadequate in the process.

"How had you planned to get by them?"

Kai looked up. Was that amusement in Uriel's voice? Damn him. "I hadn't actually gotten that far," he admitted, feeling his throat tighten in embarrassment. "I could use your help." Kai knew that was what the archangel had wanted to hear and hated having to ask.

Uriel glided off the wall to the ground. The cats in the immediate vicinity came running. They purred, rubbed, and wound themselves between his feet, altogether thrilled with his presence. The Egyptians had been right to revere cats. Uniquely attuned to the supernatural, the presence of a cat could keep ghosts and spirits away, and their saliva was poisonous to Other-kin. While the cats couldn't hurt Kai, they would raise the alarm, and having Uriel prevent them from doing so would be immensely helpful.

Kai watched from his perch as Uriel walked among them, stooping every now and then to stroke, pet, and scratch behind their raised ears. Eventually, he picked up a smoky grey one and walked a few feet ahead with it in his arms.

He turned and addressed Kai. "Come down, vampire. They will not announce your presence."

* * *

Roberta looked at the pictures of two cats on her desk, her predecessor's pets. She wondered what had happened to them. The woman who'd held the position full-time had died quite suddenly of a stroke after working there for almost fifteen years. Roberta couldn't imagine it. She'd been the third temp in as many days and, because of it, had been offered a ridiculous amount of money to take—and keep—the job. Having a reputation for being able to work for anyone, no matter how difficult they were, had its perks.

She'd been under the impression that she had seen it all, and that she could handle everything with a smile and professionalism. Gregory tested that theory within the first fifteen minutes of their meeting. He was rude, crass, and insulting. By the end of the first hour, she was in tears in the bathroom.

It was then that she realized the reason behind the forty-dollars-an-hour salary—it was a bribe, pure and simple.

The agency had finally acquired his company's business and were eager to keep it. If she couldn't handle it, they had no one who could. For forty dollars an hour, she could do it. Just the idea of that kind of salary left her thrilled. She could actually create a savings account.

That was then. Now she just wanted to make it to Friday. Once Friday came, she would refuse to continue the assignment, and they could bribe someone else. She could be bought, but only so far.

She blew out a breath and looked out the large windows of the outer office. It had surprised her to find out that Gregory's home and office were located in a sprawling estate in upstate New York. As it turned out, he was a workaholic recluse that lived and worked on his property, and he expected certain others in his employ to mimic his bizarre lifestyle.

She'd taken residence in his former secretary's cottage, an adorable, one-story, picture-book structure with a stone fireplace and exposed stone walls. A dormitory was provided for other employees. She had yet to understand why he required so many to live on-site. The main office building housed a cafeteria, a small convenience store, and a fitness room with a spa and sauna. The meals were delicious, and most of the workers were friendly, if not slightly odd. Overall, it didn't seem like a bad place to work. She had free room and board, plus a very nice salary.

Unfortunately, the person who made it unbearable was the person she had to work for.

She admonished herself for being seduced by the money, free food, and free place to live. A month had already passed. At the end of every week, she intended to quit and tell them to take the job and shove it, but she never made the call. She would tell herself it wasn't that bad, and to rest over the weekend and see how she felt on Monday morning, planning to call then if she really wanted to quit.

But she always managed to talk herself into staying. When she was first offered the cottage, she'd refused, saying she didn't want to move until she had permanent employment. It was a polite way of saying, "No fucking way." Then, abruptly, her apartment in Brooklyn had gone condo, and she'd needed to move. The Asshole's wife and personal aide, Catherine, a.k.a. the Iron Lady, had stepped in and had her things packed up and moved. Just like that. Roberta had wanted to object, but every time the opportunity arose, her reasons felt flimsy, and she felt ashamed for even thinking about complaining. Besides, living on the property was so much easier.

A couple of the cats outside chased each other past the window. Were her predecessor's cats among them? When she had asked about the cats, The Iron Lady had told her that she and her husband loved cats so much that they had made the grounds a sanctuary for them.

Roberta found it hard to believe that either of them could love anything that wasn't power or money. They had loads of both and no heirs. Maybe the cats would get it all, unless the two planned to live forever or have it buried with them, neither of which would surprise her.

* * *

"After all this time with Lucifer, vampire, it surprises me that you are still afraid of cats," Uriel said as they walked, still stroking the cat in his arms.

"I'm not afraid of them. I just don't like them," Kai countered, eyes on the ground in front of him as he navigated through the surrounding animals. "Gregory is in one of the buildings ahead. Can you tell which one?"

"No, he is hiding himself. His presence is masked and echoes throughout. I could find him eventually, but obtaining the information the old-fashioned way would be faster."

"And probably more fun," Kai added, before tripping over a large, orange tabby. "You did that on purpose," he accused. The cat blinked and chirruped back innocently. He had no doubt that both Uriel and the cat were laughing at him. "Do that again, and you'll be warming my feet as a pair of slippers," he told the cat, who continued to appear maddeningly unfazed.

"It was my understanding, vampire, that your kind is celebrated for its heightened reflexes." Uriel's lips curved, hinting at a smile. "Perhaps the centuries spent with my brother have made you soft."

Kai stopped walking and turned to face him. "You would make yourself unwelcome so soon, Uriel?"

The archangel looked it at him, assessing. He inclined his head. "Careful, vampire, lest you become thin-skinned in your old age."

Kai couldn't help the smirk. Despite his discomfort, he liked Uriel. They resumed walking.

Eventually they came to a stop at a row of hedges. There were no cats on the other side. Uriel put the grey cat he was holding gently on the ground and gave it one last stroke.

"Those runes on the edge," he pointed out a line of stones, "keep the cats from crossing the boundary of the hedge. The amount of effort, time, and expense Gregory put into warding the property is impressive. He is well protected from all but my kind—and you, of course."

Te had told Kai that Gregory had magical deterrents, which, due to Kai's protections, neither of them had taken seriously. The cats had been a surprise, but thanks to Uriel, they had been only a minor inconvenience. It all proved Gregory's guilt rather eloquently. No one went to this much trouble if they weren't hiding from something.

* * *

Roberta's stomach growled. She wondered if she could get away to get something to eat, maybe bring the Asshole his dinner as well. Bound to get yelled at either way, after a quick look around to make sure that nothing needed doing right then, she decided to chance it. On the way past the door to the inner office, she listened, trying to determine if he was winding up the phone call and would be calling for her soon. He was still engaged, so she kept moving toward the office's outer doors.

Taking a fortifying breath, she stepped out of the office, keeping her head down and eyes on the floor. Moving quickly, she passed the Asshole's bodyguards stationed along the hall. Asian in countenance, tall and lean, they wore their hair long, varying in style from a single, thick braid to many braids tied back from their faces. Dressed identically in black, with intricate tattoos in the tribal style on every inch of uncovered skin, they had an air of menace about them that always made her stomach twist. They didn't carry guns that she could see, but each had a mean-looking blade attached to his hip. She wasn't afraid of them exactly. They just made her uneasy.

Having made it through the bodyguard gauntlet, she took a relieved breath as she turned down the corridor toward the cafeteria. Once again, her eyes didn't roam as she passed the stone statues that lined the walls at regular intervals.

The Iron Lady had horrible taste in art. The hideous things were all over the place. Then there were the nasty knick-knacks on the Asshole's desk and shelves, some of which looked like they could have been made from parts of real animals—or people. Thinking about them made her shiver in disgust. Once, when she'd commented on the décor, the Iron Lady told her that both she and the Asshole loved primitive art and that they made frequent trips to forgotten places around the world specifically to add unusual pieces to their collection.

Upon entering the cafeteria, she immediately forgot her train of thought and stood frowning at the menu for a moment. Once recovered, she decided on a cheeseburger with bleu cheese and fries for herself—damn the calories—and meatloaf with mashed potatoes and mixed vegetables for the Asshole. Undoubtedly he would look at her plate and ask her if she'd "ever seen a salad, ha ha." She would laugh politely and wish she'd poisoned his meatloaf.

Of course she knew she was fat; it was obvious, like having brown eyes. But there were other things about her body that she was happy with. At six feet tall, she towered over both the Asshole and the Iron Lady, with heels and without. Her hair was long, thick, and heavy, and she loved how it accepted a curl or color at her whim. She favored a reddish-brown dye for it, believing it gave life to her otherwise unremarkable appearance. It didn't all have to center on her weight, and she was fine with that.

Unfortunately, when she'd been to see her parents last Christmas, her mother, a perfect size six, had turned her nose up at Roberta's insistence that her weight not be a topic of discussion. Since Roberta had "thrown away" her "promising career in entertainment," her mother felt that she should understand that all she had was her looks, actually putting forth the question—what man wants a fat wife?

Roberta was probably all of ten when she'd realized her mother was delusional when it came to her daughter's supposed talents. She'd suffered through dance classes, painfully aware that she wasn't graceful, a realization that sapped her confidence, which in turn made her an even worse dancer—as if that were possible. She had nightmares about singing classes. Regardless of how much she'd practiced, she could not make her voice match the music. She was hopelessly tone deaf and tormented by guilt because of her lack of ability.

Still, she'd gone along with it, enduring the embarrassed looks by the other kids and parents as her mother bragged about how Roberta would be a star. Passable at acting, she'd managed a few commercials as a young adult, but after a very frank—and private—talk with her agent, Roberta had quit.

Temp work had been her salvation. Finding that she had a knack for office work gave her a deep sense of pride—finally she was good at something. Of course, her mother never forgave her and still lamented the fact that she'd squandered her chance at stardom. Subsequently, holiday trips and the occasional phone call was about all the contact with her family that she could stand.

When the meals were ready and packaged, she gathered them and made her way back to the office, wondering whether the Asshole had noticed she was gone or not. Afraid she had been away too long, she decided to take the back way through the kitchen. It would get her back to the office much quicker than if she returned the way she had come.

When she returned, the inner office doors were open, and she could hear the Asshole yelling. Assuming he was yelling at her—she seemed to be the only person he ever yelled at—Roberta momentarily tuned him out while she placed her dinner on her desk. Standing straight and tightening her mental armor, Roberta carried his dinner to his office, prepared for a verbal lashing.

* * *

Once Kai passed the hedge border, he caught a scent and understood why the cats were confined to the lawn. Scenting the air more thoroughly told him that there were five werewolves ahead. He didn't need his nose to tell him that they were all half-breeds, as no pureblood were would ever work for a human.

Taking off at speed, he headed straight for them. They stood in a group near the second checkpoint. The shifts must have just changed; they were at ease, laughing and smoking.

Not slowing, using surprise to his advantage, Kai snapped the necks of two of them. Half-breeds only changed during the full moon, and since that was a few weeks away, the best they had to answer his challenge was heightened senses and speed. Given his age alone, it wasn't even close to being enough. They circled him, preparing to pounce. He dodged one, intending to leap at another when three flaming arrows appeared out of nowhere, taking them out instantly.

"Dammit, Uriel." Kai spun toward his offending companion.

"Come along, vampire. Don't dawdle," Uriel said as he passed, heading up the driveway.

Disarmed, the bark of laughter from his own throat surprised Kai. Implausible as it was, he was more amused than irritated. He jogged up the road and stopped alongside the archangel. Two mongrel guards stood talking near the entrance. They appeared calm, not having heard the commotion from further down the driveway.

"From now on, let me handle it," Kai said, giving Uriel a sidelong look.

"As you wish, vampire."

"I have a name, you know," he muttered, before walking up the driveway toward the guards.

"Of course. Vampire," Uriel replied.

Kai snorted and shook his head. He'd never get the last word.

Moving toward the mongrels, he felt gleeful anticipation at the opportunity to stomp out two bastards of the race. Reigning in his hatred, he strolled up the driveway, reminding himself that he was here in a professional capacity, and that called for him to dispatch them cleanly, without lingering long enough to torture. Knowing they couldn't sense him, he moved at a leisurely pace, giving them ample time to see him. Once they spotted him, the one closest to him raised his gun.

"That's far enough," he said.

"Mongrels with guns," Kai replied, not slowing his pace. "If you had any self-respect, you'd be ashamed."

"Maybe you'll rethink that," the grinning guard replied and pulled the trigger.

The round hit Kai in the upper chest. He grunted in pain even as he sprinted forward, grabbed the gun, and smashed it through the guard's head. The other guard shot him in the back.

Kai cursed, turned, and leapt, snatching the gun while simultaneously kicking out and breaking the guard's legs. The guard screamed and fell to the ground. Kai broke the gun in half and threw the pieces away.

Even now he could feel the bullets working their way back out. He didn't like being shot, and he would probably use more effort to avoid the bullets but for one thing—the look on his assailants' faces when the bullets didn't stop him. It was worth the pain every time.

"When the first bullet didn't take me down, you should have switched tactics," he admonished, squatting down to address the guard at eye level.

The shocked guard tried to shrink back and away. "Those bullets were not only silver, but they were blessed and soaked in holy water. You were supposed to go down with the first shot."

"Unfortunately for you, I didn't." The sound of the bullets hitting the ground punctuated his reply. He pulled a flask from his coat, unscrewed the cap, then took a mouthful, and swallowed. Reaching out with the flask in his hand, he poured a little on the guard who screamed and tried to move away. His terrified eyes fixed on Kai.

"What *are* you?"

"Is that really relevant considering your current state?"

The mongrel on the ground looked helplessly back at him. Kai took another sip of the holy water. "Gregory. Where is he?" The guard's eyes never left the flask.

"How do I know you won't pour any more on me?"

"You don't. What you should have guessed, however, is that I certainly will if you don't answer correctly." Following through, Kai poured another thin stream over the vampire's broken legs, eliciting more screams.

"Please—down the hall and to the left. Stop," the guard pleaded, frantically waving his arms.

Kai inclined his head. "Thank you." He recapped the flask, pocketed it, and then stood up to leave.

"Wait," the guard cried after him. At Kai's inquiring look, he spoke again. "You can't leave me like this." He gestured to his broken and melting legs.

"What would you suggest?"

The guard dropped his eyes and looked away.

"If you can't ask for it, you don't deserve it." With a dark smile, Kai turned and walked away, the sounds of the guard's soft sobbing at his back.

Torturing mongrels before killing them was a favorite pastime The idea that he could actually kill one without even a little bit of torture had been truly absurd. He chuckled to himself, holy water was like acid on mongrel flesh and even if washed away would still poison them to death. He satisfied himself with the knowledge that the guard's death would be slow and painful, even if he wouldn't be around to see it.

Uriel was waiting patiently for him at the door. Kai felt rather than saw the archangel's amusement.

"What?" he asked, unable to suppress his smile.

"Are you quite finished? There is no need to rush on my account."

Kai laughed outright. Mongrels were vermin; Uriel understood his mindset. They entered the building together. As soon as he crossed the threshold, Kai could feel the magic, old and hanging with oppressive weight in the air, but he couldn't account for its origin. Uriel pointed out the statues along the corridor. Kai looked to him in question.

"To make the uncommon seem common, to confuse and confound the mind into not asking questions," the archangel replied in explanation.

Kai instinctively wanted to smash them. Uriel saved him the trouble, launching arrows and destroying the statues as they passed. No more guards came running at the noise, which was surprising. The thought that there would be no more obstacles was slightly disappointing, until they turned the corner.

"Ronin." Kai's spoken word met an accompanying surprised breath from Uriel. Six tattooed fighters stood halfway down the hall, blades drawn. How could Te not have known that Gregory had Ronin guards?

"I cannot help in this fight," Uriel answered his unasked question. "I can do this, however."

A sword appeared in Kai's hand. He hefted it and took a few practice swings, finding it not only beautiful but nicely balanced. When he looked up at Uriel and whispered his thanks, Kai was surprised to see what looked like compassion in Uriel's copper eyes, although he said nothing. Kai turned his head back toward his opponents and took a step forward, searching his memories for everything his master, who had been Ronin-trained, had ever told him about fighting them.

First, of course, was to never engage them in a fight, because he would lose. Second, engage briefly while searching for any opportunity to run. The Ronin code of honor forbade chasing a retreating opponent. Fear drew his nerves tight and beat around his gut. Neither he nor his master was a coward, but facts were facts. Ronin were unbeatable.

The fact that Gregory had this ancient race as guards was surprising. Finding someone who actually knew the Ronin rituals was practically impossible, and even if you did, their rituals were highly precise and convoluted. One misstep and it was over—the seeker was either dead or dissuaded from continuing so thoroughly that they were unable to even speak of the experience.

Ronin never turned their violence against each other. Stories of them leaving the battlefield when opposing sides commanded them to fight each other were legend.

They were telepaths, masters of every imaginable weapon, and possessed supernatural strength, speed, and stamina—killing machines. Even the Kazat knew enough not to tangle with them.

Kai breathed deeply and let his instincts take over. His last thought, as he took another step forward, was to wonder if Luc had listened to him and not put an anti-beheading sigil in place, because he would surely die if he did.

Walking down the corridor, one Ronin broke from the group to meet him. Their code dictated that if they out-numbered a foe, they would only fight in numbers with matched opponents. Since he was alone, it was one at a time, a small mercy.

They stopped a few paces apart. Kai bowed as was ap-propriate, not missing the look of pleased surprise on their faces before the bow was returned. A beat later, he raised his sword and engaged. The two circled each other, test-ing skill. Each thrust that was parried, each swing ducked, brought them closer to the actual fight. Kai relaxed into each posture and move, muscle memory making him more confident in his skill.

Too soon, the testing phase was over, and the fight ramped up. He managed to duck a swing to his head, and followed up with a thrust to the gut that was gracefully sidestepped. Trying a disarming move, he caught air as the Ronin disappeared and reappeared behind him. He recov-ered, barely managing to prevent being split in two. They continued, neither gaining ground, nor Kai losing any.

"Enough." His opponent immediately stopped, bowed to him—deeper than before, Kai noticed—and stepped back.

The one who had spoken stepped forward. Kai had the distressing thought that since he could not beat the other, he would have to fight this one, and on and on until his strength was gone. His earlier confidence evaporated, leaving him saturated with uncertainty.

"You are Ronin-trained."

Taken aback, it took Kai a moment to answer. "My master, Aram, was, yes. He, in turn, taught me."

The Ronin nodded, a look of admiration and amusement on his face. "Aram. Ronin remember him to be disciplined and diligent, a fine student. You honor him."

Kai bowed at the acknowledgement, unsure as to where this exchange was going, even as the mention of his master tightened invisible fingers around his heart.

"The reason for your presence has been ascertained. You may pursue your objective." At Kai's bewildered look, the Ronin explained, "Lord Te is a friend. Ronin will not interfere."

Once again, they bowed deeply to Kai and passed by him on the way to the exit. As one, they stopped in front of Uriel, bowing deeply once again. The one who spoke to Kai stepped up and spoke so quietly that even Kai's sensitive hearing could not catch it. The archangel stood still, a look of astonishment on his face before he quickly schooled his features, inclining his head at the Ronin as they then passed him, exiting the building.

Kai knew better than to ask Uriel what the Ronin had said, even though he was bursting to know. He contented himself with seeing respect light Uriel's eyes when he joined him in the middle of the corridor. Kai believed Uriel no longer saw him as just Lucifer's pet or Te's errand boy, but as a warrior, and pride bloomed inside of him. Uriel could have his secrets.

They headed straight for the inner office and opened the door. Gregory, deep in a telephone conversation, looked up and frowned at the interruption.

"Who the hell are you, and how did you get in here?" he barked. "Starr? Where is she?" he asked, looking out into the office. "Pierre, I'll have to call you back," he said into the phone before hanging up. He sprang out of his chair and pushed past the two intruders to the outer office. "Starr," he called again, even though it was obvious that she wasn't there. "Stupid woman, where did you go?" he muttered under his breath. He peeked out the door, "And where the fuck is my security?"

Kai and Uriel moved farther into his office and waited for him to return, which he did almost immediately.

"I should have known those Ronin were too good to be true. Undefeatable my ass," he said, as he marched to his desk and sat down.

Although Kai knew he was far older, Gregory appeared to be a vibrantly healthy man of about fifty with a thin build and a full head of salt-and-pepper hair.

Now that the surprise had worn off, he looked them over with shrewd, brown eyes. "Well, what do you want? Who sent you? Was it the Saudis? The Russians? What-ever they're paying you, I'll triple it."

Uriel scoffed at him from his place by the window.

"I was sent by the only one who should matter to you," Kai replied, placing his sword carefully on the desk. Gre-

26

gory looked at him, considering, and then continued as if he hadn't heard.

"Well, hell, you obviously bested my men. How would you like a job? Apparently I need new security." He laughed.

Kai placed his hands on the desk and leaned over it. "Lord Te is very upset with you."

At the mention of Te's name, Gregory's eyes grew wide, and his skin paled with sudden understanding. "There must be some mistake. Let's get him on the phone. I'm sure we can straighten this out." He reached for the phone, and Kai grabbed his wrist, trapping it on the desk.

"No, there's no mistake. Apparently, you've gotten greedy in your dotage. Shortages in tributes, I believe." Kai squeezed Gregory's wrist, pressing it against the desk, making the man wince. "Did you think Lord Te wouldn't notice? He has, and I've come to collect his due."

"Of course. Let me get to my safe. You can have it all with my sincerest apologies."

Kai slowly shook his head, a cruel smile distorting his features. "In exchange for wealth, power, and immortality, you promised certain things. You signed a contract. A contract you have since reneged on. You think you can simply open your safe to make things right? You of all people should know that the time for such an easy resolution has passed." He seized Gregory by the neck, drawing him up close to his face. "The payment that's due now? Flesh and, at my discretion, *blood*," he said, licking elongated fangs.

"Wait, wait, let's not do anything rash."

"Rash? You mean like this?" Kai grabbed a flailing fore-arm and squeezed, breaking bones.

Gregory screamed. "Please, please, I'll do anything, just—just let me go. Say you couldn't find me. Please!"

"No." Kai shook him, and he went limp. "That's it?" He shook Gregory again, and the man flopped like a rag doll. "After all this trouble—you had me fight Ronin." He shook him again. "And for what?" He dropped the man, who cra-dled his arm and crumpled at his feet. "Sniveling. You don't deserve Lord Te's consideration, much less his mercy."

Rage, hot and insidious, bubbled within Kai on the heels of his dissatisfaction. He thought he'd have to do a lot more convincing, spill a little blood even. Anything but have this pitiful excuse for a mogul show his belly so eas-ily. He noticed a picture on the desk, and an idea began to percolate. For all the trouble he'd gone through Kai wanted—no, needed his pound of flesh, and he figured he'd found a way to get it.

"Is this your wife?" Gregory looked up at him with dawning horror. "She benefited from Lord Te's generosity as well, didn't she? I think I'll bring her in as a bonus." He didn't try to conceal his glee at the man's terrified scream.

"No!" he shrieked with renewed vigor. Kai planted a booted foot on his back, pinning the now struggling man to the floor. "I won't tell you. I don't care what you do to me, but not her... not her."

Finally, some life, some fight. Kai took in the trapped and sobbing figure, mentally reviewing the damage he could inflict that wouldn't be fatal, when he realized they weren't alone. Looking up, he saw a woman standing in the doorway, transfixed.

* * *

Stepping in the doorway, Roberta stopped cold. Standing in the middle of the spacious office were two men. The one dressed in black had a dark, olive complexion, long, black hair, and tattoos on his face that trailed down his neck and under his collar. The other had brilliant red hair and looked like he stepped out of a fairy tale, and was that a bow and quiver on his back?

The most astonishing part of this scene, though, was not the oddity of the men, which was par for the course around here, but that the tattooed man had the Asshole pinned under his boot. Crying.

She didn't know what to do. A small voice somewhere in the back of her mind told her to run before any of them noticed her.

Too late. The tattooed man stopped what he was doing and looked at her. The other one, following his gaze, turned to look at her as well. Both gazes fixed her to the spot, and she trembled.

"His wife?" Tattooed man asked, taking a step toward her. "Where is his wife?"

"Don't you tell this bloodsucking son-of-a-bitch, you fat fucking cow. Don't you say a fucking word." The Asshole raised himself onto his knees and shouted at her.

Even on his knees and blubbering, he insults me. She felt a tickle of satisfaction when the tattooed man cuffed him on the side of his head.

"That's no way to speak to a lady," he told the Asshole, who started another bout of crying.

"Please, you can't take my wife. Let me—let me call Lord Te. I'm sure we can work something out." He was alternately trying to grab the man's pant leg and shying away from touching him. Roberta watched, fascinated, as he did this a few times while making his pleas.

She pitied him, which surprised her, since the only thing she had felt for him since the day they'd met was intense hatred. The tattooed man drew a metal band attached to a length of chain out of his coat pocket and, grabbing the Asshole by the hair, fastened the metal band—a collar?—around his neck.

That's it. I'm asleep at my desk. There is no way something this crazy could be real.

"You were asked a question." The man out of a fairy tale addressed her, immediately dispelling her illusion. "You would do well to answer it."

He came toward her. Finally able to move, she threw the tray at him and turned to run. Vaguely she thought it odd that she didn't hear the tray hit him or crash to the floor. That thought drowned in the realization that she wasn't moving.

"Turn around."

Her body was not her own, as it obeyed without her consent. Absently, she noted the tray positioned neatly on the floor by the door, as if she'd carefully placed it there. The man was moving toward her now. Too late she realized she shouldn't look into his eyes. Her will

30

to do anything but what he wanted dissolved the instant she did. Something about him squashed any sense of self-preservation. He burned through her, and she would gladly smolder to a cinder and not lift a finger to save herself.

"Knock it off, Uriel." She heard an exasperated voice say. *Uriel? What a beautiful name.* The tattooed man brushed past the one named Uriel to come toward her, leading the Asshole by the leash.

"Do you want the information or not?" Uriel replied, never breaking eye contact with her.

The conversation flowed around her as she floated on white puffy clouds of adoration.

"Not if you make a drooling idiot out of her, I don't."

Uriel's hair is so red. It can only be what true red looks like.

"Do you actually care?"

This was the red that nature and man alike strove to capture. Vibrant fire! The truth of it will always elude them, but I see it. I know. She did and was warmed from the inside by the knowledge, knowing it was special and only for her.

"Yes, I do actually, and you should too."

* * *

Kai looked at the blank look on the woman's face and shook his head, disgusted. He'd warmed to Uriel but now felt a rush of disappointment as he was reminded how ruthless the angels were in the pursuit of their goals, innocents be damned. It galled him that they were so unnecessarily cruel.

The woman smiled in delight when Uriel raised his hand toward her. "Take my hand, child," he said. The oozing sweetness of his voice was nauseating. He watched as the woman took Uriel's hand. "Now, this one's wife is hiding from me. Do you know where she is?"

"Most likely she's in their house on the grounds," the woman replied, breathless.

"Good girl," praised Uriel. "Picture it in your mind… that's it."

They were all instantly transported to the foyer of the main house. Gregory moaned. The woman swooned and would have fallen if Kai hadn't caught her. He gently lowered her limp body to the ground, throwing a murderous glare at Uriel in the process. Once he'd released the woman, Kai turned to Gregory.

"Now, call your wife. If you try to warn her, I swear to you I will request that you be given to me, and your fate will be ten times worse than the worst Lord Te could ever do. Do you understand?"

Gregory nodded shakily. True, Kai could search the house for her, but that was tedious. He'd spent more time on this job than he'd planned and was eager to be done and gone.

"Catherine," Gregory began, the sound little more than a croak. Kai hardened his gaze.

"Do you want me to rip your heart out? I will, and Lord Te will heal you and bring you back to life so I can do it again," he hissed. Gregory paled; his eyes rolled back in his head. Kai slapped him again. "Don't you dare. Call her again."

Gregory took a deep breath, "Catherine, come here, darling. I've something to show you." He called up the wide staircase that curved up the right side of the foyer.

The woman came screaming out of a door on the lower floor, firing a cross bolt into Kai. The bolt hit with a thump and, taking him off guard, knocked him back a step. She reloaded and leveled the crossbow at Uriel.

She didn't get a chance to fire. Kai leapt at the stunned woman, grabbing her by the throat with one hand and wrenching the crossbow away with the other. He threw it against the nearest wall, smashing it to pieces. Slowly and with deliberation, he drew the wooden bolt out of his chest and waved the bloody instrument in front of her eyes.

"The only thing you've done with this," he waggled the bolt between thumb and forefinger, "is make me angry."

Her eyes widened as he squeezed, closing off her air.

"No, please, please don't kill her," Gregory begged.

Kai eased his grip when Gregory spoke and turned to look him. Uriel stood on the leash near its attachment to the collar, causing Gregory to lie prone at his feet. Gradually, he slid his foot closer to the man's throat. Gregory, lost to his shuddering, lay defeated on the floor.

Kai's disappointment at himself for letting his guard down with Uriel made him testy. He smiled into the panicked eyes of the woman in his grip and relished the feel of slowly squeezing the life from her. When she was dead, he opened his hand, letting her drop. Gregory let out a soft mewl at the sound of her body hitting the floor.

* * *

Gregory's secretary opened her eyes and looked around, obviously disoriented. Disorientation grew into panic. Kai watched her eyes skim over everyone, frantic, until they finally settled upon Uriel. She scuttled over and stopped just short of touching before kneeling at his feet.

Lucifer had told him about the angel's power to enthrall. He'd used it himself for a time. Its intent was to gain a human's attention, to impart to them the importance of the experience so that they would remember and obey. Used properly, sparingly, it was extremely effective.

Used improperly, as Lucifer and other Fallen had done, it enslaved. The intense feeling of well-being the enthrallment produced was addictive. Once it was cut off, the subjects became intensely depressed and unable to function. Lucifer had told him that the adoration was fun, but in time the enthralled grew unable to think for themselves. Unwilling to leave his presence to do even the most basic tasks of living, they had to be ordered to eat, bathe, etc. When he left, they would pine away, waiting for him to return, eventually dying when he didn't.

This woman had been in Uriel's presence and, most importantly, had felt his power while under his thrall. It worried Kai that the exposure was enough to damage her. It was his fault. Usually he took more care. He hadn't known about the Ronin, the specifics of the warding, or the possibility of involving innocents. He was better than this,

34

yet tonight he'd proved himself unfocused and sloppy. He had to make this right.

Still looking at the woman, he addressed Uriel, "What can be done about her?"

"Why are you so concerned?"

"I'm concerned because she did nothing to deserve this." It was like talking to a child.

Kai walked over to the woman and knelt beside her. She shrank away from him, scooting toward Uriel even as he moved out of reach. Kai stopped her, gently taking hold of her arm. She let him but kept her face turned toward the archangel. He carefully but firmly took hold of her chin, turning her face toward him. Her face moved, but her eyes strained to keep the subject of her adoration in sight.

"Look at me," he commanded.

Brown eyes fluttered in his direction but immediately snapped back to Uriel.

Kai dropped his head and took a calming breath. "Uriel, a little help please?"

"What would you like me to do?"

"You really don't understand, do you?" Kai looked up to the blank face of his companion, shook his head, and dismissed a reply with a wave of his hand. "Never mind. Can you put her to sleep?"

Uriel hesitated. A small crease appeared on his brow, giving Kai the impression that he was about to ask why. The moment passed, however, and he did as he was asked. Kai picked up Gregory's leash and stood. He was hungry, tired, and looked forward to getting home.

"Take us to the City, please, Uriel."

Uriel inclined his head in acknowledgement, and they disappeared.

Three

Lucifer lounged in a chair facing the door and blew clover-tinged tobacco smoke into the air. The private room in Te's club, Fallen, was currently empty, but it would soon fill up with the members of the Council of Other-kin. Since Kai was still engaged in that job for Te, Lucifer had time to kill. It had crossed his mind to just retrieve the human himself so he could have his lover back, but he'd had to quash that impulse.

The last thing he needed was for Kai to accuse him of calling him weak. They'd been down that road before with the sigils. While he'd gotten his way then, it meant he'd had to tie Kai down to do it. It had been worth it to know his lover was protected, even if he'd had to endure hurt looks and monosyllabic conversations for weeks after the fact. All the same, he'd rather not cause that reaction again if he could help it. So that meant waiting however long it took for Kai to complete the job.

Crashing the Council's monthly poker game was as good a way to spend his time as any. To be fair, "crashing" wasn't entirely accurate, as Te had put out the word that he'd be stopping by, thus giving everyone time to prepare. While there was talk of opening the Council to the entire Other-kin community, its membership currently included only the heads of the werewolf and vampire clans. Lucifer doubted it would expand further. The werewolf and vampire clans barely got along with each other and rarely came to a consensus, so adding the representatives of the other races, especially the Kazat, meant absolutely nothing would get done.

Within moments, Te entered the room. Today's outfit was a shalwar kameez, a forest green top embroidered in red and gold with ochre pants. He headed to the table in the middle of the room, looked at Lucifer, and shook a large bag in his hand, a joyously smug look on his face.

"You brought those nasty things, didn't you?" Lucifer asked, crinkling his nose and vowing to himself not to win a pot heavy with Te's booty.

Te's silver eyes sparkled with mischief while he chuckled. "We're supposed to bring our favorites. And you're one to talk," he said, waggling a large, brown finger at Lucifer.

Now it was Lucifer's turn to chuckle. He stood and walked over to the table, dropping a bag of matchstick pretzels on it.

"The best part's the salt," he said, as Te wrinkled up his nose. He hated the pretzels as much as Lucifer hated the gummy bears. They made it a point to avoid facing off against each other if they could help it, because they didn't want each other's loot.

Since the goal of the Council was to foster cooperation between the species and clans, it was determined that playing for money would be counterproductive. The richer clans would have more leverage in the games, and the resulting jealously would strain already tenuous relationships. It was Te's idea that they should play with a favored snack food. As Steward to the Other-kin, he attended the Council meetings to keep the peace and mediate when necessary.

Playing poker with them served as a reward for their attendance at the meetings. Lucifer's rare appearances, when Kai was otherwise engaged, served as further incentive. The smart ones had taken the honor of his presence seriously and had begun choosing their "money" with him in mind—as an offering of sorts—since he had a tendency to play them to bankruptcy for certain treats.

Lucifer could think of less pleasant ways they could curry his favor. His favor was about the prestige of being in his presence only. They never asked him for anything—that was what Te was for. While they knew better than to cross him, an amiable relationship with him over a game of poker was something they could brag about among themselves and among the members of their clans. Status and reputation were valued currencies among Other-kin.

Lucifer and Te had just seated themselves when Lugan, leader of Kai's vampire clan, Air, and Gwendolyn, matriarch of the werewolf clan Celesta, entered the room. Although unrelated as humans—Kai being of Persian descent and Lugan of African—as vampires sired by the same master, they were brothers. Kai, older than Lugan by over two hundred years, was technically the head of Clan Air. However, to Lucifer's delight—and hearty encouragement—he refused to lead and willingly stepped aside, allowing Lugan to take over. Each blamed the other for their master's demise, and the passing centuries served only to allow their hatred to marinate into something so toxic that they could not stand to be in the same room.

In the early days, the Celesta clan encompassed all werewolves. As time went on, restless and dissatisfied daughters of the clan matriarchs left to form their own clans. Celesta's matriarchs never forgave the perceived betrayal and worked tirelessly to either absorb or decimate the other clans.

Gwendolyn was no exception. She was physically beautiful, with long, fiery red hair, delicate features, and fair skin highlighted by green eyes, but the cold cruelty of her personality ruined the effect. As far as Lucifer was aware, she could only count the matriarch of the Zenith clan, Alana, as a friend. And that was because Alana and her mother before her were weak-minded and let Celesta blur the boundaries between their clans. At this point, they were separate in name only.

He doubted Alana would show tonight. She was terrified of him, which was prudent, but he'd never threatened her. She'd be safe as long as she knew her place. Lucifer doubted that Elizabeth, matriarch of the Lumina clan, would appear tonight either. Her clan's attempted neutrality cost them dearly, as Gwendolyn's relentless assault had driven them almost to extinction. Only by allying themselves with the Orion clan were they able to survive. The Council was working on a resolution, but for now, Elizabeth wanted nothing more than to tear Gwendolyn's throat out, which made Council meetings less than civil, diplomatic affairs.

However, Risha, matriarch of the Orion clan, was present. She entered accompanied by Jarvis, leader of the vampire clan Water. Just behind them, sullen and brooding, Mathias, the leader of the Arya clan, and the only male werewolf clan leader, slunk in.

If all went well, Mathias would utter a veiled accusation of cheating on Lucifer's part, and Risha would respond as she always did, with swift and extreme violence. It was a beautiful thing, watching her—five feet of compact muscle—pin the six-foot, bulky alpha to the ground and threaten to rip his throat out if he didn't apologize. She ruled with charm and diplomacy but was not averse to the vicious use of force when necessary.

At the moment, Mathias, like the leaders of Arya before him, lived at the discretion of the matriarchs. As with his predecessors, he would eventually insult one past the point of acceptable apology, and she would dispatch him.

Although unstable in leadership, Arya served its purpose as a repository for male werewolves who could not live under the matriarchal rule of their home clans. Males who believed in a male-dominated power structure had three choices: join Arya, join the idiots in the

Canes Inferni, or be clanless and live as scavengers. In Lucifer's opinion, none of those choices were ideal. All three choices meant that the male would never mate with a pureblood female, as no pureblood female would ever subjugate herself to a male. They had each other or human females, and as far as he could tell, none of them were truly happy with their chosen lot.

Lucifer's eyes followed Risha as she moved into the room. She was dressed simply, in jeans, flats, and a loose, white blouse, with gold mehndi shining on her honey-brown arms. As she drew near, he smiled and pulled out the chair on his right, the seat reserved for her. A smile broke out on Risha's round face, and she bowed low in return.

Gwendolyn rolled her eyes at what she perceived as an unnecessary show of obeisance. She was wrong, of course. Risha bowed to him out of a deeply held respect, but it was not only her respect that made him so fond of her. She reminded him of her mother, whom he had highly regarded when she was alive. Small in stature, Adelaide had been smart, beautiful, straightforward, fair, and deadly.

It had saddened him deeply when Gwendolyn had her assassinated. It could never be proven, but he had known and retaliated accordingly. She had robbed Risha of her mother when she was barely a hundred years old—young for a female and future matriarch—and robbed the Orion clan of a great leader. Therefore, Lucifer had seen to it that Gwendolyn would never bear another child. While Risha's line of succession was assured in her daughter, Estelle, Gwendolyn would never bear life again. And since Kai and Lugan had conveniently put an end to her first daughter—for reasons of their own—she would never pass the mantle of leadership to a daughter.

Privately, he had assured Risha that her mother had been avenged, although he had not revealed how. By this time, however, he was sure the evidence was plain and that she at least suspected. He assumed it was why Gwendolyn's barbs seemed to leave Risha so unaffected.

Adelaide's assassination had made Lucifer realize he was vulnerable through Kai, and he'd vowed that those who would hurt him would not do so through his beloved. What had begun as small tokens of affection, the sigil to protect him from the sun, for example, became, in Kai's view, ever greater expressions of paranoia. He had been adamant in his refusal of the sigil to prevent his head from being separated from his body, accusing Lucifer of believing that he was unable to take care of himself.

Kai believed, as had his master before him, that any vampire unable to keep his head didn't deserve to. While Lucifer agreed that his lover was a formidable warrior, his argument had been that Kai wasn't invincible, and Lucifer's peace of mind depended on his survival. Maybe he went too far by placing certain sigils. Even if he did, Kai wouldn't know, and the end result was the same: Kai was protected.

Once Risha was settled, Lucifer turned his eyes to Jarvis, the incorrigible flirt, who came to sit at his left. Depending on the source, when he was human, Jarvis had either been a general under Genghis Khan or a close confidante and advisor to the man. Lucifer never cared enough to find out which.

What he did know was that Jarvis was quite fond of frock coats and lace. Tonight's silk brocade number was expertly crafted and exemplified the vampire's taste in fine, beautiful things. With a coquettish tilt to his head, Jarvis swept his waist-length, platinum blond hair back, while lowering his almond-shaped eyes in a demure gesture, before passing Lucifer a joint.

"From my private stash," he said, provocatively puckering his lips and emphasizing each word.

While Jarvis was a skilled cultivator, Lucifer had no doubt that this joint would be as ineffectual and mild as all the others, but he nodded his thanks and replaced the clove cigarette he was smoking with this new offering. Lighting it with a gesture, he noticed with satisfaction the heat performing the parlor trick produced in Jarvis's gaze. Lucifer enjoyed flirting with the vampire and gave as good as he got, as evidenced by the dilation and open longing in those too-blue eyes. A flying piece of taffy hit Jarvis squarely in the head, accompanied by Risha's unabashed giggling, and it brought the elder vampire's attention back into the room.

"Bitch," he said without heat, as a wry smile twisted his lips. He tossed the candy back to Risha and then opened his bag and stacked the contents—hash brownies—on the table like miniature bricks. It was an acceptable offering. While the hash didn't affect him, it added a savory note to the brownies that made them exceptionally tasty, so Lucifer didn't mind all that much.

"Jarvis, must you bother Lord Lucifer with your skunk weed?" Risha asked, as she accepted the joint and took a drag when Lucifer passed it to her.

"Better than that dental hazard you seem to favor," Jarvis replied.

Risha laughed louder while upending her paper bag of saltwater taffy, tempting Lucifer into stealing a piece. She caught his eye and with an exaggerated gesture scooped all the errant pieces into a pile in front of her, while thrusting the joint back in his direction. "Oh no, my Lord, you must earn them, fair and square."

"As if he actually knew what that meant," Mathias grumbled under his breath.

Lucifer caught Risha before she launched herself across the table, as it was much too early for bloodshed. To everyone's surprise, Lugan cold-cocked Mathias, causing him to fall out of his chair. Maybe it wasn't too early for bloodshed after all.

"Apologies, Lord Lucifer. I know it is not my place to interfere," the slightly built, dark-skinned vampire said. "But I cannot sit here one more night and listen to this brat's insults."

Lucifer made a gesture that gave permission for Lugan to proceed, at which point the vampire reached down and, grabbing Mathias by the hair, brought the werewolf's face in so close that their noses almost touched.

"You seem unwilling to obey the matriarch. I assume that it is in deference to your race that she has been lenient. I have no such restraint." To his credit, Mathias managed to keep eye contact. "From this moment until we leave, if I deem anything you utter to be an insult to anyone at this table, I will paralyze you from the neck down. I'm sure my reputation precedes me."

Lugan, Lucifer knew, might look like an accountant or schoolteacher, but his true vocation was far less wholesome—and bloodier—than his appearance would suggest. By the look on Mathias's face, he knew it too. When he dropped his eyes, Lugan let him go. Setting himself back in his chair, Mathias kept his head down and began fussing with a bag of Mary Janes.

"Oh, Mary Janes. My favorite." Lugan smiled as he prepared his pile of mini peanut butter cups.

While everyone got settled and Te shuffled the cards before the first hand was dealt, a medium-sized black dog came into the room carrying a brown paper bag. The dog trotted over to Lucifer, placed the bag on the floor by his feet, and then rolled onto its back, barking once.

"Octavia, is that what I think it is?" Lucifer asked, leaning over and giving the dog's belly a quick tickle before scooping up the bag. Inside, just as he'd suspected, were two Jamaican meat pies. He reached in and snagged one, then broke it open, exposing its warm and fragrant insides. He handed a delighted Risha half and shared a conspiratorial look with her while taking a bite. Octavia, leader of the vampire clan Earth, barked again.

"Of course your tribute is accepted. Good health and happy hunting," Lucifer said, having quickly polished off what was in his hand. He started in on the second pie. This one, he was not sharing. Satisfied, Octavia trotted out again, barely acknowledging anyone else in the room, as usual.

"Does anyone even remember what her human form looks like?" Jarvis asked.

"She was fat," Gwendolyn said, while pouring the black jelly beans she'd brought into piles. She always brought black jelly beans. Everyone assumed that she brought the same ones to each game—she was that stingy.

Risha finished licking her fingers from her unexpected treat and cocked her head at Gwendolyn. "Hardly. She's about as fat as I am."

"Exactly. Fat," Gwendolyn repeated.

With her hair so closely cropped to her skull and her head tilted just so, Lucifer could swear that at that moment Risha was channeling Adelaide. The moment was broken when Te slammed the cards down in front of Mathias and told him to cut the deck.

"The game," Te said when he retrieved the cards, "is five card draw. The joker and the six of hearts are wild."

Now it was Jarvis's turn to roll his eyes.

* * *

"You know you want to fold," Lucifer said to Te. Despite their distaste for each other's betting pool, they were locked in battle. All Lucifer had was a pair of sevens, and

47

he was trying to bluff his way into a win. Despite Mathias's and possibly others' thoughts on the matter, he didn't cheat. It would be ridiculously easy to do so, but he preferred using his skill with the cards, and sometimes intimidation, to win. It was all extremely satisfying.

"What I want to do," Te said, before depositing a generous handful of gummy bears atop the treasure trove of snacks, "is not only call but raise you as well."

Dammit. The two of them had the rapt attention of everyone around the table. Even Gwendolyn looked interested.

"Are you sure you should continue? While it's a pair, the value is fairly low," a voice from behind Lucifer stated.

Lucifer closed his eyes and placed his cards face down on the table. "Fold."

Te whooped and slammed his cards on the table showing a pair of tens. Then he reached over and turned Lucifer's cards face up. The reveal caused him to lose it completely while managing to shovel his winnings into a pile beside him.

"Michael," he said between guffaws. "Good to see you. Shall I deal you in?" he asked, when he could catch his breath from laughing so hard.

The room had gone silent. The Other-kin present knew who Archangel Michael was, but they had no idea why he was there or if they'd even survive the night. As a result, they all fixed their eyes to the floor and pretended they were invisible. Te was still chuckling.

"A pair of sevens. You went through all that for a pair of sevens." That started him laughing again.

Lucifer sighed. "I'm never going to hear the end of that. Having a slow day, are we, Michael? Come to frighten the children?"

Te only snorted and laughed harder as a result.

Contrary to outward appearances, Lucifer was quite surprised. He hadn't seen Michael or the others for ages and, despite himself, was curious to know why he chose to show up now.

"I came because we need to talk," Michael said, moving into Lucifer's line of vision. He made sure to give the still-laughing Te a disparaging look. To Te's credit, he took the insult in stride.

Lucifer examined his brother—warm, olive skin, violet eyes. He looked the same as when they'd last seen each other. The only difference was that now Michael dressed in modern military attire. He was an austere sight in black, from his short, dark hair down to his boots. They were the same height, but Michael was more muscular and, like all seraphs, breathtakingly beautiful.

"It's nice to see your wardrobe's improved. I'm not fond of many modern fabrics, but you seem to take to them quite well."

Te, who had finally managed to compose himself, dissolved into more gales of laughter. Michael shot them both an annoyed look.

"I wouldn't have come if it wasn't important."

It was Mathias's turn to deal, but he, like the others except Te, obviously had no intention of moving until this was resolved.

"Fine." He sighed, snatched a piece of taffy from his pile, and stood. Retrieving his coat on the way, he walked toward the door, unwrapping the candy. "Proceed without me. If I'm not back in one hand, Te, you get my pile," he said, before popping the sweet into his mouth and leaving.

* * *

Lucifer sat at the bar and signaled to the bartender. Te ensured that all the staff knew to not only fulfill his requests promptly but also to never hassle him about money. The bartender, for example, knew that unless told otherwise, when signaled he should bring over a glass of Glenfarclas. The bartender placed the glass carefully in front of him and quickly walked away. Lucifer hadn't paid attention to whatever tale Te had spun about him, because it didn't matter. What did was that they were afraid to make him angry, lest it get back to their boss.

He drank the scotch because he enjoyed the taste, but like the pot, it would not get him intoxicated. Taking a sip as Michael claimed the seat beside him, Lucifer ignored him and lit another clove.

"Hey, you, blondie. There's no smoking in here."

Lucifer turned to face the young woman who spoke. She was typical for the crowd the bar attracted: young, probably mid-twenties, hip, and casual, but not a regular. They knew better than to bother him, although he did get flirted with quite a bit. She stood squarely on her fancy sandals,

50

hands on hips, glaring at him with fierce blue eyes. He stared back, took a drag, and blew smoke out and into her face.

"That is so rude," she said, glaring at him while waving her hand to clear the smoke.

"Why must you antagonize the humans?" Michael asked him.

"Because they're so reactionary," Lucifer said, still watching the woman. Her two friends rallied around her, but the staff avoided her requests for help. Disgruntled, she stalked out. He was a little disappointed. She looked like the type to cause a scene.

"So? Why are you here, Michael?"

"He's right in there, officer. Smoking in a public building, breaking the law." The young woman's voice followed the officer as he strode over to them, utility belt jangling at each step. The cop looked annoyed at being forced to deal with something so mundane but determined to do his job. Lucifer continued smoking.

When the cop reached them, Michael stood and showed him a badge. While the cop looked at the badge, Lucifer felt Michael's gentle *push*. The cop instantly relaxed.

"I apologize for my suspect, Officer…"

"Singleton."

"Officer Singleton. He's a person of interest on a case I'm working on. I bent the rules when I shouldn't have. We'll be going now."

Lucifer scoffed. "I haven't finished my scotch."

"Person of interest?" Although still relaxed, the cop's eyes turned eager, more interested. "You need any help, sir?"

"Sir?" Lucifer mocked. Michael sent him a warning look.

"No, thank you, Officer. He's not dangerous. He only thinks he is."

At that, Lucifer was tempted to play belligerent and start a fight. He and Michael hadn't fought in ages, and the idea was more and more appealing. Michael seemed to sense his intent and discreetly shook his head.

Lucifer knocked back his drink and stood. Starting a fight in front of humans, that would inevitably involve humans, would bring him all sorts of family grief he could do without. He took a drag from his cigarette, looked at Michael, and blew out the smoke. He then turned and walked towards the door.

Michael followed him outside.

"What was that badge? FBI?"

"Army Counterintelligence. It seems to play well in the South."

"I'm sure it does. Probably as well as those stupid wings used to. But who needs wings when you can have a badge."

"I think only Uriel hated those wings more than you did," Raphael said, surprising Lucifer, who turned toward him. Dressed as a typical biker—leather chaps over denim, leather vest over a T-shirt, and a rough beard—Raphael leaned against the side of the building, smiling at him. His shaggy, black hair fell over brown eyes crinkling with mirth.

Lucifer smiled back despite himself. Raphael's words elicited a wave of nostalgic camaraderie within him. Raphael laughed and nudged Gabriel, who stood nearby, to Lucifer's ongoing surprise. Gabriel twitched and drew into himself, as if to avoid having his pristine, grey suit sullied by Raphael's proximity. He too wore his rust-colored hair long, and as with his brethren, his amber eyes and stunning beauty were the only things that hinted at his otherworldly origin.

The last time these three came to see him, they'd staged what could only be called an intervention. It did not end well. Lucifer hoped they had the sense not to try anything so ridiculous again. Lighting up another clove cigarette, he crossed the street, heading toward Waterfront Park.

"We're here because we have a problem," Michael said, coming up beside him.

"We? Since when am I a part of *we*?"

"Since always," said Raphael from behind him. The sidewalks in this part of town barely held two people, forcing Raphael and Gabriel to take up the rear. "It was your choice not to act on it."

"Uh huh. So what is this problem?" Lucifer asked, stopping at the corner. A car had come up to the intersection, and he waited for it to pass before crossing.

"It would be best if we showed you," Gabriel said.

On the other side of the street in front of the park, Lucifer stopped walking and turned toward his brothers. They appeared sincere, but then, for angels on the straight and narrow, that was a character trait.

"This better be worth it," he told them.

"It is; I promise you," Michael said.

"Then lead on."

* * *

"So this is your problem," Lucifer said. The four of them stood unseen inside a hospital room with a single patient. A nurse took the patient's temperature.

There were very few things that could make him truly angry, but he could always count on the meddling of these three to do it.

"Just what are you playing at?" he asked, feeling the stirrings of a rant so fierce and vicious that they wouldn't dare bother him for a hundred years. "You drag me here with such urgency, and for what? Are you insane? Do you think I care a whit about any them? Let them suffer. Let them die."

Michael stepped in close. "Stop playing the martyr and shut up."

Before Lucifer could respond, Raphael was moving. He shot an exasperated look at Michael before he squeezed between them.

"Please, hear us out." Placing a calming hand on Lucifer's shoulder, he said, "This isn't what you think. You wouldn't be here if this wasn't absolutely important."

Lucifer tore his gaze away from Michael's defiant eyes and looked to Raphael, assessing him. Michael was the warrior, Gabriel, the scholar, and Raphael, the heart. Of them all, Raphael was the most genuine. He wore his heart on the outside with such humble sincerity that even if Lucifer thought him a fool, he couldn't blame him for it. It was this alone that persuaded him to stand down and listen.

The nurse had completed her notations and now walked on silent feet to the door, pausing briefly to lower the lights on her way out. The man in the bed was large and looked healthy except for the fact that he was apparently in a coma.

"The man is as healthy as he looks. The cause of the coma is unnatural," Raphael said.

Michael walked over to the bed and leaned over the man. "The humans haven't noticed a pattern, and it's doubtful they will, as it's not a contagion per se." He looked up at Lucifer. "What do you see?"

"A human in a hospital bed and an archangel who needs to get to the point." Lucifer crossed his arms and did little to bank his irritation.

"If you looked with more than your eyes, you would see this." Michael reached into the man's chest and pulled out a shiny, black substance, thicker than water, more viscous than oil. Wherever the substance touched him, it bubbled and spat, like acid on metal. In fact, it affected Michael's skin the same way, burning and eroding the surface. Hissing in pain, Michael dropped the substance back on the body, where it instantly disappeared, reabsorbed. Free of the material, Michael's hand was still red and raw. It only began to heal once Gabriel clasped it and loosed his holy power over it.

Genuinely surprised and intrigued, Lucifer stood stunned a moment before he collected himself. Once composed, he looked at Raphael. "What was that?"

"No idea," Raphael said. "We can't even figure out how or why humans get infected."

"There's more." This from Michael. "Seals are breaking."

Lucifer's annoyance returned tenfold. "So send your lackeys to fix them. How is that my problem?"

"Dammit—" Lucifer smirked when he caught the warning look Raphael threw Michael that caused him to stop mid-sentence and visibly calm himself before speaking again. "These seals are not ours. In fact, they seem to have been erected eons before ours. Plus, they're breaking from the other side. We can't close them because that...that goo, for lack of a better term, is oozing out." Michael thrust his still-healing hand toward Lucifer. The skin was pink and shiny, nowhere near as healed as it should be. "We can't get close enough to the leaks to close them without that stuff attacking us."

"Wait. You're telling me it's alive?" Lucifer asked, feeling both appalled and disgusted.

"We don't know for sure," Gabriel said. As usual, he'd been quietly watching his brothers' exchange, only now offering a tidbit of information. "It doesn't seem to be, but it has been known to attack. Whether it's alive, or if it has intelligence, has yet to be determined."

Lucifer crossed his arms and walked over to the bed, digging through memory. "I remember coming across one of those ancient seals." He frowned, shaking his head. "I asked Him about it, but He distracted me." He shrugged. "Then I forgot all about it when He created you lot." He waved in the others direction.

"Wait, Father knew about those seals but didn't create them?" asked Gabriel.

"Try to keep up with the class."

"But this is His creation. That doesn't make sense," Michael said.

"No. Me, you, the animals, and humans are His creation. The rest," Lucifer shrugged, "was just here."

"No," Michael said. "He created Heaven and Earth…"

Lucifer held a hand up to stop the litany, as he had no desire to hear it. "If you prefer revisionist history, so be it." Michael's lavender eyes were stormy. He was itching to argue, but Lucifer derailed him again. "Why come to me? The Old Man too busy to be bothered?" He noticed Gabriel and Raphael purposely avoiding his eyes. Cold realization flooded him, and he turned to Michael. "He sent you."

"The situation has changed," Michael said quietly. A shadow of an emotion passed too quickly over his face for Lucifer to decipher. He paused a moment to study Michael's face, but his features were once again set in practiced neutrality.

There was something they were not telling him. Had the Old Man ordered a truce of some kind between them?

Interesting. Not that he had any intention of making such an arrangement. He loved his life and would not make compromises, no matter how much He decreed or demanded.

Lucifer moved his attention back to the human in the bed. When he took the time to really see, he was both fascinated and repulsed. There, where the soul should be, was a black, roiling mass. What had happened to the soul? Was it replaced or devoured?

Curiosity spurred him to plunge his own hand into the man's chest. Grabbing a handful of the stuff, he pulled it into view. There was a faint smell of moist decay, not clean like what one would find in a forest but fetid and festering like a neglected wound. The substance bubbled as it did before; however, on him there was little effect. A good portion of it dissolved into nothing on contact, and the rest shrank away from him, using gravity and momentum to attempt to return to the body in the bed. He was too engrossed to notice the relief on his brother's faces.

Straightening up, Lucifer brushed off his uninjured hands and addressed his brethren. "Looks like you've got your work cut out for you."

"You cannot be serious. This is a threat to all of us." Michael approached him, jaw clenched and prepared for war.

Lucifer scoffed. "It may be a threat to you, but as you've seen, it's not a threat to me."

"I told you he would be selfish," Michael said to Raphael and Gabriel.

"Selfish? Is that the word we're using now?" Lucifer let his anger unfurl. "You call me selfish, yet who desired to twist my fate to their own desires and then cast me off when I refused to heel?"

He pinned them each with the weight of his gaze. Only Michael met it and glared back with matching heat.

"I led you to victory after victory over the Darkness, and I do one thing, and you punish me for it. I refuse to bow down to the naked, stinking apes, and you make sure all of Heaven despises me for it."

His voice had gradually gone low and quiet. He never wanted them to see how much it hurt, but this chance to even the score loosened his tongue, and he wouldn't stop until he'd purged himself.

"I chose one thing for myself, and suddenly, all believe I was kicked out of Heaven, disgraced for challenging the Lord God." His eyes swept his brothers and noted with satisfaction that even Michael averted his with shame. "I am selfish, but it was you who betrayed me."

"We thought—"

"And who sat back and did nothing to stop you?" He continued on, refusing to be silenced. "You turned your backs on me. The Old Man turned His back on me. If this is such a threat to you, then let Him deal with it. As far as I'm concerned, you're on your own."

He disappeared.

"Wow." Raphael blew out a breath with the word. "Hindsight says I should have expected that, but I had hoped..."

"That his sense of superiority would override his feelings for us?" Gabriel asked. Raphael nodded. "It is hardly surprising, although I admit I never realized how badly he was hurt. He will never willingly help us."

59

"He doesn't understand." Michael looked to his brothers. "Once he does, he will come around." He disappeared.

"He gets points for determination, but they're about evenly matched when it comes to being stubborn." Gabriel smiled at Raphael's attempt at humor, and then they too disappeared.

Once the room was empty, the man in the bed began to laugh.

Four

According to Other-kin lore, the City was strong and vibrant thousands, perhaps millions, of years before humans inhabited the planet. The City's fall came during the Purge, the time when the angels came and slaughtered the ancestors. It was always suspected, but never proven, that the purpose of the forced extinction was to clear the earth for humans.

In an attempt to save civilization from total annihilation, the City, along with four others, was intentionally buried, hidden underground. The stories varied on how this was accomplished. One version told of ten powerful mages who chanted for forty days and forty nights to raise enough power to accomplish the deed. In another version, the ten mages required continual blood sacrifices to raise the power. In Kai's favorite version, huge black dragons flew overhead, protecting the mages, matching the angels in power and ferocity, all but one sacrificing themselves to ensure the safety of the City deep within the earth.

Only the species most dangerous to humans were targeted for extinction in the Purge. The rest dwindled naturally as humans thrived, claiming land and resources, or were defeated directly as the humans proved more powerful. Of the five cities saved, only the City remained, its residents deciding early on that they preferred survival to fighting an unbeatable foe. Three of the other cities gave way to in-fighting, inadequate leadership, and lack of resources. The fourth became a staging ground for the holy war, which the angels would not tolerate.

* * *

Uriel deposited the little group at the entrance. The curving walls of the antechamber, carved with images of creatures from another world, always filled Kai with wonder. He knew, as did all residents of the City, that his ancestors were somewhere on those walls. Hybrids to the last, Other-kin owed their existence to experimentation, both natural and magical. Like most, he had no idea which creature was his ancestor, that knowledge having been lost long ago.

The hall was deserted except for the twelve-foot-tall Black Stone guards that stood to either side of the entrance and at intervals along the walls. Although it was ostensibly the main entrance, its purpose was vestigial. Travelers into and out of the City used dedicated portals in their respective 'neighborhoods' or paid mages for the privilege of transportation.

Kai regretted not being more specific when he asked Uriel to bring them to Te. Given the status of the prisoner, Uriel had deposited them there in order for Kai to make a grand entrance. Now Kai stood looking through the wide entranceway and into the marketplace, hoping he'd spot Te so he would come and take Gregory off his hands.

He knew better. Instead, he would have to trot his captive down the main thoroughfare in full view. Of course, the parade and display of such an important captive would bolster his prestige, but at the moment, he just didn't care. Feeling impatient and irritable, he just wanted to get this over with so he could go home.

It was fitting, given his eroding patience, that the last person Kai wanted to see would currently be mincing his way toward him. Stephan—pronounced *Stef-ahn*—was the only being on the planet that Kai wished he could repeatedly kill on sight until the end of time. He was a simpering toady who constantly tried to undermine Kai's relationship with Lucifer and Te.

Officially, Stephan was Te's personal assistant, but he aspired to more and thus only bothered to work when he deemed the work important. Then he'd parade around with an insufferable air of authority, making sure everyone knew that he was in charge. If it had been up to Kai—and many others, he was sure—Stephan would have been dead long ago.

But Te's incomprehensible fondness for him kept him among the living. According to Te, Stephan had the gift of "forging order out of chaos" or something equally as absurd.

Kai knew it for the farce it was. Stephan had been a whore in one of the brothels that Te frequented and, having recognized Te as a way out, had managed to latch on to him. Now lovers, Te indulged him to a ridiculous degree. If Te hadn't been who he was, Kai might have been worried that he was being taken advantage of.

He turned his head to comment to Uriel and was annoyed to find the archangel missing.

"Coward," he muttered, hoping Uriel could hear. Apparently he could, because a feeling of amusement touched the edge of his awareness. Kai didn't think he would ever be used to Uriel's odd sense of humor. Making sure that the woman was still unconscious, and that Gregory still cowered at his feet, Kai mentally recited his standard mantra—*do not kill him*—as the willowy creature approached.

Stephan breezed into the entryway, nose in the air and a smile on his face. An Eineu in a lavender tunic trailed a few steps behind. "You've returned. We were beginning to wonder what was taking so long."

"Stephan." Kai pronounced it *Steven*, knowing how much it aggravated the taller vampire. He held back a smile as Stephan absorbed the insult, clearly wanting to respond, but afraid to.

Stephan cleared his throat and collected himself by looking over the humans on the floor. He had an ethereal quality, more so than even the actual angels Kai knew, and a delicate bone structure that Kai usually associated with the feminine. He wore his platinum blond hair cropped short, which made his cerulean eyes seem to blaze out from his oval face. Stephan was tall and lithe, and played up the feminine in his appearance by wearing makeup and colorful, flowing robes. Kai was hard-pressed to call him attractive, although given his pureblood nature, he was objectively stunning. But his personality was so loathsome that it outweighed the beauty of his outward appearance.

"Kai, why is our property clothed and disrespectful?" Stephan snapped, self-importance fully restored. "And who is this?" he asked, toeing the unconscious woman with a dainty foot and then shaking his head in overly dramatic derision. "If I didn't know any better, I'd swear you were a novice at human retrieval."

Pompous ass. Of course Kai knew the rules regarding human captives. As distracted as he was, the last thing on his mind was proper protocol, but he wasn't about to tell Stephan that.

"I do not answer to you," he replied, daring the other vampire to make more of the issue.

Stephan drew himself up to his full height and towered over Kai. "Maybe not, but it is highly unusual, not to mention sloppy, and more work for the rest of us." He huffed, no doubt to make Kai aware of how inconvenient he was being. Then, indicating the woman, Stephan spoke again. "No matter. I'll have a Beetle put her in one of the holding cells—"

He didn't get to finish his sentence before Kai snatched him by the front of his robes and pulled him in close, dangling him by his neck.

"You will do no such thing." Kai spoke softly, but his body tensed with restrained violence. "Under no circumstances will she come to any harm. She is a guest and under my protection. If she is not treated with the utmost respect and courtesy, I will peel the skin off of your worthless body, crucify you, and plant the cross in the noonday sun. Do. You. Understand?"

Stephan, unprepared for the viciousness of Kai's reaction, immediately went limp and dropped his eyes. "Of course. But—"

"But?"

"But a human *guest*?" Stephan still avoided eye contact. "Such a thing is unheard of."

"Do you really think you're in a position to question me?" Kai asked, his eyes promising pain if Stephan continued to push the issue.

"Of—of course not. Pardon my misunderstanding." His acquiescence prompted Kai to let him go. Taking a healthy step back, Stephan straightened the front of his garment and waved a guard over. "Take the woman to a suite for honored guests."

He glanced nervously at Kai, who stood watching with narrowed eyes as the guard jostled her in its attempt to pick her up.

"Gently." Stephan's voice cracked on the word. "Gently, or I'll have your arms, and your nest will devour you before they have time to grow back." The guard managed to gingerly pick the woman up and lumber off with her in the direction of the guest quarters. Kai then addressed the Eineu.

"John, if she wakes, see to it that she has everything she needs."

The creature bowed and scurried off after the guard.

Kai felt like he was spiraling out in a wider orbit from who he was, rather than in closer. Stephan's very presence irritated him, made him defensive, and as soon as he'd opened his mouth, he regretted it.

His intent had been to consult with Te about the woman. He felt honor-bound to do right by her. What he should have done was left her and then come back with Te. Why that course of action hadn't been clear when it mattered was beyond him.

Now the City's first human guest was under his protection. Perfect. When this got around—which it would, thanks to Stephan—there would be no end to the trouble it caused, not to mention the increased damage to his already less-than-stellar reputation. Not that he cared about such things.

His anger at himself put a hard edge in his voice when he spoke to the man on the floor. "Strip."

He could tell Stephan was about to speak, so he shot him a warning look that shut him down. Gregory was trying his best, but with the broken arm, his progress was slow. Removing a knife from a sheath in his coat, Kai cut and then ripped away the material that still covered the man. Once he was bare, he retrieved the leash and jerked on it, making sure he had the man's full attention.

"You will walk behind me. You will keep your eyes lowered. You will not speak. Nod if you understand."

At the meek nod, Kai turned back to Stephan and gestured toward the entrance. Thankfully without another word, Stephan turned in a flurry of color and swept through the massive pillars, Kai directly behind.

They stepped into a large, oval cavern that covered an area roughly the size of four large airplane hangars. The marketplace always reminded Kai of the biblical story of Jonah, who was swallowed by a whale. Ten blazing, white quartz crystals, reminiscent of whalebone embedded in rock, arched up from the floor to form rib-like arches in the ceiling. The pillars, each with the bones of a long dead mage at its base, were a physical manifestation of power that still glowed after all the centuries, providing light, heat, and later, electricity.

Many Other-kin said that they could still see the bodies of the dragons turned to stone in the ceiling. As much as Kai wanted to believe, he could never see them and feared it was more fantasy and tricks of light rather than actual fact.

The City served as the primary domain of Other-kin that could not pass as human. Fixed into the walls between the crystals were domiciles and businesses. Over the years, more had been cut into the neighboring stone, which became honeycombed with them, as well as with miles of tunnels. The center of this cavern held the marketplace, where vendors sold everything from clothing to food to more personal services in tent-like stalls, tables, or dirt mounds, depending on preference, wealth, and inclination.

Two main streets cut the marketplace into quarters. The central intersection showcased the auction blocks that were run exclusively by goblins. Columns stood along the roads, and atop each stood a Black Stone guard.

The Black Stone were an insect race that, when immobile, camouflaged for the hunt, resembled giant, black, oval stones. As was common among Other-kin races, they had a true name for themselves, but they either kept it secret for religious purposes or just chose not to share it. Either way, they didn't care what others called them. Black Stone was the universally accepted name for them, although Beetle was also used derisively on occasion.

The area immediately surrounding the entrance grew silent when they entered. That silence traveled in a wave as the little procession made its way down the main drag. Kai kept his eyes on the middle distance, ignoring Stephan's annoying swagger a few paces ahead. He just wanted to get this over with as quickly as possible.

Kai's sharp eyes easily plucked Te out of the crowd ahead, the dashiki he wore making him stand out in a blaze of brilliant red, blue, and gold. In his official capacity, Te looked just as imposing as the first time Kai had seen him.

They'd met in the mid-1600s, when Kai and Lucifer had crashed a small ceremony where the humans involved intended to raise and enslave a demon. All had gone quite smoothly, until the newly raised demon walked straight to Lucifer, knelt, and declared his fealty and fidelity, which was graciously accepted.

Thinking they were there for a lark, Kai was surprised that the humans had actually succeeded in conjuring anything at all. His reaction, however, paled in comparison with that of the humans, who were properly terrified. Kai wasn't sure which terrified them more: having Lucifer among them or summoning a demon that would not be controlled. Lucifer had not been surprised. In fact, he was so composed that Kai accused him of being in on it, a stance he would recant shortly thereafter. Who knew Lucifer would react so strongly? Subsequently, Kai kept his suspicions to himself.

Under Lucifer's amused gaze, the enormous, naked, and glistening demon immediately used the ritual participant's superstition—or religious fervor, depending on perspective—fear of death, and greed to bind each of them to him. He promised wealth and immortality in exchange for a healthy percentage of the profits, and swore an eternity of torment for any who cheated or disobeyed him, thus giving rise to the legend of "selling your soul to the Devil."

Te became a part of their household then, as well as their occasional "partner in crime." Years later, he'd come to the City as its steward, fulfilling the prophesy of the dying dragon god, Uru.

A yelp and a jerk on the chain snatched Kai out of his reverie and had him whirling around, ready to lash out at Gregory for tripping. He stopped when he saw the man lying on the floor with a fresh gash on his bare buttock and a pleased Kazat licking a bloodied knife.

Upon seeing the source of the commotion, Stephan flew into a rage. "How dare you touch Lord Te's property—guards!"

Simultaneously, three guards dropped from their posts atop pillars, and Other-kin closest to the offending Kazat moved as far away as possible, leaving him standing alone. Assaults on slaves going to auction were commonplace; feuding Other-kin routinely sabotaged one another this way because injured slaves drew lower prices. Due to Kai's relationship with Lucifer, he was seen as an impostor, one whose status was given and not earned. Despite being over 900 years old—and age alone went a long way to conferring status in Other-kin society—he was constantly disrespected, especially by the Kazat. He should have expected this and prepared for it. It was another thing to add to the growing list of the night's fuckups.

As handler, it fell to him to examine and treat Gregory's wound, should he care to. The wound was deep, having slashed muscle, and without intervention, scar tissue would most likely leave him lame. As it was, he wouldn't be able to continue walking. Kai cursed aloud. He needed to put the Kazat in their place.

"Pick it up and bring him," Stephan told the guards, indicating both Gregory and the Kazat, and the procession began again.

* * *

Waiting at the main auction block, Te observed their approach. Looking at the little group, it was easy to assess

71

the situation. The Kazat had grown brasher in their disrespect for Kai. It wasn't just him either. They were dangerous, and Te was always dealing with complaints. Their participation in that stupid war after Uru left had made them bold, and his appearance, though prophesied, hadn't tempered them much. He should have culled their numbers then, as a warning. For the sake of the City, he would eventually have to do something. But all Other-kin were fighting extinction, and he didn't like the idea of hastening the inevitable, even if they were a nuisance.

Stopping within a few feet of him, both Stephan and Kai bowed formally, as was custom, Stephan attempting to one-up Kai by kissing the hem of Te's purple trouser leg. He gave Stephan an indulgent smile, being used to and generally amused by his antics. He knew that Kai's restraint regarding Stephan was a sign of how much he respected him, and he appreciated his friendship even more because of it. He reminded himself to tell him so. Te made a show of first looking confused and then enraged as he examined Gregory. With calculated fury, he turned on the captive Kazat.

"I should have your head for this damage to my property," he thundered. Turning to other members of the species grouped nearby, he issued a warning. "You may disrespect Lord Kai, but when your actions affect me, you will bear the brunt of my retribution. Is that clear?"

The highest ranking Kazat in the group moved toward the captive, stripped it of weapons, tribe insignia, and trophies, and then stepped back and bowed low to Te. "Our deepest apologies, Lord Te. This one is Unborn. May the blood of your enemies soak the ground at your feet."

The little group bowed in unison, and a rumbling sound began with the speaker and spread throughout the group. Soon it was taken up by other Kazat in the marketplace. That sound was joined by shouts from the crowd, and soon the marketplace was awash with the cacophony.

"Silence!" Te's voice reverberated throughout, immediately quieting the crowd. "There will be no bloodshed here today," he told the crowd, who loudly voiced their disapproval. "Death is a mercy, a release from suffering. Do you believe I should show mercy?"

"No," screamed the crowd, catching on and relishing the idea.

Te addressed the Kazat currently in custody. "As Unborn, you have no value to your race, but your life has value to me. For damaging my property and diminishing its value, you are now my property. I'm sure you'll fetch a fair price."

The crowd enthusiastically cheered and hollered its agreement. A few of the buyers around the main auction block began shouting out prices, furiously outbidding each other before formal bidding began. The goblin auctioneer took advantage of the frenzy, taking the bids and raising prices as the Kazat was led to the stage. It was a fitting punishment. Kazat pride made them terrible slaves; the sale was entirely about prestige. The final price was nothing compared to the rise in status and the ability to participate in the humiliation of one so dishonored.

Te knew the other Kazat would take it to heart, and he was glad for it. He turned to Stephan. "Take this to holding, call a healer, and have it marked. Then prepare me a list of the bidders."

He gestured to Gregory, now lying limp in the grasp of the Black Stone guard. Stephan bowed his head and promptly delegated. With the excitement over the Kazat highlighting the day's auction, it was easier to have Gregory prepared properly and presented at a later time. Te watched them go for a minute, then turned to Kai and wrapped an arm around him.

"You look like you could use a drink. Come."

The hostile look Stephan shot him when Te wrapped his arm around his shoulders did not escape Kai. He did, however, manage to resist the urge to look smug. Leaning into Te's embrace, he let himself be led away to a pub.

The pub they entered was quiet, the few Other-kin present scattered about in small groups. It looked like any other human pub Kai had been in. There was a bar with stools and taps at one end, a huge fireplace at one wall, and scattered chairs and tables strewn about the large room with no real deference to form or design. This particular pub was hewn directly out of the rock. Three of the walls were rock, while the fourth—facing the outside—was shaped earth and glass. The major difference from a pub on the surface was that any humans on the premises were either there as slaves or food.

They took an empty table near the fireplace.

"You want to tell me about it?" Te asked when they were both settled.

"Not right now," Kai replied, attempting nonchalance. "I'll just have that drink and go home," he said, hoping Te wouldn't press.

"Uh huh." Te raised an eyebrow, and Kai knew he wasn't done. Te wanted a full accounting, but all Kai wanted was to put it aside for the night. "Michael and the others stopped by. Luc went off with them."

Now it was Kai's turn to raise an eyebrow. "Why? Do you know where they went?"

Te shook his head. "No, I just thought you should know in case he's not back yet."

Kai laughed. "Remember the last time?"

Te joined in the laugher. "He was livid. One thing I can say about our dear Lucifer, he's inventive with his curses."

The bartender, a pear-shaped, jowly Lisatu, shouted and waved excitedly at Te. The language of the Lisatu was one Kai had never bothered to learn. In Kai's mind, Lisatu were so low in the hierarchy of Other-kin as not to even register. They were a sickly, stinky bunch, resembling two-legged, deformed elephants. Every one had multiple sores covering their large bodies. Like a fair portion of Other-kin races in the City, they specialized in one thing. In their case, it was pub ownership.

He watched as Te responded in their guttural language with accompanying hand gestures. "Excuse me, Kai. I need to take care of this. I have to hear yet another complaint about shortages in Corolon spirits."

"The satyrs?" Kai asked with a smirk.

"Of course it's the satyrs. It's always the satyrs. Anyway, this place is always stocked, if you're hungry."

Kai was indeed hungry, but eyeing the largest lesion on the bartender's face, he felt his appetite draining away. Besides, all they had was human blood. Why have that when he could have better? "Maybe later, although I would like that drink."

"Of course, my friend." Te went back to speaking and gesturing at the bartender, nodding when the bartender responded. "Due to the shortage, it'll have to be from the surface. I'll have it sent right over. Be back shortly."

Relieved, Kai watched him stride away, then relaxed at the table, and stared into the fireplace. He'd have to discuss the botched retrieval and the woman eventually, but he preferred later rather than sooner.

The Lisatu waiter—waitress?—arrived with a bottle and a glass. Kai was pretty sure it was a son or daughter. The age he guessed by the lack of facial lesions; as to the sex, he had no idea. They set the glass down and were reaching for the bottle when Kai reached up and plucked it off the tray.

"This will be fine," he said, as he poured himself a glass. The Lisatu opened its mouth to speak before glancing to the side and hurrying off. Kai sipped his drink, noting by the smell the group of young Kazat that scared the server away.

If there was an archetype of strength to which all the Other-kin races aspired, it was based on the Kazat ideal. Adults averaged seven feet tall, their thick builds ranged in color from grey to dark green, and armor-like plates protected the back and torso. Kai always wondered if the creators of that cartoon with the ninja turtles had somehow stumbled upon a Kazat and lived to make huge profits off of that waking nightmare, as the resemblance was uncanny—minus the shell, pleasant disposition, and love of pizza, of course.

The Kazat maintained their power through physical force and by willingly abandoning threats to the stability of the whole as Unborn. A dissenting member would be torn apart without sentiment, all for the glory and maintenance of the status quo.

Neither male nor female, they reproduced in cycles, members becoming male or female as needed. Such a sporadic birthrate resulted in young that were highly prized as gifts from the gods. Shortly after birth, they were sequestered for decades and put through ritualized training that emphasized the race's core values of dominance, physical strength, and racial superiority.

The group that approached him now carried themselves with the bravado that could only come with younglings out for the first time without their guardians. If this was the case, then this was their last test before adulthood: comportment in public. Kai had a feeling they were about to fail.

"Look, it's Lucifer's pet vampire," a Kazat called from the middle of the small group. Snickers from the room followed. Had the Kazat been an adult, trophies from various kills and slave captures would have been included with the trinkets haphazardly attached to the cloth it wore over its dark green body. "So, is it true?"

"Is what true?" Kai replied, going about the business of enjoying his drink, eyes still on the fire.

"That Lucifer has you on a short leash and you don't feed on humans anymore 'cause you're tame." The youngling's smile stretched in a sinister fashion over its reptilian face. Full-on laughter broke out in the room.

Smiling, Kai looked up at his questioner and leaned forward, motioning for the Kazat to come to him as if he had a secret he wanted to share. As soon as the Kazat was within reach, Kai grabbed it with one hand and ripped its head off with the other, throwing it into the fire. The firelight cast a warm glow on his hands as he took his time cleaning them on the carcass's garments before kicking it out of his way.

"I'll be glad to answer any more questions," he said, leaning back into his seat, black eyes looking up and scanning the room; his upper lip pulled into a sneer showing elongated fangs.

Nobody was laughing now. More than a few patrons remembered they had important business to conduct elsewhere. Kai heard them scurrying to leave, and it warmed his heart. They needed to be afraid of him. A slow, nasty smile spread across his features, daring the remaining Kazat to meet the threat. None did. Fear radiated from them as they quickly sobered, remembering what they were dealing with. A couple of them found the floor very interesting.

One raised his hands in a placating gesture and spoke up. "P-p-please forgive us, L-Lord. The w-wine is strong here."

Kai was unimpressed and certainly not feeling very forgiving.

Te stormed back into the room. Within seconds, his gaze took in the body and Kai's murderous face. Crossing his arms, he leveled a glare at the frightened and huddled younglings. "Well?"

Kai settled back in his seat, finished his drink, poured another glass, and then watched the scene unfold. His features hadn't relaxed, signaling deadly consequences to anyone—but Te, of course—stupid enough to approach him.

Once Te had been filled in, he lit into the small group. "Taunting a vampire who's older and stronger than you? Stupid. You're lucky he didn't kill the lot of you. Now get out. Make sure I never see you again."

Turning to Kai, he said, "Join me in my office. I'll be there as soon as I've dealt with this." He waved toward the corpse on the floor. Kai inclined his head in acknowledgement, finished his drink, rose, and left the room.

* * *

Te's office was at the uppermost level of the City. The room appeared to be scooped out of the surrounding rock or recessed into it, depending on inclination and point of view. Beautifully appointed, the wall opposite the door was made of glass. To the left of the door sat Te's huge desk, fronted by two wingback chairs. A huge tapestry depicting Uru overlooking the City hung on the wall behind the desk. To the right was a sitting area with a couch, more wingback chairs, and a wet bar nestled in the corner. Two bookcases framed a fireplace, both crammed full of books and what Te liked to call the "flotsam of centuries." Paintings and sculptures from both human and Other-kin artists filled the remaining available wall and floor space.

When Te entered his office, he found Kai at the glass wall, looking down at the marketplace. "I don't think there'll be consequences," he said, walking over to his desk and sitting down.

Kai couldn't care less. His pupils were still dilated, and his fangs were still elongated—evidence he was primed and high from the kill. He longed to spill more blood.

"Is this what they're saying now? Lucifer's vampire. Lucifer's tame vampire. Do they even use my name?" he asked, still staring out the window.

"Saying? What are you taking about? Who's saying?"

Kai turned to him. "You know exactly what I'm talking about, so just answer the question." He didn't like snapping at Te, but he was being evasive.

Te sighed. "There are some who say that Lucifer has forbidden you from feeding on or killing humans." Kai's jaw tightened. Te hastened to add, "But there are also those who say that Lucifer couldn't care less what you do."

Kai turned back around toward the window. "What do you say?"

"I say the latter, because I know the truth. What's going on, my friend? I've never seen you this touchy before."

Kai ignored the question. "I think it's time I held Court." His face finally flowed back to its more human features.

"What?"

Kai turned around again. "You heard me. I want to hold Court."

"But you hate politics. There's also the fact that you've never shown any interest in it since I've known you." He came around his desk and sat on the edge. "What's going on? Why this sudden desire? Was it those Kazat? They were just kids. Why let it bother you?"

Again, Kai ignored the questions. "It's my right. I've let them disrespect me long enough."

Te sighed again. "Okay, okay. You've had a stressful few days. Go get some rest."

Kai looked at him, knowing he was being dismissed. "I'm going, but I mean it, Te," he said as he walked to the door, determined to let the demon know he was serious.

"Rest, and we'll discuss it tomorrow."

Kai bid him goodnight and was gone.

* * *

After leaving Te, Kai walked toward a portal that would take him home. Clan Air's exit portal wasn't difficult to access. It was passing all the Other-kin on the way that was the problem. Even now, the gossip had probably spread. He was sure he saw derision in the eyes of those he passed. In retrospect, it hadn't been surprising that a Kazat had the audacity to speak to him that way, especially after the attack on Gregory in the marketplace. As a race, they seemed to enjoy pushing boundaries and causing trouble, although their targets were usually Other-kin known to be weaker than them. Obviously, they didn't think of him as a threat, and that had to change.

He hadn't wanted to admit to Te that the Kazat's taunt had bothered him so much because it was partly true. Had his association with Lucifer tamed him somehow?

He should have had the desire to feed on any human he came across. In theory, this was true. When he was among humans and smelled their blood, he found it tantalizing, but in an almost abstract way. Centuries ago, when he'd tasted Luc's blood for the first time, he'd realized that it was all he could ever want or need. Granted, he'd had to build up a tolerance to the powerful blood, which was frustrating but endurable, because Luc's blood had become his whole world. Given that, he didn't need to feed on humans.

So why did the fact that he didn't want to feed on them bother him so much?

Then there was the issue of killing. Usually, if he killed at all—the instances had become extremely rare—it was an assassination for Te or at Lucifer's request. Or was it with his permission? Tonight was the first time in a long while that he'd killed without either of those conditions, and it had felt good.

He feared he had either lost or was losing an essential part of himself. He was a killer by nature, and while he'd mastered the control of his baser instincts, he felt there was more at work here.

The worst part was that he had no one to ask. His master was gone, and although there were others his age or close to it, he didn't dare show his weakness by asking them questions.

Most likely he was overreacting, but he couldn't escape the niggling feeling that there was something wrong with him. Confused, hungry, and tired, he looked forward to Luc's return, wanting to lose himself in sensation so he wouldn't have to think for a while.

The nice thing about using the dedicated portals in the City was that they were premade. All one had to do was use the proper key—usually a drop of blood—and incantation to go to the desired destination, which was another dedicated portal on the surface. After placing it in the bowl provided—it would be consumed by the spell—he spoke the words and felt the world shift and settle with a jolt. A few moments of vertigo kept him standing in an identical activated circle in an alcove of their home. Once recovered, he exited the alcove and immediately undressed, discarding his concerns with each piece of clothing.

The house they currently called home was the Ashley House, a beautiful Queen Anne mansion overlooking the Ashley River in Charleston, South Carolina. They had first visited the port city in 1860, drawn by the promise of war. They'd been in the city for years, at odds with each other on where to settle. Lucifer wanted to live in a secluded spot along the Ashley River, but Kai and Te wanted to live fronting the Cooper River, the seedier section of town.

An unexpected earthquake in 1886 decided the question for them all. Lucifer absconded with the Queen Anne—it was assumed destroyed along with the other houses on its street—and moved it to its current location along the river. Local Other-kin lore insinuated that Lucifer had caused the earthquake to cover stealing the house. Lucifer was amused by the notion that he would go to such lengths to procure a house. Kai knew that he found a dark pleasure in most of the nefarious deeds he'd been accused of, even if they were untrue.

Lucifer might not have gone to inordinate lengths to acquire the house, but he did so to protect it, as he did with all of their homes. A glamour was placed upon the building and grounds to prevent errant human neighbors, curiosity seekers, tax collectors, mailmen, and the like from traipsing up the walk and knocking on the door.

Kai padded barefoot up the polished, English oak stairway, the red runner of some oriental design that he considered busy but that Lucifer loved scratched the soles of his feet uncomfortably—he wasn't a fan of wool. Kai liked to joke that he lived in a museum. This house, like all the others, contained various antiques and curios. From the crystal chandelier overhead to the Tiffany glass windows above the doors to the Louis the some-such dining set, if it caught his mate's fancy, it was in the house.

He smiled. The first time he'd called Luc his mate, he might as well have used the word enemy instead for the ridiculous amount of upset it caused. For a reason that Kai still did not understand, Luc had been furious and insulted.

He never referred to him that way again, and even trained himself to not think it. But sometimes, especially when he felt weary, the training would lapse, and he'd indulge in his desire to think of Luc as what he felt him in his heart to be.

In the master bathroom, he passed the clawfoot tub, which was his usual choice, headed straight for the over-sized shower, and turned on the hot water tap. He would never stop appreciating the pleasure of hot, running water.

He stood under the multiple sprays and forced himself not to dwell on anything. He washed himself leisurely, enjoying the feeling of soaping his body. When he was clean, he turned off the water, dried off, and went to bed. With Luc still firmly in his thoughts, he quickly drifted off to sleep.

Five

Lucifer sat on the porch of the Ashley House in his favorite rocking chair and gazed out at the river. Still fuming over being called selfish, he'd decided to let Kai sleep rather than wake him with his desire for his body and his company.

He knew that he was selfish. His lifestyle proved that with infinite clarity. He could control his urges, but why should he have to? That was for the mortals who actually cared what others thought of them. So why did the sanctimonious blathering of his family bother him so?

Their audacity never ceased to amaze him, Michael's in particular. He was sure the Old Man was behind it—probably some scheme of his to have them reconcile over a "crisis." As if he would set aside thousands of years of enmity so easily. In truth, he'd long ago come to terms with what had happened, but he wasn't inclined to let them think he could forgive and forget without due recompense. If they wanted his forgiveness, they would have to earn it, and he wouldn't come cheaply.

He took a deep breath and felt the air of the predawn calm him. This porch was one of his favorite places to sit and enjoy the view, residents and tourists notwithstanding. He'd placed the house to catch the breezes off the river and frequently thought back to quieter times before the boulevard and its influx of amblers, joggers, and sightseers.

He was inordinately attached to this house. Two-storied and gabled, it could easily have been on the historic register with its wraparound porch, second story veranda, and courtyard garden. And he jealously guarded its secret perfection. Thanks to the glamour he'd placed upon it, it appeared nondescript—definitely worthy of the million-dollar associates that sat to either side, but not interesting enough to stand out in any way, except for possibly the owner's apparent love for cats. A person who tried to look closer or crossed the property line would suddenly remember a missed appointment or urgent business elsewhere and rush off to fulfill said obligation. Later, when they discovered their error, they would have completely forgotten what had triggered their wild goose chase in the first place.

The black cat from the other night alighted on his lap and immediately began to purr when he stroked her soft fur. Closing his eyes, enjoying her vibrations and the feel of the morning breeze caressing his face, he felt the last of his anger drift away. In this calmer state, he could admit that the situation was fascinating. Upon further reflection, he'd surmised that the ooze had supplanted the soul completely, a daunting prospect. He was curious to know how it had gotten there and where it had come from, but not so curious as to falter in his stance. It wasn't his problem.

When Michael appeared at the gate, Lucifer was glad he had placed wards preventing him or any other unwanted family from coming any closer. Otherwise, Michael would have been on the porch, spoiling his recently repaired mood, instead of at a marginally comfortable distance to Lucifer's left across the wide lawn. He should have known that his annoyingly pedantic brother would not let this go. If it involved what Michael perceived as his duty—and everyone else's—he would be relentless, refusing to give an inch until he got his way. Of course he wouldn't accept Lucifer's non-involvement. Why should this time be any different?

"You know, I've always loved the sea. It has the unique ability to cleanse the soul of unpleasantness," Lucifer said, knowing Michael could hear him easily, despite the angle and distance.

"You are not on the sea," Michael replied.

"And you, brother mine, are tedious and predictable."

There was no immediate reply, although Lucifer knew he was still there.

"I didn't realize you hated us this much." It surprised Lucifer to hear a touch of sorrow in Michael's voice.

Lucifer sighed, tamping down the sudden wave of guilt. "I find it hard to believe that you actually care," he replied honestly, no longer wanting to hold on to pretense.

Again, Michael took a moment to reply. "At the time, it seemed like the right thing to do."

Still stroking the cat in his arms, Lucifer stood and walked with her to the arched porch entrance, down the stone steps, and then along the winding path to the entrance gate. Once there, he made no move to invite Michael in but gazed at him over the waist-high gate.

"Making me the enemy seemed the right thing to do." He looked down at the cat and gave her a particularly thorough scratch under her chin. Blissed out, her purrs rose in volume, and she raised her head giving him more access. "How does that work, exactly?"

"Things just got out of hand," Michael replied with a helpless gesture. Still scratching, Lucifer said nothing, but instead tilted his head to the side, examining the obviously uncomfortable archangel. "It was an idea. One of many, actually. It just seemed to catch hold. Before we knew it, it was out of our control. For what it is worth, I am sorry."

Lucifer hadn't expected the honest confession—or the apology for that matter. If the Old Man was indeed behind this sudden reversal, he no longer cared. Warmth bloomed in his chest, and tears stung the corners of his eyes. It surprised him that it took so little to ease his soul. He kissed the top of the cat's head and bent over to put her down. When he stood straight again, his smile was warm and happy.

"It did work out exceptionally well for me, though, don't you think?" He laughed, crossing his arms and leaning on the gate.

"If you say so." Michael's perplexed look said he was being humored.

"I do, and you're jealous." Lucifer's smile widened, and he waved away Michael's impending protests. "How could you not be? I get to do as I please, live as I choose." His voice lowered conspiratorially. "And it some circles, my power rivals that of the Old Man himself." He chuckled, shaking his head.

"Must you call him that?" The others were used to it, but Michael always looked scandalized when he used that appellation.

Lucifer toed the ground around the gate. "When I left and changed my name, He stopped being my father," he said quietly. "I'll call Him whatever I choose."

Michael took a breath to say something but luckily heeded the warning glare thrown his way. That was an entirely different argument, and Lucifer refused to engage.

Still leaning on the gate, Lucifer straightened slightly and looked off into the distance. Swept away by the momentum of truth telling, he said, "I hated you for a long time. Hated the Old Man even more for letting you get away with it. Then one day it occurred to me that I had everything I ever wanted. I didn't have to debase or compromise myself in any way to have fear and respect." He looked at Michael. "I realized that my dear brothers had given the humans to me on a platter, and for that, I cannot hate you." His tone grew wistful, "If anything, I feel sorry for you. You run around doing the Old Man's bidding, bearing the yoke of responsibility, when you could be free."

Sensing a rebuttal, he altered the topic. "True, I have the fan club of idiots to deal with." He gestured toward Canes Inferni compound across the river and shrugged. "But they can be amusing, so I can't complain." He pushed off the gate and brushed imaginary dust off his pristine cream suit jacket. He'd felt the stirrings of past affinity, and his voice held regret when he said, "Although I've enjoyed this time to clear the air, if you've come for more—to try and convince me to help—you'll leave disappointed."

"You don't know everything. Let me explain, please."

Lucifer studied him. Michael's stoic mask had slipped. He saw urgency, but also...fear? What did Michael have to be afraid of? Concern, yes, but fear? Lucifer was intrigued and decided he'd listen. "Fine. Explain."

"You asked why we hadn't told Father about the threat. We haven't told Him," Michael paused before reluctantly continuing, "because we haven't seen Him." Lucifer was about to interrupt when Michael stopped him. "Wait, let me finish." He took a deep breath. "I also told you that things changed at home. It's actually worse than that."

Lucifer couldn't conceal his disappointment and subsequent contempt. "How coddled are you that when the Old Man takes a vacation you run around like scared rabbits?"

"Stop interrupting me. It's not just that Father is gone. The Garden is gone as well, as is the entire Host of Heaven. Nothing is as it should be, and we do not know why."

Lucifer was stunned into silence. He stared at his wild-eyed brother as he tried to regain his composure. It was inconceivable. Was this some kind of trick? He studied his companion, and realized this was why he was afraid. No—terrified. But it made no sense. A shiver ran through him. If it was true... His first instinct was to go see for himself, but that wasn't wise. He needed more information.

He opened the gate and stepped through. Inviting Michael in would have meant he'd have to take down or alter the wards, and he wasn't willing to do that quite yet.

"Walk with me," he said, taking Michael's arm and steering him down the street to White Point Garden. There, he sat on a bench near one of the war monuments and his favorite live oak. "Sit," he said, patting the seat beside him.

When Michael was comfortably seated, Lucifer promptly stretched out and put his head in his lap. He barely acknowledged Michael's surprised squawk.

"What?"

Lucifer calmly looked up at him, satisfied with his bemused expression. "If not for you, I'd have a lap full of beautiful vampire. The least you could do is console me or take his place." Michael remained silent but was clearly uncomfortable. Lucifer nodded. "That's what I thought. Now get to it." He closed his eyes and settled in.

Lucifer knew Michael was debating the wisdom of shoving him off his lap. He also knew that he wouldn't, because they both needed the physical comfort. He had been unnerved seeing Michael so afraid and knew it was something his brother was not accustomed to feeling, much less showing. It was roundabout and awkward, but it was easier for both of them than asking for a hug.

Michael removed the cream, velvet ribbon Lucifer used to tie his hair back and then dug his fingers into the soft, thick hair in his lap. Lucifer, almost purring at the soothing ministrations of Michael's fingers, set about gathering more information.

"How long has everything been gone?"

It took a moment for Michael to answer, and when he did, the tension was absent from his voice. "No one is sure." He was quiet for a while, thinking, then asked, "When were you home last?"

"A few thousand years, at least. Not since...him," Lucifer answered quietly.

He heard the catch in Michael's breath. Neither one of them wanted to think about that. Michael let loose a small sigh before speaking. "I had feared as much. Azrael believes it has been at least three thousand years or more." He sighed. "He is the one that first brought it to my attention."

"Brought what, exactly, to your attention?"

"The changes. According to Azrael, they were small at first, barely noticeable, but as they grew more apparent, we were somehow charmed." His fingers stilled. "We didn't notice. To us, everything was as it should have been. Only Azrael was unaffected, but we do not know why."

Lucifer sat up and turned to him. It sounded too fantastic to be true. "How is that even possible?"

Agitated, Michael got up to pace. He ran his hand over his head. "I don't understand it myself. Somehow, everything managed to change, and we never noticed anything was wrong. It was like walking into a room and having everything be exactly as you expect it. Even though the furniture had been rearranged, you don't notice, because you believe it was that way all along." He turned tortured eyes to Lucifer. "Father had vanished, and *we never noticed.*"

Lucifer couldn't imagine it, and he knew Michael saw the disbelief in his eyes.

"I know. How could we not know? How could we?"

Ignoring the question of how it could be possible for the moment, Lucifer asked his most pressing question. "What happened? How did you find out?"

Michael came over and sank back down on the bench. "As I said, Azrael knew. How or why we do not know, but he did. He also knew fruit of the Tree of Knowledge would cause us to see as well. It took a lot of work on his part, but finally I ate it and saw for my own eyes what had happened to our beloved home."

They were quiet for a while, each lost in his own thoughts. It sounded too fantastic to be true, like an elaborate practical joke—a stellar practical joke that he would undoubtedly be capable of pulling off, but the others? Michael had no sense of humor, and Azrael had even less. In fact, none of the humorless bunch he called brothers was capable of such a hoax. Which left only one other—what was the Old Man playing at, and why? He set aside that question for the moment in favor of the other problem Michael had brought to his attention.

"Do you think this is connected to that black ooze?"

"No. Yes. Probably? I honestly do not know." Apparently unable to be still for long, Michael stood and paced again. "If they are related, we have not been able to discover how."

Feeling the need to move as well, Lucifer got up and moved around the bench to the tree standing behind it. One of its thick branches was chest height, almost parallel to the ground. He loved live oak trees; they commanded the ground around them, fierce and alive. Lifting his hand, he traced the patterns made by the bark while he thought.

There was no other decision to make really. He had to go and see for himself.

He turned to tell Michael but was prevented from speaking by the raw grief on his brother's face. Michael caught him looking and wiped his face of the expression but not before Lucifer was confident he'd read it correctly.

Was there more? He could see in the stiff lines of Michael's body that there was. A hot flash shot through him as his temper rose. Why did Michael have to be so stingy with his information? He'd been persuaded to help. What more did he want? It only occurred to him just now that he'd changed his mind. Cursing to himself, he shoved the fact that he could be so easily manipulated by his brother's pain to the corner of his mind.

"What aren't you telling me?" He snapped, easily redirecting the anger he felt for himself outward.

Michael didn't answer and still refused to look him in the eye.

"If you want my help, you will speak now, or I walk away." The last thing he needed right now was for his brother to be his irritating, stubborn self.

He felt a familiar tingling in his mind. Startled and suspicious, he acknowledged Michael's use of telepathy by opening his mind enough to let him in.

It is only speculation, but nothing else makes sense.

Lucifer crossed his arms to physically restrain himself from grabbing Michael and shaking until every last drop of information spilled out.

What if Father... is dead?

He didn't hear the last word as much as he felt the anguish the thought caused Michael. The pain of it was clear in his unguarded face and the tears in his eyes.

He scoffed despite Michael's distress. "You can't be serious." He almost laughed. "That's ridiculous." He waved it away.

Really? How can you be sure? Can you hear Him? Can you? Can you hear Him now? Michael asked.

Lucifer just looked at him. He'd closed himself off long ago. At first, he'd missed it, the connection, the belonging. Eventually, he'd gotten used to the feeling, to the hole His absence created within. Over time, he'd trained his mind to ignore it.

Now, though, to spite Michael, he opened himself fully. Immediately he was assaulted by the joy, pain, and despair of the despised humans across the planet, the voices of his brothers, and the distinctive and longed for hum of the Old Man. He looked at Michael, turned, and walked away.

He'd fallen for their ruse. Starting in his chest and moving up to his throat, the embarrassment crept through him like rust until he was choking with it. It overwhelmed him so badly that he couldn't even lash out with rage at being duped. All he could do was put his head down and walk away. He'd believed it, believed everything.

He was midway through the park when Michael jogged up beside him. "Luc, wait."

Lucifer stopped and lunged toward him, fists tight and teeth bared. "Don't call me that. You don't get to call me that. What did you think would happen? Did you think that having you, having Him in my head again would change things?" It did. The loneliness made his insides ache. He turned and continued walking. "Go away, Michael. Congratulations, your performance was stellar, and your little trick worked. Now just—" A fruit was shoved into his line of vision. He stopped and stared at it.

"I didn't think you'd be affected," Michael said, apology coloring his voice. "Try again. Please."

Lucifer stared at the fruit, his mouth watering, reacting instantly to that reminder of home. His first instinct was to shove Michael's hand away and resume walking. Even though he was upset and embarrassed, a part of him had been relieved, glad for the knowledge that none of it was true. He remembered that look of desperate agony on Michael's face, and for the first time in his life, he too was afraid.

Michael took his hand and gently placed the fruit in his palm. In their language he said, "Brother, dispel the illusion and see."

Reluctant but resigned, he closed his eyes and placed the red fruit on his tongue. Once he bit down, the effects were immediate. Whereas before he could hear his brothers, feel the Old Man—now in their place was nothing.

"You don't hear anything, do you?" Michael asked gently.

Lucifer was staggered on his feet. Opening himself only to find a void was like crossing a threshold only to find the ground missing on the other side. The vertigo made him close his eyes, but that only amplified the loss. Now the weight of the isolation became so intense as to be suffocating.

His eyes flew open, and he looked at Michael agape, still trying to understand what he was feeling. He walked with halting steps, arms stretched out with yearning, to a nearby tree to steady himself. Holding it, using its presence to ground him, feeling it vibrate with life, his eyes flooded and overflowed. For the first time in his long life, he found himself at a loss as to what to do.

Michael came over and put his hand on his shoulder. He should have been ashamed to be caught distraught and trembling, but he turned and clung to Michael because he was the only real, enduring thing left to hold on to. His soul denied the possibility of what his senses had shown him. He could do nothing but clutch his brother close, breathe, and let the tears flow. When the intensity of the emotion passed, he touched his forehead to Michael's and rested it there.

"I don't know what's going on, but I refuse to believe He's dead, because He isn't." He could tell Michael wasn't convinced. "I know what the evidence is, and I don't believe it. All I know is that He is not dead."

Michael's face crumpled then, and once again Lucifer succumbed to emotion and wept. They hugged each other in desperation, each reassuring the other while releasing their own pain and fear.

"He's not dead. I know it, and I'll prove it," he whispered to Michael, who could only cry harder in response.

* * *

"Lord Lucifer, you are a hard one to find. I see Lord Michael is with you. Good. Now, Lord Michael, please turn over your sword, and both of you come with us."

The female voice startled them both. Neither had any idea how long they'd been clinging to each other. It was long enough for their tears to dry, but not long enough that they no longer needed comfort. They parted and turned toward the unfamiliar voice.

She, or rather they, were like nothing he'd ever seen. Five identical warriors stood before them, each with onyx skin that was complemented to stunning effect by long, braided, silver-white hair. Their eyes appeared a silvery white as well, but it could have been a trick of light. They were dressed for battle; all had swords on each hip and unfamiliar but deadly-looking blades strapped in various places on their bodies. Whoever they were, they were not only beautiful but also quite dangerous.

Lucifer stepped forward and addressed the group, haughty mask in place. "Firstly, you apparently know us, but we have no idea who you are. Rules of polite society demand introductions. Secondly, neither of us will be accompanying you anywhere, nor will he be giving up his sword, so it would be best if you forget that little request, as we already have."

He was happy to be back on familiar ground. He may not know who they were, but he was more than satisfied with his and Michael's abilities, should it come to a fight. He hoped it would. Violence right now was bound to be extremely therapeutic.

"We are Onyda, Warriors of the Nammu," replied the one he assumed was the leader. She inclined her head in greeting. "It is your Father's trespass that you do not know of us."

"What do you know of our Father?" Michael demanded. He'd unsheathed and readied his sword.

"All will be explained when you relinquish your weapon and come with us." The five stood unmoving, waiting.

Upon closer examination, Lucifer noticed that they weren't actually identical. They appeared to be from different species. The leader had a deep, ugly scar bisecting the left side of her face. Otherwise she looked human. Another one had cat-like eyes and pointed ears. It was the skin, hair, and eyes—not a trick of light, he noticed—that made them seem identical. Despite the differences and the scar, they were breathtaking. All were tall and wore identical grey, efficient but attractive clothes of unknown design. The clothes, he could tell, covered sleekly muscled and well-formed bodies. Idly, he found himself wondering what it would be like to have those powerful legs wrapped around his waist as he pulled on that beautiful hair and—

Focus, Michael snapped in his head. *This is what you think about?*

Lucifer had forgotten he was still open and was reminded why it wasn't a good idea to remain that way.

First, out of my head. Second, if you weren't dead from the waist down, you wouldn't ask stupid questions. He could feel Michael mentally rolling his eyes. *Have you seen them before? Is this the machination of one of the Fallen?*

I thought you wanted me out of your head. Michael sent a wave of amusement in reply to Lucifer's annoyed mental huff. *No, I have never seen them before, nor have I heard of them. If they were a product of one of the Fallen, I would know*

The entire exchange between the archangels took seconds. Lucifer eyed the Onyda and answered her challenge.

"I don't care who you are or who you represent. I don't recognize whatever authority you may think you have. If you would like to explain yourselves, I will listen. Otherwise, I suggest you leave."

"We were advised that you might be difficult. If you will not surrender yourselves, you will be taken by force." Once the leader finished speaking, they attacked en masse, blades flashing, expertly separating the archangels.

Lucifer recovered quickly, surprised at how good they were. Obviously seasoned fighters, he had underestimated the Onyda's ability to pose even the slightest challenge. He had to work to keep their blades from touching him. There were three on him and two on Michael.

He'd never been one to use a weapon, instead preferring to rend and bleed his opponents with his own hands. It was immensely satisfying, but now it left him at a disadvantage. The Onyda fought skillfully with two blades, which meant that he was constantly ducking and moving out of reach of the weapons. They never let him get close enough to grab and were impossible to disarm. He knew it shouldn't be possible, but they seemed to anticipate his every move. Feints were countered. If he teleported, they appeared and attacked him at his destination. In combat, they were evenly matched, neither side gaining any advantage. A glance over at Michael told him a different story.

The two Onyda fighting the archangel were using very different tactics than the three on Lucifer. Those two were relentless in their assault. All three had been cut or slashed. While Michael had reach and power, they had more speed and agility. With their two swords against his one, he spent more time defending than attacking and was losing ground.

The three Onyda fighting Lucifer didn't fight with half the vigor of their compatriots, who were obviously fighting to the death. He realized that the three on him were to keep him distracted while the other two took Michael down.

While he didn't think they could actually kill Michael, or himself for that matter, there was no way to be sure. They had power. The blades were made of an unknown material engraved with unfamiliar runes.

The world of yesterday was not the same as the world of today.

Lucifer no longer felt confident in the things he could assume to be true. He didn't like it, but a retreat was the best plan of action.

Gathering his power, he released it in a blast toward the Onyda. They were hurled back but not far enough. He gathered more for a bigger blast but then reconsidered. The entire park was a war memorial—weapons were all over the place. He recalled the piles of welded-together cannonballs along the periphery. One cannonball could be effective, but how about a pile of sixty-five?

Using his power to pick up five separate piles, he sent them hurling at each Onyda simultaneously. The two he sent toward the Onyda on Michael hit the warriors squarely, having taken them by surprise. The piles he sent to the Onyda on him—two deflected theirs while the third cleaved hers cleanly in two—gave him just enough of a distraction to grab Michael and escape.

Six

Remember me.

A choked sob was all he could manage as his world gradually disappeared before him. He crumbled to his knees as the echo of the request played over in his mind. Remember me.

An unsettled Kai walked the back halls of the City, heading toward Te's office. He took the longer, roundabout route to avoid as much of the Other-kin population as he could. Currently, the only ones he came in contact with were the gentle Eineu servants who scurried out of his way when they saw him, and that was just fine with Kai in his current state of mind.

He didn't often dream of his master, but when he did, it always left him uneasy. It didn't help any to wake up in an empty bed. Lucifer was usually there when he woke, impatient to get his hands on him. Instead when he opened his eyes, he was greeted with the baleful stare and low growls of the newest cat Luc had acquired. Luc liked to call them "earthly angels," and with Kai's grudging acceptance, they were always in residence. Apparently, this particular "angel" didn't know the rules of the house yet, as it followed him from room to room, arching and hissing. Kai knew he was protected, but it still rankled that he felt chased from his own home by a cat. His list of annoyances kept growing by the minute.

He was on edge. Sex or feeding, or both, would have gone a long way to release the tension in his body and the clouds in his mind. The brothels were always open to him, but he knew he should only satisfy one of those desires there, and it held little appeal.

For all of Lucifer's boast and bluster, he was surprisingly possessive. Kai was mildly shocked when he found out, and at first was uncomfortable with the arrangement. The idea that Lucifer wanted exclusive rights to his body seemed stifling. Granted, he'd been with his master for over two hundred years before meeting Lucifer, but they both had other sexual partners—sex led to feeding or vice versa. It was a natural progression.

As their association grew, however, he was surprised to find that while the dictate seemed restrictive, it actually wasn't. Having Lucifer in his life was all-encompassing; there was simply no room for anyone else. Kai was more than satisfied. Except now. Now he wanted his lover and was annoyed that he hadn't found him already.

He entered the small antechamber of Te's office and was taken by two surprises. The first was that the usually absent Stephan was sitting at his desk, and the second was finding the door to the inner office closed. Being extremely jovial and welcoming, Te rarely closed the door. It existed mostly to finish the room. He shot a warning glance to

Stephan to keep his mouth shut and cautiously knocked on the door.

Kai was about to turn and leave when Te opened the door. Today's suit was canary yellow, the festive color clashing with his somber expression.

"Come in." He gestured toward one of the wing chairs that stood opposite the desk. Kai took the offered chair and waited for the troubled demon to speak.

Te held up one finger, signaling Kai to wait, before making a complex gesture. Kai felt the magic tingle over him and looked at Te, bemused. "Stephan has been particularly nosy today."

Kai snorted in amusement at the thwarting of Stephan's plans to eavesdrop. He settled back in the chair, eager to hear what was on Te's mind.

"We have a problem," Te said as he walked around to his desk and sat down.

"Who do I have to kill?" Kai responded, trying to lighten the mood.

"That's exactly the problem." Te's silver eyes focused on his desk for a moment before looking up and fixing on him. "That youngling you killed last night—"

"Let me guess," Kai interrupted. "The Kazat won't willingly dismiss it. The little shit insulted me. I was perfectly within my rights to kill it."

Te nodded his head. "I know, and technically you didn't break Other-kin law. But—"

"They still want vengeance," Kai interrupted again.

Te leaned back in his chair, eyeing him. "You know how they feel about their young."

"I'm sure it doesn't help matters that the youngling's killer just happened to be *Lucifer's pet.*" Te made a non-committal gesture, but before he could speak, Kai waved a dismissive hand. "Fine. We'll settle this at Court."

"I had thought that once you'd calmed down, you'd change your mind. You're serious? You really mean to go through with this?"

"I do." Kai got up, walked toward the wall of glass, and stood in front of it looking out. "They don't respect me, Te." He turned to face him. "Worse, they don't *fear* me. Even younglings feel they can insult me." Strength must be shown; he was a rightful master, and holding Court was the most direct way of reminding everyone of that fact. He knew Te understood, so why was he fighting this?

Te looked at Kai, concern plain on his face. When he spoke, it was obvious he'd chosen his words carefully. "Are you at all concerned that your long disdain for politics has placed you at a disadvantage?"

"No."

"Well, I am. Plus, you've spent the last seven hundred years traipsing about with Lucifer. You're out of touch."

"You're saying I'm weak."

"No, I'm saying you're inexperienced and possibly too much of a beta for your own good."

Kai recoiled, taking a step back as if hit. Te rose and swiftly crossed the room. When he was close enough, he placed a hand on Kai's shoulder, a gesture meant to soothe, even if the result was Kai tensing to the point of pain.

When he spoke, his voice was gentle. "I mean no insult. I worry; that's all."

Kai had forced himself to maintain eye contact throughout. "I am beta to you and Luc. Not to Lugan or the rest of my clan, and certainly not to the Kazat."

"My apologies." Te squeezed his shoulder, and Kai relaxed. Te then crossed his arms and studied him. "Remember, you are the rightful leader of the clan. If you decide to hold Court, Lugan will think you're making a play for power, and technically he'll be right. Are you prepared for the consequences?"

Kai shook his head, frustrated. "I don't want to lead the clan. All I want is to assert my position as a master."

He was out of his depth. His plan had been to hold Court, assert his rights, and be done with it. He honestly had no idea that it was any more complicated than that. Te was right; he had no idea what he was doing.

His confusion must have shown on his face because Te raised a calming hand. "In this instance, what you want is immaterial."

Kai turned back to the window, afraid Te was right. He didn't want to fight Lugan. He didn't want to have to kill his brother over something he didn't want.

Te stepped up to join him at the window and mirrored his posture looking out over the City. "Calling for Court, even if you hold it here in the City, will be a challenge to

Lugan's authority. But there is another way. It's rare, but there is precedent. Have you ever heard of a Rendering?"

Kai looked at him and shook his head.

"It was very popular during Uru's time. Court is a private affair within a clan. A Rendering, while following the basic Court pattern, is really nothing more than a public spectacle. It was designed to resolve disputes between individuals, species, and sometimes clans as an alternative to war. They were discontinued when it became apparent that the Kazat were using them to skew the balance of power to their advantage. Given the circumstances, I can decree that you and the Kazat settle your differences in a Rendering. Everyone knows there's bad blood between you and the Kazat, and once explained, it shouldn't be seen as anything else. As the Rendering will be independent of Clan Air, Lugan's leadership should remain unquestioned. But I warn you, I don't call it a 'spectacle' lightly. It will be open to all residents, and the decorum of Court will likely be abandoned in favor of rowdy and unrestrained enthusiasm."

"When I defeat the Kazat champion, it will be worth it."

Te smiled. "They do need to be put in their place. Just make sure you give the audience a show. I can schedule it for day after tomorrow, unless you want it sooner."

Kai nodded, relief and gratitude making him relax. "Day after tomorrow is fine. Thank you." Now that that was settled, he raised what was really on his mind. "Have you seen Luc?"

Te's eyebrows rose, and he turned to face him. "I thought he was home with you. You mean he's not back yet?"

Kai walked back to his vacated chair and slumped into it. "No," he grumbled. "What in the world could be taking so long?"

Te followed and stood nearby. He reached out and gently touched Kai's chin, tilting his head up so he could get a good look at his face. "You don't look good. When was the last time you fed?"

Kai tried to pull away. "It doesn't matter. Don't fuss." When Te didn't back off he sighed. "A few days," he lied. "Also, I dreamt of my master last night, and with Luc not here... I don't know. I suppose I'm just restless."

Te knew about Kai's master's sudden disappearance on a desolate Scottish road and how Lucifer had found him hours later, still weeping and waiting for the sun. Kai would have died had Lucifer not cajoled him into living one more day and then another and still another. They had been together ever since.

He placed his wrist in front of Kai's mouth. "Drink."

Kai tried to pull away, but Te wouldn't let him. Blood was blood, true, but if Kai didn't want human blood, he wanted demon blood even less.

Te sensed his unwillingness and pressed harder. "Stop this foolishness. Luc could be a while, so let me take care of you."

Reluctantly, Kai acquiesced. Closing his eyes, he bit gently into the offered wrist. Immediately, the blood's power

110

slammed into him, zinging through his body, sparking his nerve endings. He barely noticed Te's soothing strokes in his hair as his world whited out in the rush of pleasure. Once he'd drunk his fill, Te removed his wrist from the limp puddle of vampire Kai had become and walked back over to the window.

"You..." was all Kai could manage—when he could finally speak again. He was in shock and still reeling with the knowledge.

"One of the Fallen? Yes. You mean you really didn't know?"

"I was never sure. Why didn't you ever say anything?" Kai was floating on the angelic blood, and it was glorious.

"It never came up. Besides, I reinvented myself, didn't I?" Te said, his hearty laugh reverberating throughout the room.

Kai frowned, his brain still a tick behind. Finally, he collected himself enough to turn and face Te. "You were the one prophesied?"

Te's grin turned conspiratorial. "It's easy to prophesy yourself into being, wouldn't you say?"

Kai's eyes widened, and he stood up. "You were Uru?"

"Brilliant, yes?"

That his lover was Lucifer and he'd had dealings with the other archangels should have lessened the blow caused by this revelation, but it didn't. Lucifer had shattered many an illusion, and while this one had come from a different source, his feeling was the same. Disillusionment always hurt. True, it explained so much—the little inconsistencies,

Te's loyalty to Lucifer—but it instantly proved everything he'd known or believed about the City to be untrue.

"I am honored that you told me, but…"

Te looked as though he understood. "I'm sorry. I wouldn't have done it if you weren't hurting. I can only imagine how disappointing this must be. But nothing's changed. I was the dragon god. I took a… hiatus… and then came back as foretold, this time in my true form. That's pretty much all there is to it."

"Says the former dragon god." The bitterness Kai felt infused his voice, but he couldn't help it. His eyes drifted to the tapestry behind Te's desk. Every Other-kin was beholden to Uru, because without him, they wouldn't exist. The lore was deep, and rich with courage and sacrifice. It was also, apparently, all lies. He would laugh about the falsities of human belief, but not the falsities of his own.

"We'll not speak of if again unless you want to." Te's silver eyes sparkled with love and mischief. "So, feeling better?"

Te's lighter mood hijacked his darker one, and Kai laughed. "Much, as I'm sure you're aware."

"Good. We need to talk about last night."

"I know. It was one unforeseen event after another. In fact—" Kai had been walking toward Te as he spoke, but what he saw through the window cut off his train of thought. "You should see this," he told Te, indicating the unusual scene outside. Frowning, Te turned and let out a surprised whistle.

"Well, that's unexpected."

Uriel was making his way slowly down the avenue. The crowd knew who he was and stood well out of his way, watching in awe and fear as he approached. Recognition of the archangels had been ingrained in the Other-kin from the beginning. They knew who they owed their lives to and who could erase them from existence, should they forget their place.

Rooted by curiosity, they marked the passage of the regal figure in outdated dress as he made his way into the City. While most instinctively stepped back, some kneeled as he passed. His presence was unprecedented.

The archangel stopped in the center and looked up at Te. Although it was a fair distance, Kai had a feeling that made no difference and was soon proven right.

"Welcome to the City, Archangel Uriel. My house, and all within, is yours to command," Te said in a normal speaking voice. Kai could hear it amplified down in the City, enabling all the inhabitants to hear.

Uriel acknowledged Te with a slight incline of his head.

"You honor the City by your presence. Please, come visit with me in my office. John will escort you." An Eineu in a yellow tunic hurried to meet Uriel and, after bowing a few times, led him through the crowd and toward the exit that led to the ramps to Te's office.

"Wonder what that's about," Kai said.

"As do I. I haven't seen Uriel in ages. We'll meet for a drink later, and I'll catch you up, and you can catch me up on last night's activities," Te said, throwing an arm around Kai and leading him out the door. In the antechamber, he spoke to Stephan. "I'm calling a Rendering between Kai and a champion of Kazat choosing." A stack of papers appeared on the desk. "Everything you need to know is right there. Begin preparations immediately."

Te squeezed Kai in a half-hug before letting go. Kai acknowledged him with a smile and smirked at the sight of Stephan gingerly poking at the stack of paper like it was a fetid pile of rags instead of a work assignment. He supposed that in the blond vampire's mind, there was little difference. He chuckled at the absurdity as he left and headed down into the City.

The big room was alive with speculation, and Kai was as curious as everyone else. He strolled among the marketplace, listening to the gossip and mulling over Uriel's arrival. Why had he presented himself in such a public way? And what did he and Te have to talk about?

Seven

Lucifer took Michael dimension hopping—a means of escape that, if done subtly enough, would be impossible to follow. Fortunately, it was something at which he was extremely proficient, his ability honed by the necessity of avoiding notice or interference by his family.

The Onyda shouldn't have been able to follow them after the first shift, but he wasn't sure of their capabilities, so he moved them through four more dimensions before decreeing them safe enough. Then he took them through five more, just to be sure. During the last stop, he checked Michael's wounds, which, to his relief, were well on their way to being healed.

He was about to say something when the look on Michael's face stopped him. Was that awe? When Michael caught him looking, it was swiftly replaced by disapproval.

Interesting.

Michael's scowl deepened, and Lucifer laughed. "Even when it saves your life, you disapprove. You're such a piece of work, brother mine."

"There is a reason why dimensional travel is forbidden."

It was forbidden because the dimensions were only theoretical until they were visited; once visited, they became real. It was forbidden because it was the only way they could create Life. Lucifer would have pressed his point about Michael being dead if he hadn't, but he could see in the rigid line of his brother's jaw and his narrowed eyes that there was no point. He'd broken the rules, no matter the end.

Lucifer shook his head, sighed, and instead said, "Take us to the others."

Michael's eyes shifted away from him and fixed in the middle distance. "I do not know how."

Of course. In this case, to learn, you actually had to *do.* "Fine. I'll take us back to the Prime; you take over once we get there."

Michael clenched his jaw but said nothing, only nodded.

* * *

To Lucifer's surprise, they ended up in a large cavern in a cave system somewhere in China. The system was deep, and access to it had been sealed and warded to prevent accidental discovery by humans or colonization by Otherkin. Raphael, Gabriel, Azrael, and about fifty to sixty lower ranking angels from various houses were dwarfed by the vast space that once wouldn't have held a fraction of the entire Host of Heaven. The lower angels instantly drew their weapons when they saw him.

"Stand down," Michael ordered.

"Please, no need to fuss on my account," Lucifer said as he swept past him into the chamber.

116

"Why is the traitor here?" an angel asked Michael, his eyes never leaving Lucifer.

"We need him," Michael responded.

"Rumors of my traitorous nature have been greatly exaggerated," Lucifer said as he brushed the dust off a large outcropping of rock with a wave of his hand and sat down.

Michael gave him a sour look and then addressed all the lower angels in the room. "All you need to know is that he is with us."

The angel who had spoken bowed but kept his eyes on Lucifer.

"Thank you for joining us," Raphael said, approaching him with a relieved smile. Suddenly uncomfortable, Lucifer cast his eyes around the cavern—anywhere to distance himself from the hope that shone in his brother's eyes.

"We had an incident," Michael said before telepathically showing the gathered angels the Onyda and their subsequent fight and flight.

As he didn't need to relive it again, Lucifer paid little attention, his focus turned to the protections set up around the cavern that glowed with colorful, incandescent light within the ultraviolet spectrum. Moving from his perch, he strode around the space, examining its intricate warding.

Raphael whistled. "Onyda? I've never seen anything like that. Never heard of this 'Nammu' either."

Quiet speculation as to their identity and origin followed. Lucifer's attention was still on the wards as he moved about the room.

Michael walked forward until he entered Lucifer's space. "Is there a problem? Every one of your homes on Earth is warded against us. You cannot possibly take issue with this."

"I'm merely surprised you're as accomplished as you are. This work is extensive. Careful, one might doubt your loyalty."

Michael's violet eyes turned flinty as he took another step forward. Lucifer grinned—Michael was so easily riled. He stepped in so that they were nearly chest-to-chest.

When he spoke, his voice was low. "I've warded my homes against you for a reason, as you are well aware. Assassination attempts by overzealous lackeys have a tendency to become tedious."

"I will not spend the rest of my life apologizing to you," Michael replied, his voice matching Lucifer's in pitch.

"You should," Lucifer replied with a smirk. "Groveling suits you." Stepping back and turning away, he surveyed the group in the chamber. It was time to take charge. If Michael had a problem with that... well, it was in Michael's best interest if he didn't. "Is this it? Are you all that's left?" he asked, addressing the group.

Michael answered him. "Yes, this is it."

"Where's Uriel?"

"Uriel hasn't been taking this well," Raphael said. "He's been in and out of touch. We can rely on him when necessary, but…" He trailed off and shrugged.

Given Uriel's nature, it wasn't surprising. He would want to act, not sit around talking about action. "What about the pantheons of the Fallen? Do they know what's going on? Are any willing to help?" *Fallen* was a misnomer used for convenience among them. They used it because it was easier, not because it was accurate.

"Since Azrael is considered neutral, he was asked to approach our Fallen brethren," Michael said.

That was a good choice. Death had no hidden agenda. Azrael's house served all humans, no matter who they worshipped. Dressed in grey robes and somber as the grave, when Azrael spoke, his deep voice resounded in the cavern, causing vibrations in the stone.

"Of the Hindu, Vishnu, Krishna, and Kali are all that is left. They are in hiding, much like us, but have pledged their support. The remaining Loa are convinced Father is not only testing them but also meting out judgment. They will not help. The Fae and Sidhe fled this world centuries ago. The Aztecs refuse to speak to me; thus, I have been unable to ascertain how they fare. The Greeks, Norse, and Egyptians appear to have been destroyed, although I have no confirmation on this. The rest have either been destroyed, fled, or are in such deep hiding that I cannot find them. I will continue to search."

"What about Other-kin?" Lucifer asked.

"We were hoping you'd speak to Te," Raphael replied. "He's bound to be more receptive to you."

Lucifer nodded in agreement, "Azrael, it's imperative that you find the others and get as many as you can to join us."

"Of course." The archangel bowed and disappeared.

Even though this was the worst situation they'd ever faced, Lucifer was enjoying himself. Leading his brothers in battle during the Purge had been exhilarating, and he looked forward to doing it again. He glanced at Michael and was pleased to see he seemed content to step back. A fight for control would be messy and inconvenient.

His eyes traveled around the cavern, inexorably drawn to the deficiencies in the warding that he'd noticed earlier. While the warding was the best his brothers could do, there were lapses because they were unused to hiding. Their sanctuary wasn't as safe as it could be. He would have mentioned it had Michael not come at him with hackles raised.

Not that he acted any better, since his immediate response had been to taunt rather than explain. At some point, they would need to stop treating each other like enemies. The enmity between them was a habit. There was no real feeling behind it, not anymore, but like all habits, so easy to fall back into without thinking.

Solving the problem of the wards would be easily fixed, but unfortunately, he knew Michael would fight the idea—even if it was the only way he knew of to keep them truly safe during the planning and subsequent operations. "We need a more secure location."

"I know what you would say, brother, and the answer is no."

"This place is not safe. Even now I can see gaps in the warding. It's only a matter of time before it's breached."

"Then fix them. The other is out of the question."

"Michael, stop fighting me and think. You heard Azrael. If he can't find the others, the Onyda won't be able to find *us*."

Lucifer saw when realization struck both Raphael and Gabriel, but it was Raphael who spoke first. "You would hide in another dimension."

"It is forbidden," Gabriel said.

"But he's right, it would be impossible to find us," Raphael countered.

"I will not agree to breaking the law."

Lucifer crossed his arms, put his head down, and counted. When he reached ten, he was still angry. By fifteen, he was resigned.

"Fine," he said, raising his head. "Stay here. I'm going to find us a place. Anyone who wants to survive long enough to fight back is welcome to join me."

If his brothers were willing to die rather than break the law so they could live to fight, then so be it. He walked toward the nearest gap in the wards, intending to shore it up. If they were going to stay, he'd do his best to protect them, even if he knew it was a lost cause.

Speaking of lost causes, ever since meeting the Onyda, he hadn't stopped to really think about their situation, but instead let each piece of information gather within his consciousness. Now, as he stood reinforcing the wards, he saw the reality for the first time with vibrant clarity.

They knew nothing about the Onyda—where they came from, their strengths, weaknesses, where they were based. This wasn't a war. At most, it was a siege, with them on the defensive, always trying to retain what little they had. The skirmish with five Onyda had nearly bested two of their most powerful fighters.

He stopped what he was doing and looked over the assembled angels—Raphael was still trying to convince Michael and Gabriel that a retreat into another dimension was their best option—and knew that if the Onyda had even half their numbers, they would lose.

"I would like to accompany you, if you don't mind," an angel said, breaking into his thoughts. Looking up, he saw the angel who'd challenged him earlier.

Lucifer turned and studied the angel closely for the first time. "What is your name?"

"Kadrael."

He felt an uneasy prickling sensation. "Tell me, Kadrael, why is it that I don't know you?"

Close enough to hear the question, his brothers stopped arguing.

"He is of Uriel's House," Michael said.

"No, he's of my House," Raphael said.

All eyes turned to Kadrael, who smiled—until his face melted.

The features of the angels around him changed as well.

In moments, an unknown male replaced Kadrael. An unknown female stood next to him. And at least twenty Onyda flanked them in a loose circle. There was something oddly familiar about the couple, but Lucifer had no time to think about why.

"Retreat," he yelled, moving to help cover the lower angels' escape. Understanding his plan, the archangels moved to do the same.

"Retreat now," Michael yelled, reinforcing Lucifer's command.

"That will be quite impossible," the male said, loud enough for everyone to hear.

Murmurs rippled through the assembled angels as it became clear that no one was able to dematerialize.

"You can only be the fabled Nammu I haven't heard so much about," Lucifer said, addressing the man and woman.

"I am called Anu," said the male. "And she is called Ki." He gestured to his companion. "We are fables only to the uneducated." The man's smile grew wide, and he walked the few steps toward Lucifer.

Recognition was a handful of puzzle pieces away as Lucifer's eyes swept over the Nammu. Anu and Ki could have been twins. Except for their gender, they appeared identical. Generic and bland, their faces were perfectly symmetrical, and Lucifer supposed that underneath the ankle-length, white shifts they wore, they were just as generic, just as unremarkable. He also supposed that it was the universal one-face-fits-all quality about their appearance, and that grey skin...

Shock zipped through him as the last piece slotted into place. It took a considerable amount of effort to keep his composure. He had seen those nondescript features and that grey skin that wasn't really grey, just every skin tone flashing by on a revolving loop, before. A glance to his brothers told him that they had seen the same thing and were using just as much effort to remain outwardly calm. His entire worldview had upended on the appearance of these two. But unfortunately, this would not be a happy family reunion.

"Somehow, I thought you'd be taller," he said, leaning back into the familiar territory of haughty bravado.

Anu chuckled. "How rude you are."

He seemed scandalously delighted, like an adult whose toddler uttered its first curse word. When he spoke again, it was with the kind of condescension the superior bestow upon the eternally dull-witted.

"Your Father has been remiss in your education."

The insult to their Father burned and made Lucifer want to rip into that perfectly uninteresting face. "Really? Then would you be so kind as to enlighten me, enlighten us?"

He gestured to the angels and archangels present.

"You wouldn't speak to us in that manner if you knew exactly whom you were addressing. That alone grants you a temporary pardon for your disrespect," Ki said.

Lucifer had a feeling he knew exactly whom he was addressing, and it changed nothing. He would face his death with nothing less than a contemptuous smirk on his lips before he'd cower to anyone. He crossed to the seat he'd held earlier and sat down, disrespect clear in his body language. Once seated, he produced a clove cigarette, lit it, and took a few leisurely puffs. While he smoked, the tension in the room rose, and he smiled at the Onyda shooting murderous glances his way.

"I'm sure if I knew to whom I was speaking, I'd be grateful for your pardon. At this moment however, I remain... unimpressed."

"Is that so?" Anu asked, the apoplectic look on his face telling Lucifer that he might have pushed too far. Secretly, he readied himself for violence but was still caught off-guard when a bright, blinding light flooded the cavern. His head was suddenly too small, too close.

He fell off the rock, screaming and clutching at his head, terrified his eyes would pop out of their sockets and his skull would burst like an overripe fruit.

Time passed—he lay unaware of how long, a few seconds or many hours—before he was finally able to open his eyes again. When he did, he was on the floor, his face wet with tears. Managing to sit up, he saw that the lower ranking angels were gone.

Fear threatened to overwhelm him, and it took more will than he thought he had to beat it back and then lock it down. Once he did, he was able to see that Michael, Raphael, and Gabriel remained. Catching Michael's eye, he saw a mirror of his own panic before Michael managed to get himself under control. It was apparent that the Nammu had, in an action faster than thought, incapacitated them and killed the lower angels. Remorse jockeyed for position with his outrage.

"Has this small display impressed you?" Ki asked. "The lesser of you," she said that as if they were bugs that needed swatting, "were destroyed by a mere fraction of our power. I warn you to think on that before you speak again."

The four of them exchanged looks. While Lucifer could see sadness, he also saw helplessness, and it was that that angered him the most. With dignity as his anchor, he wiped his face and got to his feet. The others stood as well. Gabriel glared at him in warning, and if he hadn't been so humbled, he would have ignored it.

"You honor us with your mercy," Gabriel said, bowing his head, his voice still shaky as he recovered.

Lucifer hated hearing the quiet reverence in his voice.

"Such lovely obsequiousness as befits your station. We are pleased," Ki said, beaming, before walking over to Gabriel and smoothing his long, red hair back over his shoulder, lifting his chin, and wiping the tears from his face. "This place is not so barbaric after all." She shot Lucifer a foul look.

"We are unworthy but humbled in your presence, as we remain in the presence of our Father," Gabriel said, his head lowering once again. Ki continued to stroke him as she would a beloved pet.

"An astute observation. You notice the resemblance and wonder why." She looked at Lucifer with undisguised contempt. "You may thank your brother for your continued existence and for the gift of our introduction."

Lucifer forced himself to look away. It was either that or say something inappropriate.

"We are a race of Creators—Gods of worlds far beyond the scope of your imagination and comprehension," Anu said, looking at each archangel with theatrical intensity.

Lucifer wanted so much to heckle him, to peel back that arrogant veneer. These two were much easier to take once the mask of civility had been stripped away. He preferred to feel terror instead of contempt.

Anu's voice rose with authority. "Paired with a complementary counterpart, male or female, our purpose is order. Order exemplified by our creations, each a mirror of our divine perfection. The inhabitants of each world in every universe live perfectly prescribed lives of classified productivity, each individual secure in the knowledge of his or her place in the scheme of things. The Perfection of Order—that is how We live, that is how it must be." He paused and eyed them each in turn, as if making sure they understood. Once satisfied, he resumed the lecture.

"Among Us however, there is a faction. This group—erroneously, mind you—believes that the chaos known as free will could somehow enrich Us, that We could possibly learn from the choices and experiences of Our creations. Utter nonsense, of course—as if We, the creators of untold worlds, were lacking in some way. With

Our most perfect love for them, We tried to dissuade the faction from this most destructive path and make them understand that no good could come of such a backward way of thinking. It was, unfortunately, to no avail, and We had to accept the inevitable—that they had turned away from the righteousness of Order." Visibly distressed, he stopped. Ki drifted away from Gabriel to embrace him.

Despite himself, Lucifer was fascinated. Why hadn't the Old Man ever mentioned any of this? It was obvious that He'd been a member of this faction, but at least if his brothers and he had known, they could have been prepared. They could have mounted some defense, but as it was, they'd been blindsided.

Damn that fool! Now they were all to die because He had to keep secrets. It didn't surprise him in the least, just made him more resentful. He watched with the others as Ki murmured softly to Anu before he disengaged, once more fit to continue their instruction.

"We are constantly in the process of rooting out these heretics and destroying their creations. The universes are vast, with so many places to hide, but we are vigilant. The chaos must not be allowed to continue."

He paused mid-stride and took a deep breath.

"So here we are. We had been searching for your heretic Father and his mate for a long time. But they were clever. This solar system was not only isolated but had been created by another heretic long ago. It had already been found and destroyed, its Creators imprisoned."

His eyes were shining now, a feverish expression that looked out of place on a face that seemed designed to carry only neutrality or the occasional smile.

"It was brilliant, incredibly brilliant of them to use an isolated and dead system—but it was also their downfall. Because the system had been left to the Darkness for so long, it needed a sudden, massive infusion of Light for any creations to survive. It was that sudden, massive infusion of Light that acted as a beacon that drew us right to you."

He walked over to Lucifer and stood nose-to-nose. Lucifer locked his knees to prevent himself from recoiling at Anu's proximity and washed his face clean of betraying emotions so he could stare back.

"You should be asking yourselves, what was that sudden, massive infusion of Light?" Anu murmured.

When Lucifer still did not react, he smirked and turned away.

"I'll tell you what it was. It was the unthinkable. It was the unholy sacrifice of your Mother merging Herself with the planet in order for it to sustain life. Your Father's most heinous crime was to persuade Her to sacrifice Her most precious Self for His creation." Anu spit the last words on a voice tight with heightened emotion. He wanted vengeance, and Lucifer knew once the story was told, he would be taking it out on them.

"Actually, what was undoubtedly His most heinous crime," Ki said, her tone of voice suggesting her fatigue at continually having to correct her mate with this argument, "was in creating beings, yourselves included, with the blasphemy that is free will. It was unfair and a disservice to you to create you with the freedom to make your own choices, fully aware that such an inherent imperfection would cause your lives to be chaotic, pain-filled, and unproductive. All of your lives, a shameful waste. It breaks my heart; it truly does." For her part, she did look adequately regretful. "Your Father's crimes warrant our worst punishment—imprisonment in Hell."

She had to be lying, as there was no such place. There had been rumors among some of the Fallen of a place beyond the Old Man's reach, but he'd never believed it. But why lie? Why not just admit he was dead?

Lucifer didn't have time to try and make sense of it. A plan was taking shape in his mind. It was desperate and, by that definition, stupid enough to fail, but he could tell that the Nammu's tale was almost complete, and they were out of time. Hours before, he'd told them they were on their own, and now here he was trying to save them. It was almost funny.

I have an idea. Trust me and don't resist. He dismissed their curious expressions. *I need some time. Keep them busy.*

Slowly and gently, he drew upon his power.

"We are ignorant and beg your consideration. There is a black substance unknown to us. Would that be your doing?" Gabriel asked.

"Yes." The Nammu responded together. "No."

With a look to his counterpart, Anu spoke. "Both yes and no, actually. That 'black substance,' as you call it, is the Essull, the essence of the Old Ones, beings of Darkness that We banish as We expand the universes. No doubt your Father created His own seals. Did He ever tell you their true purpose? Seals are used at weak spots to shore up the integrity of Our creation. They are breaking now because We have weakened them to facilitate the destruction of this abomination. We are giving it back to the Darkness, returning it to where it belongs."

When he finished speaking, he stood opposite Ki, and the look they shared was nothing short of satisfaction.

Gabriel raised his hands in a show of prayerful obeisance. "My brothers and I thank you for your merciful indulgence."

The Nammu were smiling.

"We are beneficent beings, after all." Ki bowed her head to her mate. "We saw the lengths you went to, to unravel this mystery. We were surprised, quite frankly. It is a rare thing to discover the ruse." They chuckled in tandem. "It was the least we could do before killing you."

Lucifer sent a silent *thank you* to Gabriel. They'd all be dead now if they had to rely on anyone else—him specifically. He refocused on his task. He knew it was possible, having done it to himself and to Kai, but at that time, he'd had more time to get it right. He told himself that they would die today regardless, so if he failed, his brother's deaths wouldn't be on him. It was a small comfort.

Keep stalling.

"As your infinite knowledge has no doubt surmised, we have many questions. We ask your continued indulgence."

"Why, of course. We understand that you are in no hurry to die, and we welcome the chance to educate," Ki said, preening under the respect in Gabriel's manner and tone.

How could they be so cheery in the light of his and his brother's imminent execution?

"The Onyda, who are they?" Gabriel asked, gesturing at the warrior women still silently gathered in the cavern.

Anu beamed with pride at the question. "They are your equivalent, actually." He turned his beatific smile on the ones closest to him. "They are recruited from all the worlds in all galaxies, some across universes—many races, but one uniform standard. Aren't they magnificent?"

"Yes, most magnificent and worthy to serve your Grace," Gabriel agreed. "But…" He hesitated, and Anu urged him to continue with a nod. "If your worlds are created with order, why do you need them?"

It was time. Gabriel was out of questions.

"I was hoping you'd ask," Anu responded happily. "They are Our liaisons with the world's inhabitants, a visible reminder of Our glory. They are the priestesses in every temple. Through them, We are accessible to the populace in every way."

Relax and trust me.

Lucifer unleashed a massive burst of power, once again washing the cavern in blinding white light. The release wrung him out so badly that he sagged on his feet. When he raised his head, his brothers were gone. A chuckle tickled through his exhausted form and grew in strength until it was a full belly laugh. He didn't know if they were safe or destroyed, but he had robbed the Nammu of their prize—and that was enough for his soul to sing with satisfaction.

"What did you do?" The Nammu thundered in unison, the air vibrating with their anger.

"Denied you your vengeance," he replied, lightheaded and drained. He'd used more power than he ever had before. Although unsteady, he remained standing, intending to meet his end like any warrior should—on his feet.

The Nammu recognized his posture and shook their heads. "Do you think We would reward you with death? No. Now it is We who will deny you. The Essull that await you in Hell will covet this prize, although you may not feel as fortunate."

Their power hit him hard. For the third time, blinding white light filled the cavern. Lucifer felt himself moving fast and gaining in velocity. Then he felt nothing at all as blackness enveloped him and he lost consciousness.

Eight

Stephan sat in a chair by the woman's bed, puzzling over Kai's guest. Who was she, and why did Kai threaten him over her safety? He remembered his reaction, and it made him cringe. He'd all but rolled over and showed his belly. As it was, it took a huge amount of will not to bare his throat. It was embarrassing. Kai would pay for that and for so much more.

If only he could taste a drop of her blood, then he'd know everything. He couldn't risk Kai finding out, though—she'd been uninjured when she arrived. He jostled the bed. She continued to sleep.

Why won't she wake up? If she was awake, he could get her to tell him everything he wanted to know just by looking into her eyes. He bumped the bed harder—still nothing.

The Eineu he'd shooed out of the room when he'd entered peeked its head in. At least he thought it was the same one; fuckers all looked alike.

"Master must not disturb Miss," it said in a sibilant whisper. "Miss must rest. John to keep watch over Miss." He spoke without looking directly at him.

"Just what are you insinuating?" Stephan responded, eyes narrowed. The skittish creature jerked into a bow.

"John mean no offense, Master. John has duty to watch over Miss." It gave another jerky bow.

"You make me repeat myself, *John*." The inflection made the creature flinch. "I do not like to repeat myself. Leave. Now. If you bother me again, I will peel you like a grape. Is that understood?"

If he were able, Stephan would have purred in satisfaction at the sight of the terrified creature's hasty exit. One thing marred his pleasure: those creatures took what they perceived as their duty seriously. He had no doubt that it would go tattling to Te. It was a good idea for him to make his exit.

He stood up to leave, studying the woman once more. What was it? She was old—probably in her late thirties or early forties—and too fat to be attractive. She couldn't possibly be a trophy. It made no sense. He crossed the room to the door and glanced back, because he couldn't help himself. Te would tell him. Given time and the right encouragement, he would tell him anything he wanted to know. Satisfied for the time being, he exited the room, quietly closing the door behind him.

Flashing his fangs at a passing Eineu, Stephan smirked as it scurried out of his way. He was feeling particularly gleeful today, because the obstacle that was Kai would soon be removed. He had looked forward to this for so long.

Originally, the problem that had continued to vex him hadn't been how to kill Kai, but how to kill him and get away with it. His a-ha moment came when it occurred to him that actually killing Kai wasn't necessary. Stephan literally smacked himself when he realized he'd forgotten the obvious.

He merely needed to make Kai unappealing to Lucifer and Te, and the easiest way to do that was within Kai himself. All the vampire clans had advantages and disadvantages, and while they weren't flaunted, they weren't exactly secrets either. Clan Air had what everyone considered the worst disadvantage—they did not regenerate. They healed, but any piece, from a chunk of skin to a limb that was separated from the main body, did not regrow. The best part was that Kai's extreme age would ensure that he survived his injuries.

Once he'd realized the solution, the new problem had been how to have Kai maimed. Stephan felt like he'd been stumped on that for ages.

The Rendering was the revelation he'd been waiting for. The champion chosen to fight Kai, conveniently hopped up on steroids, would tear him apart, and Kai's defeat could not be traced back to him.

The genius and simplicity of the plan made Stephan giddy. Steroids were all the rage when he was turned; otherwise, he was sure he never would have thought of it. He assumed that since they made humans stronger and more aggressive, they would do the same for a Kazat.

By nature, the Kazat were strong and savage fighters—and dumb as posts, in his opinion. What they lacked in speed and agility was made up for by the fact that they were extremely hard to kill. The extra strength and aggression from the steroids, combined with their stamina, should negate any advantage Kai had.

Then the champion would be free to literally tear Kai limb from limb, making sure to badly scar him in the process. The sexual advantages of fucking a torso notwithstanding, Stephan was sure Lucifer and Te would move on, and he would be there to step in and be the perfect companion and mate. He'd then stash Kai away in the same brothel he'd toiled in, to be used, abused, and forgotten. But he'd be sure to visit from time to time, reminding himself—and Kai—how far he'd come.

That lovely image stayed with Stephan as he strolled into Clan Water's district to use their portal to travel to the Clan Seat in Los Angeles. He may have been persona non grata with the clan, but his status as Te's consort overrode whatever restrictions he may have had.

Acquiring the steroids would be a fairly easy process. Jarvis held a fascination for all things humans deemed illicit and illegal. While a portion of the clan's fortunes came from legitimate entertainment industry ventures, the majority came from activity that was far from legal. Jarvis had his pleasures, and they were housed in vaults throughout the city.

Stephan wasn't supposed to know about them, but then he wasn't supposed to know a lot of things. Gathering and trafficking secrets was a skill honed in his last life that saved his new life and helped set the stage for him to create a better one out of less than ideal circumstances.

In the late '80s, he'd been a lawyer at one of the most prestigious and lucrative law firms in New York. At that time, he'd managed to acquire everything he'd ever wanted, and that only opened up his mind to want more. Being comfortably in his prime, white, talented, straight-acting, and gorgeous meant that anything he wanted, he'd soon had. Ruthless, but always charming, he'd spent his days tearing a path through corporate law for his clients and his nights in a coke-fueled frenzy of parties and sex.

It was at one of these parties where he'd met Valerie. The minute he'd smelled her perfume and looked into her strange, bright blue eyes, he'd been hard, and fucking her had become his hallowed goal—a goal that was achieved less than five minutes later as they rutted in a dim corner of the Limelight. In retrospect, it seemed fitting that the encounter that would change the course of his life would happen in a church-turned-dance club—as if God had symbolically turned his back on what he was and what he would be.

They'd partied and fucked their way through club after club. Not once had he questioned this odd attraction. By the end of the night, she'd told him that if he stayed with her, the party would never end.

"If you could do this forever, would you?"

Building to his sixth climax of the ecstatic night, he'd locked eyes with her. "Yes," he had answered truthfully.

It was that simple. She'd turned him. He had left his human life behind and never looked back. They had spent the next five years together, and she'd introduced him to a world he never knew existed and indulged his every whim. He'd been deliriously happy.

That delirium had ended in 1992 when they were caught and slated to be executed. She had turned him without sanction, flouting the law and then running from the repercussions. At the time, Stephan had thought they moved around so much because she was restless and easily bored. She must have known that being caught was inevitable; the only question was when and where. Valerie had been executed for Crimes Against the Clan, never once trying to defend herself or to plead for Stephan's life.

Aware that he had been created illegally and that death was his certain future, Stephan had used all of his charm—supernatural and God-given—plus a few revealed secrets in his bid to stay alive.

In an unveiled moment, Valerie had revealed that he had not been her only unsanctioned progeny. There were two others whom she had abandoned shortly after turning. She had intimated where and when. While on his knees servicing Jarvis, he had offered to find these others and dispatch them in exchange for his life. Jarvis had laughed and called him a fool but allowed it and, in a humoring gesture, gave him a clan member—Alice—funds, and a year's reprieve to get the job done. Alice's main job had been to kill him when he failed. Since Stephan wasn't a fighter, a side deal with Alice had been necessary to secure her cooperation and ensure that she'd do the killing when the time came.

Together, they had managed to complete the job in six months. Impressed, Jarvis had stayed his execution and instead banished him from the protection and aid of the clan for "no less than one hundred years."

The life of a scavenger was hard and short, and without proper mentoring from the clan, he was not expected to live. Of course, once again he'd defied expectations. Life in the brothels had been unpleasant, but Other-kin, like humans, shared things they shouldn't in front of those they deemed invisible. He'd collected enough secrets to trade his way into a position where Te couldn't help but notice him. His charm and *other* skills had done the rest.

* * *

Vials acquired, he hurried back to the City and immediately made his way toward the Kazat section. There were times when Stephan was annoyed with his heightened sense of smell, and this was definitely one of them. The Kazat were not big on hygiene. He was sure he'd have to burn his clothes once he was finished here, as he doubted the smell would come out of the silk, even with a good soaking. They were like magpies—there were piles of interesting-only-to-them garbage everywhere. Kazat didn't wear clothes for modesty; they wore cloth solely to display the crap that was small enough to carry around with them.

He approached a youngling.

"Take me to Ru'uk," he commanded, giving the youth a handful of shiny glass and metal beads. The youth examined them and him and then nodded for him to follow. The smell grew thicker as he followed it further into the complex. He was definitely going to need a bath after this.

The Kazat tunnels were designed to be confusing to outsiders. Besides the trash strewn across the path, the corridors folded back on themselves and dead-ended without notice. Stephan needed a guide to lead him to the war chief because he would have been lost soon after entering. He had a feeling that the youth was fucking with him, though. It felt like they had passed the same malingerers in the same passageways a few times now. He resigned himself to letting the youngling have its fun, knowing his status with Te would keep them from doing him serious harm. Keeping his mouth shut and head raised, he followed the youth deeper and deeper into the tunnels.

Nine

Te's mind was buzzing with questions as Uriel entered his office. He didn't know what to make of his sudden appearance but was looking forward to having him as a guest. He gestured to a chair in the sitting area and then sent Uriel's Eineu escort for refreshments.

"Haven't lost the taste for Ambrosia, I hope."

Caught off-guard, Uriel's neutral expression turned delighted before he caught himself and retrained his features. "Do not tease me."

"No, I'm serious. Been hoarding it for ages. I think the only reason Lucifer has me around is to discover where I've hidden it," Te said with a wink and a smile.

Uriel gave him a small smile in return. "He has not managed to wheedle the knowledge from you yet? Surprising."

"He's easily distracted." He gave Uriel a conspiratorial look. "Besides, every century or so I give him a taste." The tension in the room eased.

The Eineu came in then. They watched the tall, thin creature gracefully pour two glasses. The yellow tunic complemented the light green iridescent scales that covered his body. John-yellow placed the bottle gently on the table and quietly left.

"Is it true they all call themselves John?" Uriel asked.

Te nodded, smiling. "They don't see themselves as individuals. I had to call them something, and John was just as good a name as any. Used to drive Luc crazy. It was his idea to have them all wear different color tunics."

"What about the females?"

"I've never seen one that's noticeably female."

"Oh."

The Eineu were a fairly recent addition to the City, previously having managed to live isolated lives in small communities in the rainforests of the world. Vegetarian and nonviolent, they spent their entire lives in trees. As the rainforests dwindled, so did they. Of the forty or so left in the wild, he'd managed to persuade about half to live in sanctuary in the City under his protection. He had planned it to be temporary while he searched out a suitable dimension for them, but they had no interest in leaving this world.

The two angels drank and lapsed into an increasingly awkward silence.

"I've missed you, Uriel," Te said quietly.

Uriel focused on his glass and drained it before speaking. "And I you. I called you friend once."

Te frowned and leaned forward in his chair. "You were more than that, you were—no, *are*—my brother. I was a part of your House, for pity's sake. I never stopped feeling that loss."

"You were a part of Samael's House first. You've always favored him."

"Don't make this a contest. I love and was loyal to Lucifer, just as I love and was loyal to you."

Uriel placed his glass gently on the table, then stood and walked to the fireplace, keeping his back toward Te. He stood there a moment, watching the flames. "And you showed that love and loyalty by leaving."

"I never left you. You could have joined me; I asked you to."

"Leave and do what exactly? Parade around as a god?"

Te couldn't suppress a flinch at the dig. "You could have done anything. You could have been anything. That's what Lucifer taught us—that free will was for us as well as the humans. He gifted us with the knowledge of choice. Why can't you see that?"

Uriel turned to face him. "This place was never for us. Lucifer's *gift,* as you call it, caused the fracture and division of what had been united in purpose and duty. All of you not only turned your backs on our Father but set yourselves up as his equals."

To the ones who stayed behind, that had been their greatest sin. Te looked at his untouched glass, the precious contents grown sour.

"I will always love Father, as I will always love you." He placed the unwanted drink down and looked up. Uriel's eyes, the color of burnished copper, bore into him. Tension weighed heavily in the room, and Te didn't last long under the assault of his accusing stare. He deflated a little.

"I wanted to explore my existence. To know more. To do more."

"Like Lucifer, you thought you were better than the rest of us. Those of us content to serve as we were meant to."

Te looked away, unable to continue to face the raw look of betrayal in Uriel's eyes. "Father has forgiven me. Why can't you?" Uriel didn't answer. Te let the moments pass and then gave up. "Why are you here?"

"Change is inevitable, even for us." It was like flipping a switch. Uriel returned to his more stoic disposition.

"I'm not in the mood to play twenty questions. Say whatever it is you mean to say."

Uriel looked puzzled at the reference then moved back to his vacated chair and sat down. He didn't speak right away. More moments passed, and Te was about to repeat himself when Uriel finally began speaking.

Twenty minutes later, Te wished Uriel hadn't spoken at all.

"I took you in once. I had hoped you would return the favor."

"Of course. Rest assured, you are welcome here." It went without saying. "But there are others left. We have to organize, do a thorough search—"

"Tamiel, stop." Uriel cut him off, and Te was taken aback not only by the tone of the command but by the use of his given name. "Do you think we have not done these things already?"

"But—"

Uriel cut him off once again. "Do you not see? Or are you in denial like Michael and the others?

"What are you talking about?"

Uriel responded without expression. "All of it—the mysterious black ooze, the disappearing angels, the shrinking then disappearance of Heaven—all of it points to one thing. Father is dead."

Decisive and focused, he had always been able to see what others could not. Te knew he spoke the truth, but knowing was one thing, accepting it as fact, another.

"How can you say that when not five minutes ago you accused me of turning my back on Him?"

"It is the only thing that makes sense. The sooner you accept it, the sooner you can move on."

"Is that what you've done? Moved on?" Te's voice was bitter with hurt.

"No," Uriel said, voice low and defeated. "But I will not drag you into a fruitless search as Michael has done with Lucifer." He sank further into his chair and stared into space. "If you feel the need to do something, you will do it without me."

Te didn't know where to go from there. He'd never seen Uriel distressed and defeated. The thought that Father was dead was horrifying, true, but it was also distant. It was Uriel's distraught state not three feet from him that moved him to action.

He opened up the link between them, gently prodding Uriel to do the same. It took some work, but Uriel slowly opened to him. Te was overwhelmed at first by the intensity of Uriel's emotions—the terror, loss, bewilderment, and resolute determination to keep it all to himself. Te held him. Even fearing he'd succumb and be swept away with the fierceness of it, he held fast, sending waves of love and remembrance of unity.

It was into this now-peaceful space that a frantic Eineu burst, and immediately felt calm and safe. "Pardon, Lords," the Eineu bowed. "John is not meaning to interrupt."

Reluctantly the two seraphim released each other. Te turned and addressed the Eineu, this one dressed in lavender. "It's okay, John. What do you need?"

"Is Master Stephan." John bowed again, and with his eyes firmly on the floor at Te's feet, he spoke. "John understands is consort but is afraid for Miss. John has duty to care for Miss."

"Miss?"

Uriel explained, and Te cursed, causing the skittish creature to jump.

"I'm not mad at you, John. You did the right thing. Thank you for telling me. Did he scare her?"

"No, Lord. Miss still sleeps."

"Good. Find Lord Kai and ask him to meet me in her room." John bowed a final time and backed out of the room.

Uriel raised an eyebrow at Te in question. "Consort?"

Te rolled his eyes and shrugged. "I let him think what he wants. Sometimes it's just easier."

"Sounds to me like you spoil him." Uriel showed a rare smile, the link between them still active and comforting.

"Yeah, I do that too. You should get yourself a plaything. Then we could commiserate." He winked.

Uriel's face screwed in disgust. "Continue to make such suggestions, and I will take my leave."

Te laughed and waved Uriel out the door. "You really don't know what you're missing." He laughed even harder at the hardy helping of revulsion on Uriel's face as the two of them headed to the guest quarters.

Ten

Stephan stood waiting for the Kazat war chief to accept his plan. Ru'uk's painted white head was tilted as it eyed the vial with suspicion. The hesitation wore on Stephan's already frayed patience. He'd spent at least a half an hour walking the Kazat's foul tunnels before the youngling had brought him to the war chief. Now he stood in a room with ten other Kazat while Ru'uk took its sweet time mulling over his proposal. The stench was even stronger in here, something he hadn't thought possible. It was making him irritable.

"Look, do you want to win or not?" He really didn't have time for this.

"Why do you care who wins?"

Stephan caught himself before he rolled his eyes. Why wouldn't they just do what they were told?

"Did Lord Te send you?"

He mentally shrugged and figured what the hell. "Of course he did. He's friends with Lucifer and, as such, can't be seen talking to you. Everyone would assume you were plotting against Kai, and if it got back to Lucifer, Lord Te would bear his wrath. This way, Kai is defeated, and even you can't be blamed, because you were following the Law."

It was a shame that the Kazat couldn't be charmed. This meeting would be over by now if they could be.

"This magic will make my champion strong? My champion is strong already."

"Kai belongs to Lucifer. Do you think he left him unprotected? This magic will make sure your champion wins." Why was the stupid Kazat not getting this simple concept?

"Where did you get this magic? Why is it unknown to me?"

"It's human magic."

That had been the wrong thing to say. "Humans have no magic."

Which was true. He had to salvage this. "They have a kind of magic that's different from ours. Some of them are very good at potion-making." The war chief was scowling but hadn't attacked him yet, so he kept going. "Humans are weak—"

"But tasty," a Kazat in the back interrupted, laughing. Ru'uk and the others joined in, everyone commenting and agreeing or disagreeing on their favorite parts.

Stephan plastered a smile on his face until they'd exhausted their commentary. God, this was tedious. "Because they're weak, they create things to make them stronger. Have your champion take this, and—*anie* will be stronger." Kazat took offense at being called "it" to their faces, and since every other language had a gender pronoun, they got called 'it' a lot. Stephan almost fucked up entirely, but at the last minute remembered to use their term, *anie*, when referring to the champion.

Ru'uk considered and then crooked a long, thick finger at the shadows. A hulking figure stepped forward and bowed. "Drink it."

Stephan snatched the vial away, "It won't work if anie drinks it."

Ru'uk looked about to change its mind.

"Wait. Let me show you." Everyone watched as Stephan drew a needle out of his pocket. "I need to stick anie with this."

Ru'uk came close to examine the needle. Stephan wondered if they believed their strength was connected to body odor. It would explain a lot. As it was, the war chief had the most trophies: ears, fingers, noses. Stephan was sure it all added to the stink.

Slowly, Stephan showed them what he needed to do with the needle. Luckily, he had thought to bring extra, as a test prick broke two needles before he figured out how to stick them correctly. The champion huffed at him with each attempt but otherwise stood quietly and let him get on with it. The dose finally administered, he prepared to leave.

"I'll be back to administer a dose tomorrow, and anie should have another one right before the Rendering."

Ru'uk moved into his space again. "If this does not work, Lord Te will have to find another consort."

"It will work," Stephan assured him, concealing any possible doubt.

The trip back to the marketplace took little time. When he reached it, Stephan almost broke into a run. The desire to burn his clothes and spend an hour scrubbing his skin was strong. He refrained, however. Thoughts of finally entering Lucifer's bed gave him the strength to stride with dignity and purpose during the too-long journey to the quarters he shared with Te.

* * *

"Anie lies." M'ok, the clan shaman said, as they moved out of the shadows. M'ok's head was painted black, from the missing eyes to the back of the skull. The trinkets that adorned their cloth—beads, discarded bits of polished glass—were more about station than they were trophies for captures or kills. God-Touched, M'ok was gifted with Sight—the eyes had been removed as they were not needed to See—and great magic.

"Leave us." Ru'uk told the rest of the room, needing privacy should M'ok reveal any God-Speak.

"What do you see?" asked Jol'un, the clan chief, as they moved out of the shadows to join the other two. Much like Ru'uk and M'ok, the clan chief's head was painted from the eyes to the back of the head. Jol'un's color was red.

"Lies, some truth."

"Explain," Jol'un commanded.

"Anie believes the potion will work. That is truth. Anie lies about why anie comes to us."

"The vampire has reasons. If the potion works, those reasons do not matter," Ru'uk said.

Jol'un nodded their head and crossed massive arms. "Agreed. The vampire's request to maim and not kill?"

"Ignored," Ru'uk said. "We fight to the death. Always." All three smiled, thick, wide lips pulling back over sharp teeth.

"I will meditate until the challenge, even though the Gods remain silent," M'ok said, instantly dulling the mood.

"When will this silence end?" Jol'un asked. By now, the question was rhetorical, having been frayed and worried over by all Kazat for years.

The Gods chose M'ok yet hadn't spoken through them in seventy-five years. At first, it had been merely unsettling. It didn't become worrisome until the mating cycles stopped, and their petitions for young were continually ignored or denied. This halted reproductive cycle made the loss of Om'sau that much worse.

All agreed that Om'sau had been stupid in confronting Kai, but while unfortunate and unwanted, their death had provided the ultimate real-world experience—a dire lesson for all younglings. That death would be avenged partly as gratitude for the sacrifice. But mainly Om'sau was being avenged because Kai took advantage. Had one of the seasoned warriors been the one to confront the vampire, the outcome would have been much different. Ru'uk didn't need M'ok to know that.

Whether the Gods deserted them or were testing them, M'ok could not say. Ru'uk believed they'd been deserted when longer sleeps had begun. What was usually a seasonal hibernation cycle happening no more than twice a year had, for some, turned into one cycle lasting months.

The three of them carried the brunt of the stress of that extended cycle. They were the ones who had no answers when the clan looked to them for guidance. M'ok had suggested for Jol'un to bring the issue to Lord Te, but Jol'un refused. While Lord Te, like Uru, was respected, the matter was too personal to bring to outsiders. Their Gods would have answers, and Jol'un decreed that Kazat would wait until the Gods told them what to do. They were strong; they would endure. In the meantime, Kai would repay the life he stole, and every Kazat would rejoice in the deed as if it were their own.

Eleven

Three figures stood at the foot of the sleeping woman's bed. Te looked at Kai. "Uriel told me, but I'd like to hear it from you. Why is this woman currently occupying one of my guest suites?"

Kai appeared uncomfortable but answered anyway. "Gregory's secretary. She walked in on his retrieval. Uriel enthralled her so she would give up the location of the wife."

"Who is now dead," Uriel interjected. Te didn't miss the frosty look that remark earned from Kai.

"The wife is unimportant," he said, still looking at the woman in the bed. "Nice to have but not necessary." He looked back over at Kai. "So collateral damage then. This is unlike you."

Kai looked away, embarrassed.

Te looked at him closely. He had said that it had been two days since he'd last fed—two days since he'd last had Lucifer's blood. When he'd posed the question, Te would have guessed much longer. Even though it had only been a few hours since he had given Kai his own blood, Kai still looked... off.

No doubt his blood wasn't as powerful as Lucifer's, and Kai had been having that regularly for centuries. Although he'd kept it to himself, over the years, Te had wondered if there was a downside to Kai feeding from Lucifer exclusively. It appeared that there was, if Kai's poor performance during this retrieval and possible questionable health were any indication. Lucifer's blood must burn through him quickly, especially if he had to have it every day. A vampire Kai's age should have been able to go for weeks, if not months, before having to feed. He wondered if Kai knew. What disturbed him more, however, was wondering if Lucifer knew.

With all that was going on, the question of when Luc would be back circled both of them. Kai might not be able to wait. "When you go home after this, if Luc's not back, you need to come to me. You need to feed."

Kai looked at him for a while before speaking. "Sure," he said, but Te wasn't convinced.

"Promise me."

"I promise," Kai replied with the look of one backed into a corner. It was enough to satisfy Te.

"Touching," Uriel noted, "but if you have no further need of me, I shall depart." He disappeared without waiting for either of them to reply.

"We'll talk again soon," Te said to the departed archangel, unbothered by his typical evasion of pleasantries. He pulled a chair close to the bed and sat down, leaving Kai to hover at the foot. Resting one hand on the top of the woman's head and the other on her lower abdomen, Te examined her.

"How long was she under?"

Kai shook his head. "Not sure, although she did feel Uriel's power when he transported us to the wife's location."

"She's deep within herself," Te said. There was something else, but that could wait. He removed his hands and produced a small jar from nowhere.

"Wait, you're going to treat her with that?" Kai asked, incredulous. "Since when could Stardust treat anything?"

"Moondust." Kai rolled his eyes at the correction. "The youngest generation calls it Purple Passion or P2," Te said, smiling when Kai's face wrinkled in annoyance.

"Leave it to those pretentious mutts to come up with something so insipid." Kai stopped. Te knew a rant was forming and watched, amused, as Kai mentally redirected himself. "Fine. It won't kill her?"

"No, it won't. P2 is fascinating, really," he said to Kai's scowling and unconvinced countenance. "It actually has more uses than getting the weres high." Kai still looked skeptical. "Honestly. In vampires, for instance, it acts as like a strong aphrodisiac."

"I didn't know we needed such a thing."

Te gave him a smirk of his own. "It comes in handy."

Kai shuddered and playfully covered his ears. "Enough. I don't want to know."

Te chuckled. "In humans, the dominant effect is calming. There is a euphoric effect as well, but the strength varies with the individual. It seems to only be addicting with them though. To treat the thrall—in mild cases—we've found that it helps with the anxiety of the separation. For those firmly enthralled, of course, there is no hope."

"So her case is mild."

"Yes, and this will take the edge off of the withdrawal." Te rubbed his hands together causing a slight halo of light to shine between them. Then he replaced his hands in their original positions.

The woman woke with a start. She looked around, disoriented.

"Can you tell me your name?" Te asked gently.

"Roberta," she answered, eyes unfocused.

Te snapped his fingers quickly in front of her face, bringing her attention back to him. "You were enthralled, and you also had a magical spell on you before that."

She looked puzzled. "What? I don't understand."

"I know this is confusing and that you have questions, but for now, just relax."

Her eyes were sluggish as they roamed the room. As soon as they rested on Kai, however, they grew alarmed as memory overtook her, and she shrank back, cowering against the headboard of the huge bed.

Kai held his hands out, palms up, trying to be as non-threatening as possible. "I won't hurt you."

Roberta moaned, curling into herself.

Te reached over and touched her lightly on the head. "Calm." She immediately relaxed, her breathing slow and even. "No one in this room means you any harm," he told her, smoothing her hair back from her face.

Her eyes wandered the room once more, alighting upon John.

"That is John. He will acquaint you with your rooms and take care of any basic desires." He held up the jar. "You'll also need to take this. He'll administer it to you when you need it."

John came forward, bowed, and gave her a wide smile, showing black gums at the top and thick, blunt teeth on the bottom.

"Sleep now," Te said, and her eyes closed as she fell into a comfortable, natural sleep.

* * *

Te leaned on the wall outside Roberta's room and eyed Kai. He would not like what he was about to say.

"That woman in there was Gregory's property."

Kai, who had been leaning on the wall next to him, stood up straight. "Shit." As the implications hit him, he slumped back on the wall. "I had hoped..."

"You had hoped that I could wipe her mind and somehow she could go back to her old life."

"Yes." Barely a whisper.

"Well, if you hadn't run into Stephan and if she was actually a free human, that might have been possible. As it is..." Gregory had signed a contract. Everything he owned when the contract was revoked now belonged to Te. Kai understood, and for the second time in as many days, Te felt his disappointment and was sorry for it.

"What are you going to do with her?"

"I'm giving her to you."

"What?" Kai was off the wall again. It was apparent that he hadn't expected that.

"Having a slave will make an excellent impression at the Rendering."

"I can't do that." Kai turned away from him and walked down the hall.

Te walked after him, easily catching up. "Then she goes to the block. Slave or food, it doesn't matter to me."

Kai whirled and was instantly in his face. "You would do that? Save her and then throw her away?"

"I could ask the same of you. Your code of honor—the very thing that prevented you from leaving her—condones turning your back on her now?" He didn't like hurting his friend, but Kai had started this. He would either step up or get out of the way.

Kai turned and resumed walking the hall. "I know what it's like to be helpless to the whims of others. I can't make her a slave, can't take away her free will. And food is out of the question," he said. Te didn't miss the note of helplessness in his voice.

"Free will? She'd already lost it to Gregory, then temporarily to Uriel. It's been a long time since she had free will."

"How long?"

"Five years, give or take."

Kai let out a breath. "Damn."

He was tired and feeling more agitated by the second. How did he get himself into this mess? He needed to go home and find Lucifer, needed to feed. It was beginning to be hard to concentrate, and his muscles were starting to hurt. He led them down a branching corridor, which was deserted, and stopped midway, once again leaning against the wall. Roberta was a problem he couldn't focus enough to solve.

"I rescued her from slavery just to make her a slave."

They stood in silence a moment, and then Stephan swept around the corner. His face broke into a wide smile upon seeing Te. Was this happenstance, or had Stephan been following them?

"There's my consort. I've been looking for you."

Te returned the smile, ignoring Kai's look of disbelief. "Well, you found me," he purred.

Consort? Kai mouthed the word at Te, who shrugged as Stephan threw his arms around the big angel's neck and wrapped his legs around his waist.

"Take me to bed, lover," Stephan cooed while burying his face in Te's neck.

Kai sniffed the air once and cocked his head at Te in question. If he didn't know better, he'd think Te looked a tad sheepish. Slowly shaking his head, Kai backed up down the corridor, intending to get far away from the two as quickly as possible.

"We'll talk later, Kai," Te said almost absently.

When they started making out in the hallway, Kai didn't answer, choosing instead to turn and hurry toward the nearest exit—hurrying toward the archangel waiting for him at home.

* * *

Te carried Stephan toward their rooms, intending to dump him in the bath because he stank.

"You stink of Kazat. What have you been up to, little vampire?"

Stephan wrinkled his nose. "I went there ages ago to make preparations for the Rendering. I've taken one bath already."

Te frowned, because he was lying. Te knew Stephan had sent a messenger to the clan leaders and matriarchs, and yet he expected Te to believe he personally went into that foul Kazat warren to make preparations for the Rendering. Te stopped walking and pressed Stephan into the wall.

"Remember who you talk to, little vampire. You do not want to cross me."

Stephan pouted then licked his lips. "Maybe I do."

Te spanked him, hard. The jolt sent pleasure zinging through their bodies, making them moan simultaneously. He did it again and was about to do it a third time when Stephan pulled him in, and they kissed with the abandon of horny teenagers.

He pulled off the wall and resumed course for his rooms. As he walked, he occasionally raised and lowered Stephan on his hips, availing them both of the delightful friction the movement provided. Te would have passed Uriel if not for his heightened awareness of his brother's presence in the City. He didn't want to stop, didn't want to postpone

162

his lovemaking. It was with regret that he let Stephan slide from his arms, giving him a lingering kiss of promise as they separated.

"You seem to think you're done here," Stephan said, arms tightening around Te's neck, refusing to let him go.

Te smiled down at him. "For now. I need to talk to Uriel."

He kneaded Stephan's ass in his big hands, eliciting a delicious whine that made him less inclined to stop.

"I can change your mind," Stephan said, licking his lips.

"I know." Te laughed. Why pretend? He knew it was true. But Uriel had dropped some serious news at his doorstep, and as much as he wanted to ignore it, he couldn't. "Go on, take another bath. I'll see you later." He turned Stephan toward their rooms and slapped his ass to get him moving.

Stephan looked at him over his shoulder, lips twisted in disappointment. "I'm important too."

"I know you are. Now, my little vampire, go." Te shooed him away, and Stephan reluctantly began to walk. The walk turned defiant when he added a switch to his hips. Te shook his head and watched Stephan as long as he could, losing sight of him when the vampire turned a corner. Te was still smiling when he stepped onto the balcony outlook on which Uriel was standing.

"I hope you'll find the hospitality of the City to your liking," he said, moving past Uriel and stretching out on the wide stone railing.

"Michael and the others are dead."

Te put his feet on the floor and made a gesture with his hand, sealing them off from eavesdroppers. "What?"

He hadn't digested the news from earlier and instantly regretted leaving Stephan for this conversation. Uriel glanced at him and then returned his gaze to the complex below.

"They are gone. Check for yourself and tell me what other explanation there could be."

Te did as Uriel suggested. There was nothing. Earlier, when he had connected with Uriel, he could feel the other archangels in the background. They had been alive then. Now they were gone. He and Uriel were the only two left.

"We are the last," Uriel said, echoing his thoughts.

Te looked at his impassive face. He could gain no clue as to what the archangel was thinking or feeling. A knot formed in his gut. He stood up and leaned his forearms against the stone rail. "What do we do?"

"Nothing."

Te straightened so he could meet Uriel eye-to-eye. "Nothing." Now it was his turn to play echo. "But there has to be something."

It always amazed him how much Uriel could say with just a look. The look he gave him now told him he was being foolish.

"Michael, Raphael, and Gabriel would not let it go. They dragged Lucifer into it. Now they are all dead." His eyes momentarily flashed red, and his expression grew even more resolved. "I do not want to die."

They stared at each other. Although Uriel's face was closed, his essence begged Te to let it go, let them live. If it had been anyone else, Te would have put more effort into arguing. But Uriel, who was no coward, who would never shy away from vengeance, was prepared to let it go for obviously sound reasons.

Lucifer... *Luc*... was dead. Sorrow and a longing for retribution ignited within him, as well as a heavy helplessness. How could he hope to defeat anything that could kill Lucifer? His instincts told him that he would live a lot longer if he listened to Uriel and let it go.

"I have to tell Kai." He spoke aloud before scrubbing his face with his hands and then absently scratching at the oath-binding on his chest. Uriel frowned but remained silent. Te faced the City again and clasped his hands behind his back. He knew better than to look to Uriel for assurance. True, he loved his brother, but eternity would be long with only Uriel for company. He slumped into a nearby chair. "I'll have John set aside rooms for your use."

Uriel, still staring out over the City, said nothing.

* * *

Roberta floated into consciousness, her psyche wrapped gently in cotton wool. She stretched and allowed herself to gaze around the room. She wasn't in her bedroom on the Asshole's property, so she hadn't been dreaming. Her eyes landed on the creature—she'd been told that John was his name—and she stared unabashedly at him.

She prided herself on being practical, never driven to believe in fantasy or outrageousness. That being said, she wasn't the type to deny the evidence of her own eyes. It was what bugged her most about most horror movies—once the protagonist was presented with evidence, they spent half the movie wasting time by denying it instead of trying to find a solution.

She clearly remembered the events of the previous night and wasn't about to spend any time trying to fit it into reality by denying it. There was no precedent, no frame of reference for her recent experiences, though, and she was scared. The best course of action would be to appear compliant while looking for a way out. The way to survive this was to keep calm and be alert.

Her stomach growled, and the creature in the corner—John, she reminded herself—giggled. The sound startled an answering giggle from her.

"Sorry." She didn't know why she was apologizing.

"Miss is hungry," he said through his wide mouth. "John brings food, yes." He nodded.

John appeared to be a gentle, delicate creature, but she wasn't letting her guard down just yet. He approached her slowly. It occurred to her that he was approaching her as if she were the wild animal. His eyes were huge; they reminded her of a gibbon or the sugar glider a high-school friend used to have as a pet. If she touched him, would his skin feel smooth and silky like a snake? When he was close enough, she almost reached out to test her theory but managed to restrain herself. He poured her a glass of something and handed it to her with a little bow.

"John brings Miss food now." He glided toward the door. She watched him go, captivated by his grace and economy of movement.

She sniffed the glass of liquid in her hand. It could be orange juice. It smelled sweet and maybe a little citrusy. She put it on the nightstand, not feeling brave enough at the moment to taste it. What she would do when he brought food back, she didn't know. If they were going to poison or drug her, they would have.

Speaking of, the big black guy had said something about her having to take a drug because she'd been enthralled.

What the hell? Not likely.

What that was about she didn't know and would make it a point to be gone before it became an issue.

Roberta got out of bed to explore before John came back with her food. She was in a large, nicely appointed bedroom with a queen-sized bed. One door led to a small bathroom with a shower stall, sink, and toilet. Another led to a decent-sized closet. She was surprised to find that the third door led to a living/dining room. It was a small apartment, and a rather pretty one too—the purple and gold color scheme was quite inviting. There was a comfortable looking couch on one wall, with a low table and chairs around it. Further into the room was a very expensive looking table with an ornate chair on each side, and behind that, in front of the far wall, was a full bar.

Facing what she assumed was the door to the suite, a balcony opened to the outside. There was no door, just an opening draped in curtains, and a warm, slight breeze blew in from outside. She parted the curtains, walked out on to the balcony, and was stunned by what she saw—a city, and from the looks of it, it was underground.

Where the fuck was she?

The calmness she woke with bled away as she stood there. Her room was at the highest point against the wall of the cavern. She'd guessed that it was hewn directly from the rock. The cavern was a big, oval shape, and her room was close enough to the apex that she could see down the length of the city. There was no noise, but she could see activity down below.

Her throat got tight, and tears blurred her vision. She was trapped. But hadn't that man said she was a guest? Her thoughts started to unravel, and she shook harder. She was a prisoner in an underground cavern.

Casting her mind back to last night, Roberta searched desperately for a reason. It had to have been the Asshole's fault. Why the hell hadn't she quit? She hated working for him, so why had she stayed so long? If she'd quit, she wouldn't be a prisoner now.

How was she going to get out of here? If her room was any indication, there had to be miles of tunnels. Miles!

What was that bastard into that those scary guys would come at night to snatch him away, and why had they taken her? She remembered the guy with the tattoos. He had an unusual name she couldn't remember at the moment. She didn't want him anywhere near her. He scared the shit out of her. But his friend… Uriel was kind and would take care of her. He would save her. He'd saved her already, hadn't he? Just looking at him made her feel warm and safe. That's all she needed.

Uriel. Uriel. UrielUrielUrielUriel…

* * *

When John knocked and entered some time later, he found the woman curled up and rocking in a corner of the balcony, sobbing and chanting Uriel's name. She didn't move or resist when he administered a dose of P2. Not knowing what else to do, he set off in search of Lord Te, hoping he would know how to help her.

* * *

Te sat in the chair, elbows on his knees, avoiding thoughts of Lucifer or Kai. Instead, he contemplated his shoes. The canary yellow wingtips matched his suit perfectly. He really liked yellow; he didn't wear it more often because there were so many other colors he liked just as much. Fuchsia—now there was a color. He let himself build the outfit—fuchsia with yellow pinstripes and bowtie, or maybe a zoot suit—as further distraction from thinking about how and when he would break the news to Kai about Lucifer's death.

He glanced up and saw John-lavender standing at the entrance to the balcony, shifting from foot to foot. The soundproofing he'd placed not only kept sound in but also kept everyone out. How long had he been standing there? A gesture brought the barrier down.

"What is it, John?" he asked, surprised by how weary he sounded.

"Pardon, Lords," John-lavender eyed Uriel and quickly bowed a few more times. What could be wrong now? While timid, the Eineu were usually competent and only came to him with problems they couldn't solve. Maybe he needed to have a sterner talk with Stephan, one without him in his lap. He felt a twinge of longing at that image. The Eineu stepped onto the balcony and bowed once more.

"It is Miss, Master. She is…" John-lavender wrung his hands, and his oval face distorted in despair. "Unhappy."

Te instantly understood why John was so distressed. The Eineu were highly empathic creatures, so much so that intense negative emotion easily made them ill. He stood and addressed Uriel. "You coming?"

"I have no intention of ever seeing that woman again."

Te was still tuned in enough to feel Uriel's discomfort when he mentioned "that woman." "You're getting feedback."

John-lavender's fidgeting increased at the delay, but Te ignored him.

"I am not familiar with the term."

"The enthrallment." Uriel looked concerned but didn't say anything. "Are you hearing her? Feeling her emotions?"

Uriel deflated slightly and looked away. "Both. At first it was merely echoes. It has, however, gotten stronger."

Te reached over and squeezed his shoulder. "I'm sorry. I hadn't realized that she was your first."

Uriel closed his eyes and bowed his head. "Her pain shouts in my head."

Te brought their foreheads together. "I know, brother. I know."

Uriel pulled away, pain still tainting his eyes. "You know how to make it stop."

Te sighed. "Once she's completely weaned, you'll only be aware of her if you want to be. If she'd had longer exposure, the only way it would stop would be if she died."

Uriel did not look relieved. "You would be disappointed in me, should I kill her."

He sounded so petulant that Te wanted to laugh. Wisely, he did not. "It will be over in a few days. Killing her would be a bit heavy-handed, don't you think?" The look Uriel gave him said that he didn't agree. Te tried another tack. "Besides, I gave her to Kai. She belongs to him."

Uriel stepped back and leaned against the wall. That, apparently, had been the wrong thing to say. Te could feel him closing himself off again. "You would choose a vampire over me." Uriel's eyes bore into him. "No. No, once again you choose Lucifer over me."

Te could only imagine what it was like for the archangels when Lucifer left. Uriel still burned with that betrayal—there would never be enough reassurances to salve and heal that wound. He was tired of apologizing. "I think you should come with me. I think you should get to know her, I think—"

Uriel leaned his head against the wall and closed his eyes once again. "Go away, Tamiel."

Dismissed, Te did as he was asked. He addressed John-lavender when he stepped back into the tunnel. "Have one of your brethren prepare a suite of rooms for Lord Uriel and inform him when they are ready. I'll see to the woman."

John-lavender bowed. "Yes, Lord." He glided away to follow his orders.

Te set off toward the guest suites, happy that he had such competent aides in the Eineu. In general, Other-kin valued aggression and physical strength over intelligence, and because of that, they did not take the Eineu seriously. Their demeanor had a tendency to ignite the prey instincts in the more dominant members of society. Despite his protection, the close confines of the City meant they were a constant temptation to carnivorous Other-kin. So for their safety, most were stationed as housekeepers, caretakers, and gardeners in his homes around the world. The two to three working for him in the City were just rare enough as to be a reminder of whose wrath would be incurred should one disappear.

When he arrived at Roberta's door, Te knocked out of courtesy before entering. Sensing no one in the rooms, he walked toward the balcony. Roberta sat at the stone table, looking at her hands, which were spread flat on the surface.

"What would it be like to have flippers?" she asked when he stepped onto the terrace. She bent her fingers, touching the tip of her first fingers to her thumbs. "Picking up stuff would be a bitch."

Te sat on the stone bench across from her. "True. It would be an interesting change, but you'd regret it once the novelty wore off."

She looked at him. Her eyes were still puffy and swollen. "I want to go home."

"Do you understand what happened to you?"

"I understand that you are drugging me and holding me against my will."

Her pupils were dilated, and her voice was flat, but she was otherwise calm, the P2 having taken effect. The only other indication of her distress was a slight tremor in her body. The P2 appeared to have pulled her out of the agitation she was feeling at Uriel's absence but only slightly muted her overall fear of being trapped somewhere she didn't want to be.

"You cannot go back. Your life is here now. It belongs to me, and I gifted you to Lord Kai." Te regretted those words as soon as he spoke them. Everyone from waiters and shopkeepers to the ones bound to him like Gregory responded to him without questions or the look of hurt and denial the woman was giving him now.

"No one will decide my fate but me," she whispered. The woman was terrified, but there was a look of determination in her eyes. She wasn't going to accept her lot so easily. In that moment, he decided he liked her.

"The world you know is only part of the truth." Thus began his explanation and her induction into the world as it truly was.

* * *

"They're all real."

"For the most part, yes. The mythology is wildly inaccurate, but the participants are real." Te wasn't sure how much of her reaction was due to the P2, but the woman accepted the news better than he'd expected.

"But why can't I just take this P2 with me and go home?"

The earnest look on her face reminded him of how simplistic humans could be. "You would be unable to get more. Besides, ultimately you are here because you are my property."

"You can't do that. You can't just own people."

He didn't reply but waited her out.

"But… why do you want me?" Her voice sounded near tears, but her eyes were clear, the P2 again muting the intensity of her misery.

"What year is it?"

Roberta was nonplussed, finally answering when she figured out he was serious. "2010."

He shook his head slowly. "The year is 2015."

She didn't answer. He could see her mind working the problem. "But—"

"How long did you work for Gregory?"

"A month, give or take. It was a temp assignment. I was gonna quit." Her voice rose slightly, but the drug didn't let her spike too high. "Five years." It was a whisper. "I worked for that son of a bitch for five years? How?"

"Binding magic. To your credit, you hadn't fully succumbed." He let her hear the admiration in his voice. "You were stuck in a loop of sorts—that talk about quitting.

At some level, you knew something was wrong, and you fought it."

"For five years."

"Most people wouldn't have lasted more than a few months."

"Yay me." Fat tears rolled down her cheeks. "Why?" She'd huddled back into herself, looking lost and miserable. "How can I believe that I worked for him for five years? That I've lost five years of my life?"

"Why? I honestly have no idea, but you became his property. What was his is now mine."

"I don't accept that."

"You will, or you will die." She started to argue, but Te cut her off. "If there is one thing about living here that you must understand, it's that humans are not dominant. You are chattel—at best, a treasured pet, at worst, a disposable laborer." They were also food, but she didn't need to know that right now.

"No." Roberta wiped her face and sat up straight, but her hands shook. "No…"

He had the sense that she'd wanted to say more, but that was the only word she could manage.

She took a deep breath and started again. "No. I'm not staying here. This is insane. I will not allow myself to be treated this way."

The outburst built in intensity, the momentum lifting her from her chair and propelling her from the balcony and into the middle of the suite. She paced the room, the determination from moments before morphing into des-peration.

"Let me go. Please, let me go. How can you talk about humans that way?" She paused, looking at him. "Wait. You're not human, are you?" She shook her head, backing away from him with a warding gesture. "I don't want to know what you are. I don't care. I promise to forget you, this place, *everything*. Just… don't do this."

Te had followed her inside and stood watching her throughout. She'd guessed he wasn't human. He liked it when humans were smart. She would accept it, eventually. How she came to accept it was not his problem. It was Kai's, who should be thankful that he'd laid the ground-work.

"You no longer have a choice about what does and does not happen to you. Understand this." He walked toward her and raised her chin with his forefinger, catching her eyes with his to drive the point home. "Do not try to es-cape. There are no exits to the surface from within the City. If you try, you will be captured by beings far less benevolent than Lord Kai or myself. You may be eaten out-right, raped, or a combination of both."

Kazat loved hunting escaped slaves. If they were re-turned at all, it was with pieces missing.

"But you said I was a guest." Her trembling voice was small, almost inaudible.

"I did, but only within these rooms. Outside of them, you are property. Now, if you would like to see the City,

I could take you, but you'd have to wear something more appropriate." He stepped back, effectively letting her go.

Her eyes dropped to the floor, and her body slowly followed until she was sitting cross-legged. She didn't look up at him when she spoke. "Maybe some other time."

He sent out a call, and within moments there was a knock on the door. "Come."

John-lavender entered the room. Te walked over to the forgotten tray of food on the table. The stew had gone cold. A light touch to the bowl set it steaming again.

"John, make sure she eats and changes into the garment on her bed."

John bowed. "Yes, Lord. John will take care of Miss."

Satisfied, Te then addressed the woman seated on the floor. "If, after you've eaten and dressed, you desire to see the City, I will take you out. Let John know, and he will tell me."

Roberta didn't look up but nodded in understanding. "What about those memories? Will I get them back?"

"Your mind put itself in a loop as a protective measure. I can restore the lost memories if you'd like, but from what you know of the man, do you really want those five years of memories back?"

She raised her head at this, the horrified look conveying her answer.

"If you should change your mind, let me know." It was a small thing, and he had no good reason to refuse her.

He exited the suite and walked the short distance to his rooms. If he was lucky, Stephan had already worked himself up into a state of jealousy and was just dying to prove his worth. One look at Stephan when he entered his rooms told him that he was very, very lucky.

Twelve

A soft, fragrant wind caressed Kai as he walked along the Ashley River toward the park. Lucifer hadn't been home, and while Kai had promised Te he would return if Luc was still absent, he found himself walking the boulevard instead, deciding to go hunting with the hope that it would take the edge off until Luc got back. He also needed time to think, as his actions in the past day had entangled him in situations with no simple solutions.

There hadn't been an occasion in centuries when he wished he could turn to his master for guidance, until now. Aram had had the ability to navigate the conundrums of life with a facility that eluded Kai. His convictions had streamed out of every pore as if merged with his very essence. Kai was clumsy and inadequate in comparison. Taking responsibility and caring about one's actions and how they would affect others had been the core of Aram's teachings—teachings passed down from the Ronin that had taught him. Kai had found the fighting easier to digest than the philosophy. He tried nonetheless. Kai felt that he owed it to his master's memory to strive to live up to those difficult standards, even though to do so meant that those closest to him, Lucifer and Te, mocked him for it.

When it came to Roberta, his intent had been honorable. Saving her, having a duty to protect an innocent, had felt good. For that brief time, he'd felt anchored to something meaningful.

He mentally redirected himself, not liking where this train of thought was going. There were only three choices where she was concerned: continue her enslavement, kill her, or turn her. Killing her had to be noted as an option, even though he had no intention of doing so. Turning her was also something he had to acknowledge as an option, even though that, too, was impossible. If he did that, it would be without sanction, unless he received Lugan's permission or fought him for control of the clan.

He bristled. Neither of those paths was one he was willing to take. He was content to ignore Lugan and be ignored in return. It worked well for the both of them.

With two options off the table, the only choice left was to continue her enslavement. It went without saying that Lucifer would not take Roberta's presence well. Even the argument that she'd raise his status for the upcoming Rendering was a weak one. Nothing could bolster his status more than Lucifer himself, and they both knew it, even if it simultaneously hurt that status as well. Of the three possibilities, keeping her was the least abhorrent of the lot. Kai didn't feel as if he had a choice and hoped Lucifer wouldn't be too unreasonable.

Level with the park, Kai stopped walking and turned to lean over the railing. Night had just fallen, and the river was dark, the swirling, briny water lapping at the bulwark. It had been a long time since they swam in that water. He made a note to drag his cohorts on an expedition to do it again soon.

Letting his eyes drift toward the mouth of the river, he let his mind drift as well until a slightly agitating thought bobbed to the surface. It was possible, in hindsight, that he may have overreacted in killing the Kazat youngling. A beating would have sufficed. Had he not let his emotions push him to rash action, he wouldn't be faced with the Rendering, which might or might not be as detestable a custom as holding Court.

Like Aram before him, Kai hated Court. He hated the spectacle and pompous ritual, the polite disdain, and most of all, the constant jockeying for position and subsequent bestowing of favors to beings that would try to kill him if given half the chance. Supposedly not as genteel as Court, the Rendering may not be as bad—Kai had no idea.

But there was no backing out. The Kazat were calling for blood. He could either put an end to it now or have a Kazat blood feud that lasted indefinitely. He was locked onto a specific course and had to see it through no matter how much he would like to avoid it.

He turned and leaned his back against the railing, tuning in to the humanity that passed. The night was warm and attracted a fair number of people strolling the boulevard. He needed to get back into the habit of hunting.

Te had offered his blood out of loyalty to Lucifer, and that was fine. But Kai wasn't helpless. He would feed on humans until Luc returned. Besides, it had been much too long since he was left to follow his own whims and desires, and he was surprised to find himself excited at the possibilities.

Moving away from the river, he walked across the park to King Street. Whenever he encountered people, they automatically cleared the sidewalk, crossing the street in most cases, although a few edged around him. He wasn't actively hunting at the moment. If he was, he'd make more of an effort to appear nonthreatening by tying his hair back and wearing a glamour to hide his sigils. Even dressed simply in a black button down, trousers, and shoes of quality, his regular appearance caused all but the hardiest of humans on the street to instinctually want to avoid him.

As he walked the deeply shadowed, tree-lined streets, a smile slowly grew on his face as he remembered the early days when he first became aware of his abilities. Picking a spot, he jumped, startling a pair of humans, who apologized for not having seen him. Of course they hadn't seen him—because he hadn't been there a second ago.

He waved them off smiling; he'd forgotten how much fun shadow-jumping could be. When he was younger, he had marveled at the ability to seemingly vanish into thin air and reveled in all the havoc that he could cause because of it. Learning about his new abilities had been a source of endless wonder for him—and caused a fair amount of trouble for his master. He couldn't wipe the smile from his face. Feeling a joy he hadn't felt in a long time, he shadow-jumped his way up the block.

Avoiding Te was paramount, so he stayed on King Street, far enough away from Te's bar, Fallen, which was located off East Bay Street toward the Cooper River. Kai snorted in amusement, only now realizing how apt the name was. Doubtless Te and Lucifer thought themselves very clever. Clan Orion owned a club called Mist in the upper part of the peninsula, and he headed there, thinking that if he was going to play politics, he might as well get started. Besides, Lucifer had an unusual fondness for the matriarch, so showing his face there couldn't hurt.

Mist was located on Upper King, near the Ravenel Bridge overpass. The area was slowly being gentrified. What had been a blighted neighborhood of low-income housing and abandoned storefronts had turned into bustling shops and renovated apartments for the up-wardly mobile—a perfect spot for the young and hip to gather to party.

At the curb, a large sign in black and chrome displayed the name in sleek lettering. The building itself was a non-descript metal affair with a wide door facing the street. An obligatory red velvet rope cordoned off the entrance, and large bouncers tamed the would-be entrants, the line of which snaked up the street.

The humans waiting to get into the club watched him, some outwardly gawking, others taking surreptitious peeks. Unlike the residents in his neighborhood, these humans were keen on his presence and what they undoubtedly considered his exotic appearance. In Lucifer's orbit, Kai easily forgot about his own charisma. Luc shined brighter than the sun and always pulled the focus to him. It was only on the occasions that he was alone and garnering a certain reaction while not actively using the Seduction that he remembered he was not without his own charms. Without breaking stride, Kai walked through the entrance, nodding at the were doormen as he passed.

The Orion Clan called Charleston home. While they had other businesses, Mist was their most visible presence. He could see the matriarch and her mate holding court in the VIP section and headed in that direction.

Technically, his age and status meant that he was above her. However, snubbing her in her territory would be impolite. It would also make Kai an embarrassment to Lucifer, his actions poorly reflected, and that was the last thing he wanted. Although it wasn't mandatory, a gift would have been proper etiquette, but that was just too much. All Kai wanted to do was the minimum this side of rude. He navigated through the crowd. The VIP security parted, letting him enter the small enclosure.

"Lord Kai. The Mother blesses us with your presence!" Risha exclaimed as she rose to greet him.

"The Mother blesses you in all things," he replied with an incline of his head.

Her already beautiful face lit with surprise and joy at the traditional greeting. She offered him her seat, choosing the now-vacated seat of her alpha for herself. Her mate moved to stand behind her chair, and as the matriarchal rules of the pureblooded werewolf clans dictated, Kai neither looked at him nor acknowledged his presence. The matriarch noted his behavior, and approval shone in her eyes.

"How are things, Risha?" Kai asked when seated. He spoke informally, as he could only stand on ceremony and follow tradition to the barest limits of propriety without becoming impatient and rude.

She relaxed at his informal tone. "Good. The clan is strong."

It appeared she was going the traditional route, even if she spoke informally. He half listened, choosing instead to fully appreciate how beautiful she was, all grace and power packed into a petite frame. Her manner was warm, belying the fact that she could fight and kill with savage efficiency when the occasion called for it.

He'd only ever dealt with matriarchs in his youth, cold bitches every one. Risha's mother had been the exception. Kai had liked Adelaide. She'd lacked the cold-hearted, superior manner of the other matriarchs. Ahead of her time, she'd had a permissive live-and-let-live philosophy. In her eyes, there was room for all Other-kin, both on the surface and below. The resemblance was so remarkable that Kai couldn't help but wonder how much of Adelaide Risha carried within her.

"But you're not here to talk shop," she said, sensing he was done with formalities and not appearing offended by it. "So, Lord Kai—"

He raised his hand, cutting her off. "Please, Risha, call me Kai."

She smiled and began again. "Kai, what brings you to my little corner of the world—slumming?" she asked, eyes sparkling with mirth.

Kai smiled in response and with mischief replied, "I'm hiding from Te."

"Hiding in plain sight, then?"

"Well, I'm not trying too hard." He winked at her.

"How is your mate? He was most upset when he departed our company."

Kai shrugged. "As the sun rises and sets, he is eternal."

She seemed unfazed by his retreat to noncommittal formality. "There are those that would deny you your due because of your association. I'm not one of them. Love blesses us as she deems fit, and the Mother knows she can be a fickle bitch." They both laughed. "Not all of us are so blind or so stupid. Lord Lucifer would not choose a plaything as a companion for over half a millennium."

Despite his reservations, Kai found that he liked Risha very much. As a rule, he didn't like weres and so never bothered to accompany Lucifer during his visits, regardless of Lucifer's assurances that Risha was much like her mother and that Kai would enjoy her company. He was just now noting his error.

"I'm sorry. I'm acting like I've never received guests before," she said, visibly upset. "Have you fed? Please, my club is at your disposal." Her graceful gesture encompassed the club.

Kai shook his head, ignoring his body's pleas for nourishment. "I'm honored by your hospitality, Risha." He reclined in his seat and crossed his legs. "However I'm not in such a hurry to leave your company."

She laughed. "Flatterer. The offer is open, should you change your mind." She gestured to one of her courtiers. "Share a drink with me?"

Kai inclined his head in agreement. "Of course. A whiskey will be fine." The courtier scurried off and quickly returned with whiskey for him and a glass of wine for Risha.

She raised her glass. "To those who have gone before."

"And to those who will come after." He finished the traditional toast, and they drank.

She lowered her glass to look at him intently, "I mean no disrespect," she put her glass down, "but you are, um…"

"Surprisingly well-mannered for someone who was raised by a savage?" He laughed at her shock at his candidness and then waved it away. "No offense taken. My master wasn't such a savage after all."

The crinkles of worry dissolved from her lovely face. "I had heard… well, we all assumed—"

He raised a hand, cutting her off. "I know. Aram had a keen dislike for lies and deceit—in other words, what passes for court behavior. He was not ignorant, however, of proper etiquette, which he passed on to me."

"A very few know the difference," Risha responded, intent on his face. She paused, considering him. Her expression turned serious.

"We know you hate us and why." Kai, who had been leaning close, began to draw away, but she grabbed his arm. "Please." He let her pull him back. "You've carried this for a long time. Life was hard then, but it does not excuse the way our clans treated yours."

She referred to the practice of werewolves posing as vampire hunters. While by Kai's time, the Orion Clan had pulled out of such activities, the other clans would move from town to town selling their services to scared and gullible humans. The vampire clans would retaliate, of course, but they could never work together long enough to form lasting partnerships and, subsequently, were never as effective in the long term as their enemies. In the modern age, of course, such activities were impossible, but that didn't mean the grudges of the past were forgotten.

"We fought for much but gained little." Her gaze turned inward for a moment; there was pain there. He knew she had lost as much as he. "I know no amount of apologies can return what you've lost, what we've all lost, but please know that I am truly sorry."

In a move that took his breath away, Risha closed her eyes and bared her neck to him. She had to know that his vendetta was specifically with Gwendolyn and the Celesta Clan. She also had to know that Gwendolyn would never seek to make amends. She was giving him a remarkable gift.

It had been so easy to let his hatred for Gwendolyn bleed out to taint all the were clans, but with this gesture, Risha caused him to not only confront his bigotry but to feel ashamed of it.

He could sense her clan tense, waiting for his reaction. Even her mate did not move. She commanded enough respect that none would intervene, even though it meant potentially losing her. It could, of course, mean that they wanted her to die, but looking around at each of their faces, he knew that wasn't the case.

His eyes lingered on a female that could only be Risha's daughter the resemblance was so strong. Her shuttered gaze spoke of promised retribution, even knowing it would be counter to her mother's wishes. Risha offered her life to atone for the injustices perpetrated by the race as a whole. She expected that her clan would accept it and move on. Kai could tell, however, that while some might be willing to do so, the daughter who would undoubtedly succeed her was not.

It wasn't that knowledge that inspired his reaction, though, but a deep desire to get to know this matriarch who could command so much love and respect. Returning his eyes to Risha, he brought his hand up to caress the exposed flesh and then slowly and reverently, he leaned over and placed a kiss on her neck before reaching up and turning her face toward his.

"Thank you, but I have no quarrel with you or yours. And I have no desire to deprive your clan of one so beloved. Lucifer has been telling me for years just how remarkable you are, and to my detriment, I have not listened. I would remedy that, Risha, and look forward to the day I may call you friend."

Kai saw more respect on her face than relief. "You honor me—us," she said, gesturing to her clan and clasping his hand.

"The Mother's Hand guides me." He covered her hand with one of his own, acknowledging her and her conviction to reconciliation and building the bonds of would-be allies.

She reached for her glass. "That calls for another toast."

"Another time, perhaps? I'd rather not wear out my welcome." He could tell she was disappointed, but he needed to get about the business of feeding. "Besides, there is a tempting morsel in blue on the dance floor." He gave her a wicked smile, which she returned.

She shooed him playfully away. "Go feed. Enjoy yourself."

"That I shall. Thank you, Risha. I will visit again." He raised the hand he still clasped to his lips and pressed a kiss upon it before releasing it.

"Thank you, my Lord." She bowed her head. When she looked up again, he reached out and caressed her face. Once standing, Kai acknowledged her mate with a nod, who bowed his head in response.

He also caught her daughter's eye once again. He saw relief and respect in her gaze as well, and something else. Desire?

Interesting. He wasn't sure what to do with that, given that the relationship with her mother was still in its infancy and so merely nodded in acknowledgement before turning and leaving the area.

He could just hear Luc's *I told you so* when his lover learned of this change of heart. He would never hear the end of it.

* * *

Kai sat near the dance floor watching the woman in blue dance. Risha had sent over a bottle of Corolon brandy that did a very nice job of taking the edge off his screaming nerves. It also disconnected him from the writhing ball of need in his gut. He didn't remember ever feeling so disjointed when hungry. Every cell pleaded for Lucifer's blood because only it could truly satisfy.

Each moment he resisted going to Te was a victory. He had no doubt that if Luc didn't return soon, he'd give in to the addiction—because at this point, there was no denying what it was. He wanted to be angry, but he didn't have the room. The force of will it took not to give in took up any space he may have had for anger. He should have been ashamed, because it made him a slave, rudderless without his master.

He took a sip of the brandy, effectively disconnecting the thought before it took deep root. The Corolons were the sole producers of alcohol for the Other-kin commu-nity—sole producers because Corolons had trouble grasp-ing the idea of friendly competition. The Other-kin called it alcohol and gave it names like brandy and wine, but no one but the Corolons knew exactly what they were drinking. Fermented dung or water and magic—it was anyone's guess.

What they did know was that if human alcohol didn't do the job, the Corolon equivalent would. Kai was grateful for it and savored each mouthful. He would ignore the craving as long as he could and instead concentrate on hunting. He used to enjoy the anticipation, the seduction, the sensations, and he longed to enjoy the experience again. The brandy would help him relax and get into the right state of mind.

The woman danced with abandon, clearly immersed in the music and barely attentive to her partner. She wasn't particularly graceful or attractive in the conventional sense, but he was drawn to her anyway. Those were the things that he loved and only now realized how much he missed about the hunt—the little intangibles that made him choose one delicious treat over another.

He knew he was being watched. After all, it was widely known that he didn't eat humans. While the purpose of the hunt was to fill his belly, the performance of it in such a public place would provide a satisfying bit of gossip to be spread throughout the Other-kin community. It would be a boon for Risha and the Orion Clan to be the purveyors of such a juicy tidbit of information.

Intoxication was an unfortunate side effect to the calming influence of the brandy. Because of the hunger, every ounce of human blood in the room called to him. Because of the intoxication, he was on the precipice of losing control and giving in to the desire to rip, tear, and drink without end—a desire he hadn't felt since he was young and blood was his entire world.

When had he lost the ability to see that Lucifer's blood was changing him to the point that its absence would turn him feral? Did he ever know? Did Luc know? A sudden chill accompanied that last thought. He refilled his glass and quickly drowned that thought with another healthy mouthful.

His thoughts were finally coalescing around a plan when he noticed Risha's alpha coming his way. Kai cursed, emptied his glass, and refilled it, watching as the powerfully built young were advanced. Did Risha send him, or was he was there of his own accord?

"My Lord, I was hoping I might have a word," the were said upon reaching the table. He was about five foot nine, handsome, but unremarkably so, and dressed casually in jeans and a T-shirt that molded to his large, muscled torso.

"Of course." Kai motioned to the empty seat across from him and offered the alpha some brandy.

"Thank you, but, no. Corolon spirits have a way of going to my head," he said, confident blue eyes sparkling above an easy grin as he sat down. Kai didn't reply but waited for him to state his business.

The alpha looked to be about thirty, but looks in weres, as in vampires, were deceiving. Risha was around six centuries old and had been clan matriarch for five of them. Due to a number of factors, males didn't live as long, so

Kai put his age somewhere between one hundred fifty and two hundred.

"My name is Julian. I have been the clan alpha for going on two hundred years."

Impressive. A matriarch rarely had an alpha that long. He must have been successful in thwarting the challenges against him by younger males, or he was respected enough that they left him alone. Kai supposed it was even possible that it was a little of both. Julian's longevity was rare, and that made him interesting.

"Go on," Kai replied, in spite of his discomfort and desire to leave and feed.

"I wanted to thank you personally for not killing Risha."

Kai immediately revised his assessment and just managed to keep his temper. The fact that Risha would go on living was thanks enough. There were many accusations implicit in a simple expression of gratitude, as Julian was undoubtedly aware. Mercy was not seen as a virtue in Other-kin society. Kai hadn't fought a pureblood were in almost seven hundred years. Maybe it was the kind of exercise his overextended nerves needed.

"You realize I could take offense to that statement."

"You could, but you won't. You're not like them," Julian said, brushing his shoulder-length dark hair away from his face and lounging back in his chair.

"What makes you so sure?"

The alpha's easy smile turned into a laugh. "You're not Lugan."

An answering laugh escaped, surprising Kai. "Lugan's a brute."

"Exactly." Julian's eyes twinkled.

A sober Kai would have proceeded with more caution, but then a sober Kai wouldn't have waited for Julian to explain himself.

"Look," Julian said. "We are not animals, and I refuse to act as one. We all react on instinct and emotion, but we possess language and the skill of communication. We have intelligence. I refuse to walk around living as if I were a mere animal just because I can turn into one. I say what I feel, and I feel extreme gratitude to you for not killing the one that I love. Therefore, I will thank you for it."

Being Other-kin—literally human/other hybrids—too often meant actively ignoring the human influences in favor of the other. Kai could blame his feelings on the brandy, but he liked the young wolf's candor. He raised his glass toward Julian. "You are wise and long-lived. May you continue to walk in the Mother's favor."

Julian bowed his head, accepting Kai's blessing.

"If I may speak frankly?"

Kai chuckled. "As if you haven't been. Continue."

Julian conceded the point with a shrug. "There's a good many of us that are looking forward to the Rendering. It's obvious that you're testing the waters of leadership. We look forward to the day you reclaim your clan."

Kai frowned. This was exactly what he didn't want. If the Orion Clan jumped to that conclusion, chances were good that Lugan would as well. *Dammit.* "Why is it the business of weres?" His tone might have been a tad threatening.

Julian didn't appear fazed. "The Council should be moving us all into the future. For all of Jarvis's hedonism, he's remarkably forward-thinking. Octavia rarely shows, and when she does, she remains in her dog form and doesn't vote. Elizabeth is absent as well—too busy trying to keep her clan together after their war with Celesta. Alana follows Gwendolyn as if on a leash. And Mathias," his mouth twisted in a sneer. "That piece of trash is all bravado. He left because he didn't want to follow a matriarch, but all Gwendolyn has to do is cut her eyes his way and he votes as she does. The way things are now, progress is rarely made. If you take your rightful place as clan leader, the voting outcomes would be more favorable. Mathias, given his open acceptance of the Canes Inferni, would undoubtedly vote to gain your favor instead of Gwendolyn's."

It wasn't unusual for alphas to make deals behind the scenes. They were enforcers, whether their methods involved blood or actual negotiation. Kai took another sip of brandy.

"I find it rather hard to believe that Lugan votes with Gwendolyn. He hates her as much as I."

"He doesn't vote with her out of a mutual like or respect. They share the same views. That is their common ground."

Kai was reminded with acute clarity why he hated politics. He took another drink. "I will tell you what I will say to Lugan, should he ask. The Rendering is to satisfy the bad blood between myself and the Kazat—nothing more.

I have no designs on the leadership of my clan. As such, your Council will continue as it has, without me."

Julian opened his mouth, about to protest, but Kai cut him off with a look, closing the matter. He was reaching for the bottle of brandy when the scent hit him. Kai stopped and turned his head toward the hated stench, throat tight. Julian growled low in synergistic response. The newcomers sent his arousal spiraling so quickly it outpaced the brandy. He knew his eyes had gone solid black and was glad of the dim light of the club's interior.

"You've noticed our new guests," Julian said as Kai took a healthy swig of brandy forgoing filling his glass for drinking straight out of the bottle.

"Guests?" he said, voice raspy with emotion and the burn of the alcohol.

"As Lord, you have set no bounty," Julian replied. Kai caught the admonishment and let it slide. "Besides, their money is good. We let them stay as long as they don't cause trouble."

"Their very existence causes trouble." Everyone—the delicious woman in blue and Julian included—faded out of his awareness. The newcomers were now held in the spotlight of his attention.

Even the youngest of pureblood vampires could detect another vampire or Other-kin; it was a survival instinct. Mongrels lacked this ability. The only survival skill evident in them was the ability to breed like rats. Their blood was weak. Kai could walk right up to one, and it wouldn't have the good sense to run. Beyond the act itself, there was almost no sport in killing them. Almost. After all, sport was what you made it.

There were four of them: two mongrel males, a female, and a young human female. He watched them move through the crowd, sometimes picking a partner to dance, always flirting. The human female was either being groomed or toyed with—he doubted they were strong enough to make a thrall. Not that it mattered. For the time being, he was out of the business of trying to save people.

None of the mongrels had seen even a half-century of life. It was in their manner, in the cock-of-the-walk air they had about them. The two males were thin, with fine, almost feminine features. Both were dark-haired, dark-eyed, and dressed in the goth style. Kai identified the slightly shorter one as the leader of the group, as the other three constantly looked to him for permission or approval. The female was shorter and plumper than the two males, her white-blond hair messily styled, as was the fashion, over kohl-lined blue eyes. She could have been cute, if not for her overly made-up face. The human female had red hair and looked uncomfortable and out of place in her goth costume. Kai wondered what she would have chosen to wear if not for the obvious influence of her three companions.

Currently, the two mongrel males were dancing with the human female while the mongrel female watched smiling from the side. She'd just turned her gaze away when she saw Kai and stared. Kai immediately reversed the change, waiting to see how she'd react. She stared at him for a moment longer and then bolted for the door. Taken by surprise, her companions took off after her but didn't manage to catch her inside the club.

Kai was up and out in a flash. He heard Julian whisper, "Happy hunting," from somewhere behind him and smiled.

* * *

Te was moving leisurely in and out of Stephan when the oath-binding sigil on his chest began to burn. He stopped moving, which earned him a protesting groan from his vampire. He slid out, lay on his back, and urged Stephan to straddle him, so he could pay attention and do less work. With a particularly fetching grin, Stephan spread his legs wide, showing off for Te.

When he was satisfied Te had an eyeful, he grabbed Te's cock, slid it along the glistening labia a few times then started a nice slow glide engulfing it in his slick channel to the base. Te grinned. Giving Stephan a vulva was genius as far as he was concerned. It was probably twisted, as Stephan didn't ask or insinuate in any way that he wanted different genitalia. He did, however, want to be Te's consort. In the business of making deals, Te had made his proposal. To say his little vampire didn't get off on the slight humiliation of exchanging his sex organs for the title and privilege would be false. As deals went, Te figured he'd made out pretty well.

While Stephan rode him, he focused on the sigil. It wasn't a particularly unpleasant sensation, more a warming than a true burning, now that he was paying attention.

It was the first time since Lucifer had placed it that it had come alive. The sigil was his oath of loyalty to Lucifer. Implicit in that oath was his promise to protect Kai, should he need it. He knew that its activation meant that Kai was in some kind of trouble. By the feel of it, he assumed the trouble wasn't too bad. It was more of a *suggestion* that Kai may need his help. Knowing how tetchy Kai had been lately, he thought it best to wait it out. He didn't want Kai to think he thought he couldn't take care of himself. Te decided that if it didn't go away by the time he was finished, then he'd seek Kai out and help him get the situation sorted.

Seconds later, the sensation subsided.

* * *

The Corolon brandy had done its job, and for the first time in hours, Kai felt free. All that had encumbered his mind—longing for Lucifer, the Rendering, concern for Roberta—was gone, replaced by a more primal and welcome desire. The excitement of the impending kills tingled along his spine as he melted into the shadows, and then he moved on silent feet toward the back of the alley where the little group had gathered.

Male mongrel number two held the female mongrel in a loose embrace, whispering in her ear as she cowered against him. The redhead, slightly drunk, leaned against the wall and preened. Kai shadow-jumped to the top of the nearest building so he could watch and listen from the low roof.

"Are you sure he's one of us?" Male mongrel number two asked.

"That's just it, Frankie. I don't know what he is. He just scared me, okay?" she whined.

"Scared you, huh?" cooed the one Kai assumed to be the leader, male mongrel number one, while coming up and embracing her from the other side. "Whatever he is, he's not gonna get away with it," he soothed and then showed his fangs in a feral smile. "Ain't that right, Frankie?"

Kai thought the look Frankie threw his way was hardly convincing.

"Look, Vic," Frankie said. "I know Rosie don't scare easy, but if she's freaked, I say we just leave and don't mess with it. I don't want this to be Chattanooga all over again."

Vic let go of Rosie and grabbed Frankie by the neck, slamming him against the wall.

"You throwing Chattanooga in my face again, Frankie? I thought I told you it was an accident. What did I say about you getting all sensitive save-the-whales-bullshit on us? Huh? What did I say?"

Kai was thrilled—but also angry and sad that Luc wasn't there calling for popcorn and a flashback to Chattanooga.

Frankie dropped his eyes and went limp in Vic's grip, but Kai could tell he wasn't giving up.

"It took me two months to heal, Vic, and who knows if your dick would have grown back if it got cut off? This feels like trouble is all I'm sayin'."

"All I know is that everything feels like trouble." Vic let go of Frankie, and he slumped against the wall. "And I'm sick of it. Get over it already."

Vic stepped back and turned toward the females.

"Okay, we won't go after the dude. Whatever. As long as we do something. I'm bored and hungry."

"You guys go ahead. I'll catch you later," Frankie said, putting distance between him and the others and not looking convinced by Vic's declaration. He backed away down the alley, moving in the opposite direction than the one the others intended.

Vic cut his eyes away, turned his back on Frankie, and walked away, the human girl hurrying along behind him.

Rosie, looking torn and clearly waiting for Frankie to say something else, lingered. "Come on, Frankie. Don't be like this," she begged.

"You could come with," he said, still walking backward down the alley.

"Asshole," she hissed at him, and then she too turned her back and trotted to catch up to Vic.

Kai watched as Frankie's companions moved away. Then he jumped down to join him in the alley.

"Remarkable. A mongrel with a sense of self-preservation." His voice startled Frankie and caused him to spin around.

"Shit." Frankie's face started to change.

"I would control that, if I were you." Kai referred to the mongrel's facial disfigurement in response to the urge to feed or fight. "If you stop now, your death will be quick and easy," he said, reveling in the cruelty of the request.

With effort and a lot of deep breathing, Frankie managed to stop the metamorphosis, unwittingly further impressing his tormentor.

"That is rare. Did you know that?"

Frankie, although visibly distressed, shook his head. He'd started backing up, unfortunately he was going in the wrong direction, and the wall stopped his progress. He lifted his hands, placating. "I wasn't going after you. I don't care who you are. Can't you just leave me alone? Let me go?"

Kai moved in. "For reasons that you will never understand, no, I cannot let you go. I can, however, keep my promise." He reached up and tore Frankie's head from his body. It wasn't clean, but it was quick, just as he'd promised.

Troubled, he dropped the head near the body and left the alley, leaving the clean-up for the weres he knew were following him.

* * *

Te was basking in the afterglow and contemplating checking in on Roberta—John hadn't come to get him yet—when the sigil once again came to life. What was Kai doing? It was warm, just like before. There appeared to be no urgency to it, just like before.

He left Stephan to sleep, cleaned up, dressed, and left their rooms. He barely noticed when the sigil's warmth vanished a few minutes later.

Kai's emotions were all over the place. For a moment there—granted, it was brief—he'd considered letting that mongrel go.

Frankie. His name was Frankie.

Mongrels were an abomination and always killed on sight. It wasn't a question. Yet he felt guilty. Now he was angry because a mongrel, of all things, made him feel guilty. He would enjoy making Frankie's companions pay for the indignity. It didn't take much effort to find them. They weren't being especially stealthy.

"Oh shit, don't tell me we lost him," he heard Rosie complain from a few streets over.

He chuckled as a shadow-jump had him appearing in front of a corner store. "By the way, Frankie was right." He spoke, knowing they could hear him. "His death was easy. Yours?" He sidestepped into shadow, disappearing and then reappearing behind them, close enough to whisper in Vic's ear, "Will be *fun.*"

"Shit!" Vic yelled and spun around. Kai was gone.

The human girl screamed and took off down the street.

"What the fuck, Vic? What the fuck?" Rosie shrieked, looking to him for answers.

"Calm the fuck down!" he shouted back. "Look, we get Monica and get the fuck out of here." He took off, Rosie close behind.

They found the girl a block away, crying and hiding behind a dumpster. Vic gathered her in his arms.

"Frankie is dead," she bawled. "Don't let him kill me. Please don't let him kill me!"

"Guess no one's bored now," Kai said, leaning on the opposite end of the dumpster.

The girl burst into tears and was dragged away by a fleeing Vic, who followed Rosie, this time in the lead.

"Where'd we park the car?" Rosie shouted.

"Fuck! I don't remember."

They ran. Kai laughed. He let them gain a little ground. Keeping up was easy, as they were so very slow. It would be prudent for them to leave the girl. He hoped they would.

The little group stopped on a corner, and Monica gasped for breath.

"Grab that car." Rosie pointed to a car moving down the street.

Frankie stepped in front of it, making it stop. He then ran around to the driver's side, flung the door open, and pitched the protesting driver into the street. Rosie hustled Monica, then herself, into the back seat. The car took off.

Kai almost danced, happy to prolong the chase. He ran and shadow-jumped after them.

Following a car on foot was not an easy thing, but even so he found fun in the challenge. He doubted the trailing weres felt the same. Lucky for him, the traffic on I-26 was light and the shadows plenty on that end of the highway. His quarry apparently thought they'd gotten away, for they exited on Spruill Ave at a pace that suggested they were no longer being pursued.

He followed the car through the empty streets, past rundown and sometimes deserted houses. Finally, the car slowed and stopped in front of a sad-looking house at the end of a dead-end street with numbers and dashes instead of a proper name. Both females, visibly calmer, entered the building from the back. Monica was smiling. Vic drove away, no doubt to ditch the car. He appeared again, about a half hour later, cautious, looking over his shoulder every now and again. Once he reached the house, he took one last look and then went around back, out of sight.

From the looks of it, no human who cared had lived in that house for a while, probably taken from homeless or scavengers. The mongrels could squat here in relative safety until they were ready to move on. Boards covered the windows, and from the front, the house was dark.

Kai followed the path around to the back, easily picking his way through the overgrown yard. Dim light streamed through the cracks between the boards on the kitchen windows. The latch on the screen door was broken and moved on surprisingly silent hinges when opened. The back door wasn't locked. The kitchen was small and lit by one camp stove on the dirty counter.

He hadn't made it completely through the door before Monica came at him with a stake. He grabbed her and let her momentum force the stake through his heart, all the while his eyes locked with hers. It was extremely painful but worth it to see the terror in her eyes when a smile that promised death spread across his lips. He released her, and she backed away, staring.

Keeping eye contact, he pulled the stake free, the wound immediately closing. He shut the door. "Let's not disturb the neighbors."

The commotion brought Vic and Rosie to the kitchen just in time to see Kai licking his blood off the stake.

"He didn't die, Vic. He didn't die!" Monica sank to the floor, whimpering.

"What the fuck are you?" Rosie whispered, eyes watching with fascinated horror as Kai finished cleaning the stake with his tongue.

Kai dropped the now clean piece of wood and reached into a shirt pocket for his flask. "I am what you don't have the sense to fear."

Drawing a mouthful of holy water from the flask, he spit it into her face. Rosie screamed as the holy water burned through her skin. Kai wiped his mouth and emitted a dark chuckle. "Now that," he gestured to Rosie, "will most likely scar." He giggled, feeling the world tilt and his sanity sliding away.

Vic looked torn between the desire to help Rosie and the desire to run. Kai ignored him for the moment. He turned to Monica, who was still crouched in the corner.

"You will stay there. If you do not move, I will not kill you. Nod if you understand." The redheaded girl nodded, tears streaming out of her red, puffy eyes. Since he wasn't about to give her his blood to enthrall her, he relied upon forceful command, something humans seemed wired to obey.

Apparently having made up his mind, Vic charged Kai—but ended up grabbing at the air.

"Found your balls, have you? Excellent," Kai said from the next room.

Vic snatched a knife from his boot and followed. He stepped over Rosie, who was on her knees, wailing. The room appeared empty. He hesitated and then took slow movements toward the interior.

Kai delivered a hard blow from his left. Vic was knocked off his feet and into the wall. He sat on the floor, stunned. Rosie crawled over, managed to find him, and grabbed his leg, moaning. Her face was a mess. The holy water had caught her full on and was burning the flesh away. Soon it would start on the bone. The smell of suppurating flesh coated the back of Kai's throat. With his lips twisted in disgust, Vic kicked at her until she let go.

"She wasn't bad-looking before. Maybe you should put her out of her misery." Kai appeared, crouched in front of him.

"Whatever you are, you're gonna die," Vic spat, enraged, fangs snapping. Still holding the knife, he roared, lunging at Kai, who easily dodged the attack.

"What I am, is a vampire," Kai told him. He lowered his voice conspiratorially. "I would say that I'm like you, but it's not true. You are nothing."

Vic came at him again. Kai gutted him with a graceful swing of his arm, and Vic collapsed, moaning.

"Nice trick with the stake," Kai said. "Did you teach her that?"

He kicked Vic, breaking his ribs and propelling his body across the room to thud on the opposite wall.

"If I was a mongrel like you, it would have worked." He said, strolling over, and then grabbing the slumped figure by a leg. Vic struggled, trying to hold his guts in and escape Kai's grip.

"Purebloods, however, are not so easily dispatched." Holding Vic's foot, Kai twisted hard to the right, dislocating the leg at the hip. Vic screamed. Kai released him and watched him turn on his belly and try to crawl away.

"Purebloods are a myth," Vic yelled.

Kai straddled him, grabbing the knife Vic remarkably still held. He jammed it through the prone vampire's neck, separating the vertebrae.

"You know, every mongrel I've killed thought I was a myth." Kai giggled and then moved close, so he could whisper in Vic's ear. "How does it feel to know you'll be killed by a myth?"

The giggle turned to laughter as he stood and then grabbed Vic by the shirt, dragging him to the couch, entrails trailing his now-limp body. Dropping the body in a seated position, Kai sprinted to the kitchen. He rattled through the drawers and cabinets hoping that he'd find... yes! An entire drawer of eating utensils—forks, spoons, and blunt knives.

Kai let go a whoop of joy before sprinting back into the room with the drawer. Positioning the drawer on the couch for easy access, he grabbed a fork and skewered Vic through the shoulder, pinning him to the couch. Then he did the same thing with a blunt knife through his thigh. With his face frozen in a manic smile, he grabbed various utensils at will and proceeded to pin Vic to the couch in random places.

"It's a shame you can't feel any of this, and for that I'm truly sorry," Kai said. "But you have to admit, it's so much easier this way." It was then that he remembered the intestines. "Damn," he groaned, hanging his head.

"How old do you think I am, Vic?" He didn't expect an answer; he'd severed the vertebrae too high. Kai sat back on his heels and looked into sad, terrified eyes. "I was born in the twelfth century—in 1110? 12? AD—I was no one, and so my birth went unrecorded. But anyway, my point here is that I've seen a lot. Know a lot." He absently toyed with a coil of gut. "What I should have done," he said, gesturing with the fork he held in one hand, "was break enough bones to make you compliant and then tie you up with these."

He indicated the soft tube in his other hand. He didn't fail to notice the relief in Vic's eyes.

"You're lucky I'm out of practice. But," he punctuated the word with a fork through the thigh, "you'll need a good seat for this next part, and I suppose how you get it doesn't matter."

He stood then and went back for Rosie, who was by now barely conscious from the slow erosion of her head. If he didn't hurry, she would be dead soon.

"Well, at least one of you suffers," Kai commented, dragging her body over to the couch.

He propped her up next to Vic and impaled her, easily ignoring her feeble attempts to get away. The only sound out of her ruined face was a constant mewling that heightened in pitch with each stab. Once the drawer was empty, he stood and opened the front door, removing enough boards to duck outside.

He noticed the young weres in wolf form across the street, keeping a respectful distance. Smiling to himself, he managed to suppress the urge to wave them over. Instead, once he'd cleared the front window of the boards protecting it, he waved at the two figures on the couch before coming back in.

"The sun will be up soon. Tell me, Vic, when was the last time you saw the sun?" Kai asked, walking over to stand in front of the newly revealed picture window. The sky was pink, signaling the dawn.

He turned to face the paralyzed and panicked vampire. "I know what you're going to say. No need, really. You're welcome." Kai walked toward the kitchen. "You enjoy your last sunrise. In the meantime, I think I'll get acquainted with Monica," he said as he left the room.

* * *

"I am not wearing that," Roberta declared once again, defiant.

Te sighed and wondered where the sad, scared woman he'd had to reassure had gone, because this version was getting on his nerves. He'd met John-lavender in the tunnel; apparently, she had sent the Eineu in search of him.

He'd been slightly amused to hear that he'd been summoned.

That amusement had evaporated as soon as he'd entered the room and seen the look of rebellion on her face. He was confused as to what exactly her problem was. He picked up the garment from the corner she'd thrown it into. He'd had to straighten kinks in a few of the chains, but once he had, he held it up for both of them to see.

"This is beautiful. You'll look pleasing in it." He looked at her and confirmed it. So what was her problem?

"That's… it's… obscene," she sputtered.

Any slave in the City would have been honored. They felt that way because it meant they were valued. But those slaves, he remembered, lived very harsh lives. Lives that taught them to appreciate any niceties bestowed upon them by their masters, no matter how dubious they deemed the niceties to be. Roberta did not have that same frame of reference.

"Besides, I am nobody's slave." He'd tuned her out. When he tuned back in she was glaring at him, arms crossed over her ample chest.

It was only in deference to Kai that he did not slap her. She would have to learn, and however that happened would be up to Kai.

"I have informed you of your place here. Your tantrums will not change that fact."

"Then let me go. Take me home. I will not be a prisoner or a slave," she shouted.

The sigil on his chest flared to life. The pain was so intense that it forced him to his knees. The woman was still talking at him. He had to fight to focus enough to hear her over the pain.

"Are you all right? Should I call someone?"

"No, call no one. Do not leave this room."

And then he vanished.

Thirteen

Te stood across the street from the sad little house and wondered what Kai could be doing that had brought him there. The sigil on his chest had calmed somewhat, but it still burned. A couple of werewolves from Risha's pack trotted over and reverted to human form, unaware that it was unnecessary, as it would have been no trouble to pluck the information from their minds while they were in wolf form. It was just as well. The extent of his power had a tendency to make Other-kin nervous. As a courtesy, he placed a glamour over their naked bodies to prevent them from attracting undue attention in the fairly deserted but slowly waking neighborhood.

"What's the situation?" he asked when they were close enough to converse at a normal tone.

"Sir, thank you, Sir." The one closest to him stopped and saluted, acknowledging the glamour. Te didn't hold it against him; he was a young wolf who obviously never expected to be face to face with him and, therefore, improvised.

His companion caught up, nudged his younger counterpart and bowed. "My Lord."

Abashed, the young were copied the bow but kept his mouth shut. The older one, eyes fixed somewhere around Te's nose, answered his question. "Lord Kai followed three mongrels and a human to this house before dawn. He has not come out."

Te pointed to the younger were. "You. Keep watch on the street." He watched while the were transformed again and took up a position nearby. "You," he pointed to the other, "come with me."

He strode across the street and up to the door. From across the street, the sun's glare obscured the view through the front window, but up close, he could clearly see the gruesome scene inside. But Kai was not visible.

"Go around the back, but do not enter." The were quickly trotted off and disappeared around the corner of the house.

A touch to the door had the remaining boards falling away, and Te walked in. The vampires on the couch were still smoldering. It was doubtful that they'd ignite the couch, though. Once he was through, he'd send the weres in for cleanup.

The smell of blood and Corolon brandy beckoned him to the kitchen, and he stopped at the door, halted by the fact that he did not expect what he saw. He could see the were outside the back door, also stunned by the sight within. He would have to edit his memory before he sent him back to his pack.

Te's eyes came back into the room. There was blood everywhere, but mostly pooled in two areas. A naked Kai lay in one. A girl, who was the apparent source, lay in another. The girl was young—he doubted she was much past twenty—and barely recognizable. Te walked into the room, noting with disgust that his creamy beige suit, matching shoes, and maybe even his coat would need extensive cleaning after this and was slightly annoyed. Incredibly, the girl was still alive. He knelt beside her ruined body and touched what was left of her face.

"Rest," he said, releasing her essence.

"You could have healed me," a voice said from his side.

"What happened here?" he asked the dead girl.

"Pretty obvious, isn't it? Why didn't you heal me?"

"I'm not a cosmic janitor; that's why. Answer my question."

She sighed heavily, a feeling more than a sound, since she had no breath. "Whatever."

"If you'd prefer, I can put you back. Your choices led you here." He gestured with his head toward the two dead vampires in the living room. "They would have killed you eventually. Play victim to someone who'll believe it."

"They were gonna make me like them."

"Exactly. Dead. Don't make me ask you again."

"Whatever." She huffed. "I thought he was gonna fuck me, but then he couldn't get it up. Then he bit me and puked all over the place. It was pretty fuckin' pathetic. Bit me then puked, bit me then puked, bit me then puked—over and over. He's supposed to be a vampire, right? Then I guess he got mad, 'cause he started hitting me. Asshole."

Te had the impression that, had she been corporeal, she would have kicked Kai, but without a body, the action came off as less effective.

"You can go now."

"Go where? Isn't there supposed to be some fucking light or something?"

None of Azrael's house had come to escort her, solidifying his fear that what Uriel had told him was true. There were none left. He did wonder where she would go, where anyone who died would go, since Heaven no longer existed. But that wasn't currently his problem.

"Go anywhere. Just leave my sight." Thankfully she obeyed, slowly and bitching all the while, but soon he was left alone.

He then turned his attention to Kai's naked and unconscious body lying in what was apparently his own sick—Corolon brandy mixed with blood from the girl. Te cursed Lucifer in their native language, feeling both guilty and relieved that he wasn't here to hear him. He stood and walked to the back door.

"You may report back to Risha," he said, omitting Kai's condition from the were's mind. "Given the dawn and with it your increased visibility, the glamour will remain until you return to allow you ease of passage."

"Of course. Thank you, my Lord." The were bowed, transformed, and left.

After setting the house ablaze, Te vanished with Kai in tow, satisfied that rumors of Kai's viciousness, but not his weakness, would soon circulate among the Other-kin community.

* * *

Back at their house, he deposited the still-unconscious vampire in the tub. He turned on the shower and, using the handheld spray head, washed away most of the blood. Then, using a straight razor from the medicine cabinet, he opened his wrist and put it to Kai's lips, hoping instinct would innervate him enough to drink.

Te needn't have worried. The blood had barely passed Kai's lips before he came to life, grabbing ahold of his arm as if it were his lifeline and pulling the blood so hard and so fast that Te wondered if he would actually pass out. He didn't, of course, but it crossed his mind. As Kai drank, the sigil on his chest rapidly cooled until it became inert once more.

Eventually, Kai opened his eyes. When he did, Te pulled his wrist back. Kai fought the withdrawal but acquiesced when he realized he would not win.

"What happened?" Kai sounded a bit groggy but fine otherwise.

"Clean up, and then you can tell me," Te told him before rising and leaving the room.

He walked into the main bedroom and shed his clothes, burning them away until he was naked. Then he donned a pair of white silk pajama bottoms from Lucifer's closet—something he would never have done while Lucifer was alive, but he was angry enough that this little transgression felt justified.

Te opened the doors leading to the veranda and stepped onto it. It was a beautiful morning. The breeze off the river was delicate and cool. He leaned on the porch railing and forced himself to relax.

He didn't know whom he was angrier at—Kai for not coming to him for blood or Lucifer for putting Kai in that position to begin with. It was obvious from the scene at the house that Kai could no longer tolerate human blood. To be fair, maybe Lucifer had no idea that that would happen. But knowing Lucifer, Te doubted it.

A noise from the bedroom called his attention back to the room. He turned. Fresh from a shower, Kai had put on a dark blue robe and was striding toward him. Te was struck by how alluring he was. It didn't happen often, mostly because he'd trained himself not to think of Kai in that way because of Lucifer.

But Lucifer was gone, and Kai was… free.

He felt ashamed of the betrayal in his heart, but the desire wouldn't go away. There was no reason for him to deny it, not anymore. Kai frowned at him, and he realized he'd been staring.

Te leaned against the railing, bracing his arms on each side. "Want to tell me what happened?"

Kai's frown deepened, and he shrugged. In the morning light, the sigils on his face and the ones visible around the robe shimmered and danced. It was Lucifer's powerful gift to make their written language appear as though it had a life of its own. To his kind, the only ones who could read them, it would always be so. The sigil on Kai's face—where

Lucifer signed his name for all with eyes to see—mocked his desire.

He longed to cover that one with his hand and trace the others, in defiance of his oath, with his lips. Lucifer had damned Kai, and now he was gone. It just wasn't fair.

"It gets fuzzy after I followed the mongrels into that house. I think I drank too much of that Corolon brandy." Kai's lips twisted, embarrassed by allowing this lapse in control. He shook his head. "Don't remember. Then I woke in the tub. Wet." His mouth curled in amusement, but his eyes looked concerned. "I must have had a good time if you felt the need to clean me off while I was still unconscious." He stretched. "I don't even remember calling you."

"I made Lucifer a promise. No, more than a promise. An oath bound with my essence." He pointed to the symbol etched into the flesh in the center of his left pectoral muscle. "This is the symbol of that promise." Kai's eyes grew wide in surprise. He drew aside his robe to reveal a similar symbol on his chest in the exact same place. "They connect us." Te told him.

"What does it mean?"

"It means that no matter where you are, I will find you. If ever you are in mortal danger, I will know. Lucifer's idea of an insurance policy."

"Last night I was in 'mortal danger?' I would have thought fighting Ronin would have qualified before tussling with a few mongrels," Kai said, incredulous.

"Wait. You fought Ronin—and lived?" Te didn't mean to be insulting, but that just didn't happen. From the look on Kai's face, he knew it too.

"I held my own," Kai said with more than a touch of pride. "Gregory had hired them. They knew why I was there and let me take him."

"Impressive." Te smiled when Kai preened at the praise. But then he grew serious. "It was the blood. You needed blood. Not just any blood, *my* blood. I'm sure that Corolon swill didn't help matters any either. Why didn't you come to me?"

Acknowledgement colored Kai's eyes. "I thought I was addicted, but…" He turned away, walked into the room, and sat on the edge of the bed. Placing his elbows on his knees, Kai dropped his head onto his hands, his still damp hair falling down and hiding his face. "You weren't going to tell me."

"My blood was an acceptable substitute until Luc returned."

"Speaking of, where is he? Why isn't he back yet?" Kai had closed his hands and was now pulling on his hair. It was only then that Te allowed himself to wonder how much of the love Kai felt for Lucifer could be explained by the addiction to his blood.

Kai was enthralled.

Something he himself refused to do to that woman, Lucifer had done to him. He wondered if he should point out that fact but decided against it. Kai was looking at him. Te must have given away something on his face. He looked fearful.

"You know something. Did he leave me? I told him he would tire of me. He did, didn't he? That's why he put that sigil on you, bound you to me. Even when he doesn't want me, he won't let me go."

Kai had sunk to the floor. The sun streamed into the room, framing his shuddering body. Was this how he had looked to Lucifer on that abandoned road so long ago, as he wept for his lost master? Vulnerable. Exquisite. If he did, no wonder Lucifer captured him.

Te walked into the room and knelt beside him.

"He didn't leave you willingly." Although he didn't know the circumstances, Te was sure about that. "Uriel believes he's dead, and I'm inclined to agree."

The disbelief in Kai's eyes was clear. Te would have gotten the same look had he said the moon was actually made of green cheese.

"Apparently, things have been going on for some time now. All the angels are dead, and Heaven no longer exists."

"Uriel talked about changes. I thought he was being cryptic to appear more mysterious."

Te chuffed a laugh, and Kai's lips curved into a wry smile. "Uriel isn't the best communicator; that's why he appears mysterious."

The laugh they shared at Uriel's expense soothed any hurt feelings between them.

"You really believe him?" Kai whispered. Te could tell he hadn't wanted to ask the question but felt compelled to know the answer.

"Yes. Uriel and I are the only ones left. Something or someone has killed them all."

"What are you going to do?"

Te shrugged. "What I've always done. Uriel will stay in the City. Life will go on."

"What am I going to do?"

"Take over your clan and join the Council, apparently."

Kai rolled his eyes and shook his head. "When hell freezes over," he said, eliciting a chuckle from Te. "Wait, how do you know about that?"

"I hear things." He shrugged. "Risha has been hinting for years that I should talk to you about it."

Kai accepted that with a nod and then looked off into the distance. "I meant what am *I* going to do?"

Te didn't know if it was love for Lucifer or the blood addiction talking and decided he didn't care. He reached out and smoothed his hand through Kai's hair, grabbing a fist full and pulling enough to cause a low sound to erupt from Kai's throat. Te brought their lips together gently, giving Kai ample time to pull away should he desire to. It was Kai who lunged at him fast and hard and allowed Te to plunge his tongue into his willing mouth. The kiss that began as an exploration turned into a challenge and finally into one of claiming.

When Te pulled back, they both were breathing hard. "What do you want to do?"

* * *

Kai would never believe that Luc was dead. But Luc was not here, and he needed to be undone. Vampires in general liked violent sex, and he was no different. Erotic foreplay had its proper place and time, but that time was not now. So he panted in delight and encouragement as Te tore into him, broke him, and scattered pieces of him to the winds. Loving Te was no hardship and maybe a little bit of a relief. The core of him ached with Luc's loss and would hang on until he returned. Until then, he would survive. Luc had ensured that, and he was grateful.

* * *

Afterwards, Te was surprised and pleased that Kai let himself be cuddled, for now he lay spooned, comfortably sated, in his arms. Stephan would have nothing to do with such gentle moments. A few of the braver cats crept slowly back into the room after having fled the earlier violent commotion. Keeping their distance from Kai, they planted themselves on Te's side of the room. It was a truce both sides kept for their beloved seraphs.

"The Rendering is tomorrow night." Kai sighed and remained pliant in his arms.

"Not a moment too soon."

Te hummed and kissed Kai's neck. "Once you solidify your position, things should calm considerably," he said, twirling a strand of black hair around in his fingers.

"Now that Luc's gone, it's more necessary."

"True." Te nudged Kai to roll around so that they were face to face. "But why not be more? Why not lead your clan? Join the Council?"

Kai looked at Te for a long time before answering. "It would mean replacing Lugan. He's my only connection to Aram, and while we don't get along, killing him would insult his memory. I don't want the clan. I just want respect and to be left alone."

Even though Te believed differently, he knew pushing the issue would push Kai away, and he didn't want to do that, so he left it alone.

"I know what you did to Stephan, by the way. Don't even think of doing that to me." Kai told him before rolling over again.

Te laughed. "You want to know a secret?"

Kai's laugh joined his. "Sure."

"It was my price for his title."

"He got off cheap." They both dissolved into giggles.

"I don't mean to replace him," Kai said, when he was able to speak again.

"No." Te grew serious. "He has his uses, and the title of Consort gives him enough power to act in my stead when necessary."

"I'd rather he didn't know." Kai gestured between them. "About this, I mean. He'll try even harder to kill me and be even more annoying than he is now."

Te made a noise, signifying assent. "That's fine, because then I'd have to kill him, and I'd rather not, if I can help it." Frowning, he raised an eyebrow. "But won't he smell me on you?"

Kai shook his head. "No, he's much too young to distinguish your power scent from the scent that distinguishes you."

"Power scent?"

He shrugged. "That's what I call it—it's the dominating scent. Come to think of it, I wonder if due to certain circumstances, I'm the only one that can distinguish between the two."

"Intriguing. What does power smell like?"

Kai rested his head on Te's chest. "Ozone is the best word I can think of. Your true smell is closest to cedar."

"Cedar, hmm? Masculine without being obnoxious. I like it," Te said before rolling on top of Kai and kissing him, effectively dismissing any further conversation.

Fourteen

Roberta picked up the offending garment with two fingers and threw it back into the corner. The novelty of the man's sudden disappearance had worn off soon enough. She had her own problems to deal with. One thing she knew for sure was that she had no plans to walk around mostly naked.

She looked at the hated thing piled in a heap. It wasn't even clothes. It was nothing but straps and chains, and how was she even supposed to put it on? She squinted at it from her vantage point in the middle of the room. He'd held it up for her, but looking at it now, she couldn't tell the top from the bottom. Maybe a porn star or a prostitute would wear something with so much negative space—but not her.

It wasn't that she was a prude. She would wear lingerie—in private, with a lover. She would not, however, flounce around in public wearing that. It was doubtful that the thing would even fit.

She plopped on the couch and crossed her arms, not wanting to think about the fact that maybe, just maybe, if she weren't so fat she wouldn't be so freaked out by the idea. Skinny women liked flaunting their bodies if the clothes they wore were anything to go by. The thing winked at her in all its strappy glory. If she were skinny, maybe she'd wink back and take it for a test drive. Maybe the idea of wearing it wouldn't terrify her. Maybe.

Roberta could barely wrap her mind around the whole slave issue. Given the nature of the thing she was supposed to wear, she was pretty sure she knew what that meant, and she didn't want to think about it. Wrapping her arms around her body, she fervently wished she could go home, even though she no longer knew where home was.

Five years. She had lost *five years*. In her mind, it still seemed like she'd worked for the Asshole for only a month. The circumstances around getting the job had always been strange, but she'd thought it more serendipity than anything else. She had just come off of a long job and had planned to take some time off when Bree, her contact, had called.

"I know you wanted to take some time off, but we're in a bind, Roberta. We'll totally make it worth your while if you could help us out."

"I don't know."

"Look, he's run off two temps already. No one's ever complained about you. If we can put you in with him for a few weeks so you can get things running while he looks for a permanent secretary—that would be perfect. You'll be doing us a real favor. Losing his business would be bad."

"Two weeks? I guess I can postpone my vacation."

"You're a lifesaver. Look, we'll sweeten the pot for your vacation too. How's forty an hour sound?"

"I'll take it." She'd almost fallen out of her chair when Bree had quoted the salary.

The interview with the Iron Lady had been odd. She'd been asked questions that she was sure were illegal—did she live alone? Did she have a lot of friends or a boyfriend? How was her relationship with her parents? The questions had been asked during what Roberta thought was a brief chat after the interview, but still—hindsight, of course, told her why. Maybe there were warning bells. Looking back now, she could see the red flags, but then, she'd thought of the money and the gold star on her resume that would be working for the Asshole's company, and whatever hesitation she'd had evaporated.

The black guy said that he could restore her memories of those years. Did she want them back?

Her body spasmed with a sudden spike of anxiety. She remembered a month of his abuse. Did she really want to remember five years of it? Her gut reaction was no. As to her friends, she assumed they'd just given up on her, and she had no boyfriend.

But what about her parents? Granted, she wasn't close to them, but she sent them the usual Christmas and birthday greetings. At least she had five years ago. What did they think happened to her? Were they still alive? The oddness of having dropped out of time left her feeling raw, and the only way she knew how to fix it was to again move her thoughts along to the next crazy thing she had to deal with.

P2. Best. Drug. Ever.

After rehearsals and classes, she'd smoked pot with her actor friends, gotten drunk at the occasional party, but this stuff was totally outside her frame of reference. The high was amazing. It was like nothing she'd ever felt and everything she longed to feel for the rest of her life. So far, the downsides appeared to be irritability, mood swings, and a ravenous appetite.

But then, all of that could easily be attributed to suddenly finding out she was a slave held captive in an underground city and not having eaten in who knows how long. What day was it, anyway?

It was easier to think that it was the drug's side effects that had made her go ballistic over that stupid thing she was supposed to wear. Because that really wasn't like her. The man was trying to be helpful, and despite his condescension, he didn't deserve to be yelled at like that. He was certainly better than the Asshole, and she'd never gone off on him. She really needed to apologize.

While she thought, Roberta paced the room. She could feel the agitation rising within her and took deep breaths to try to calm down. She was trying her best not to think about Uriel.

What if he hadn't enthralled her? Gregory would have disappeared, and maybe she'd still have her life. Okay, she'd lost five years and probably would have continued to lose more—but at least she wouldn't know. As disgusting as that thought was, it was better than her current reality.

She could feel her desire to bask in Uriel's presence warring with her desire to scream at him for ruining her life. What really hurt was that she knew he didn't care now and hadn't cared then. He'd gone right on about his business, intending to leave her like that. Bastard. He was an angel, for God's sake. Didn't he have a conscience—some kind of holy code that said fucking with human minds was wrong?

There was a knock at her door.

John came in, bowing low. "Please excuse. Miss, has visitor."

The words were barely out of his mouth when Uriel strode into the room and her mind went blank. He no longer looked like he'd stepped out of a fairy tale. Uriel was dressed in an impeccably tailored suit so black it seemed to absorb the light from the room. But then again, he was so bright he glowed.

Seeing him was like coming home. His red hair was pulled back into a tight braid that hung heavy over one shoulder. She wanted to cry out at the injustice of binding such beautiful hair.

"You have something you would like to say to me?" His face was unreadable. He walked over to the couch and sat down, crossing one leg over the other and resting his hands in his lap.

She came back to herself in an instant, fury burning bright, as if indignant at being dampened by his arrival.

"How dare you!" Rage consumed her. The black guy had merely been the kindling it needed to ignite; in Uriel it found its fuel. "Is this what you angels do? Run around fucking up people's lives?"

He remained unmoved, an implacable statue unimpressed by her emotion. It only made her madder, but she'd lost her words. She did the only thing she could do: she screamed.

Roberta dropped to her knees and wailed. Fists balled tight, she threw her arms in the air and brought them down, pounding her fists against the floor. Then she rose up and flung them down again. She did this more than a few times, throwing all of her frustration, hate, rage, despair, and love—yes there was love in the mix, which only made her hate him more—into the rhythmic beating. When she was empty and there was nothing left but exhaustion, she sat on the floor panting.

Embarrassed, she stared at her pulsing, swollen, and red hands. There was movement to her right. John stood hovering a few feet away, drawn into the room by the commotion. He looked as if he would burst into tears at any moment.

"As you can see, your charge is only bruised," Uriel waved a few fingers of the hand that rested on his knee, healing her hands, "and is now healed. You may go."

He looked pointedly at the shivering creature that seemed reluctant to leave, even though he had witnessed the healing. Roberta nodded, and John hesitated a beat longer, bowed deeply, and left the room.

"Intense emotion counteracts the effects of the enthrall-ment as well, it seems."

She looked at him, exhausted, but feeling the most clear-headed of the entire time she'd been there. He was right. Slowly she got to her feet, walked over to an opposing chair, curled up in it, and studied her newly healed hands. While grateful, she wasn't inclined to thank him for the healing.

"Why have you come? Why now?"

Uriel didn't answer right away but just sat looking at her. He got up after a while, strolled over to the balcony, parted the curtain, and stepped out. She remained where she was, waiting. It took him so long to answer that she was unsure he would.

"Using enthrallment has always been a convenient way of gathering information or ensuring compliance." He spoke from the balcony, still turned away, yet she had no trouble hearing him clearly. "The expectation was that you would comply immediately, our interaction lasting mere seconds. Longer exposure causes... complications."

So, there were consequences. Good—the satisfaction warmed her. It served him right for fucking up her life.

He turned, his gaze lancing into her. "I am not bound to you or any such nonsense. However, I have found myself rather... attuned to your existence."

He stood there, hands clasped behind him, a dark figure silhouetted by the light coming from outside. He did not fidget or use any wasted movements. She admired his self-possession. She, on the other hand, had changed position more than once while listening to him speak.

"You ruined my life."

Roberta heard a distinct snort from his direction.

"I did no such thing. You had already doomed yourself." She stood up at this, ready to have another go at him. "The minute you consented to work for that man, your life was forfeit."

She stopped, suddenly afraid to hear more.

"The compound contained magical objects which produced a compulsion in the humans that worked there, a compulsion triggered by consent. You no doubt signed a document, an agreement."

"It was required."

"You did not read it."

"Well, no. I was told it was a standard nondisclosure agreement, that sort of thing." She felt her heart drop into her stomach at her stupid inattention to something so basic.

"You signed your life away. But your will is stronger than most. You found a reason to not completely lose yourself to the magic, to the abuse."

"I lost five years of my life. I didn't deserve that."

He made a noncommittal gesture; she had no idea if he was conceding or dismissing the point.

"I want my life back."

"Humans," he spat. "Your sense of entitlement never ceases to amaze me."

She wanted to hit him.

"I would advise against that. While the enthrallment has given me what could be called an affinity toward you, it would be unwise of you to test me in such a way."

"Get out of my head!" Roberta really wanted to hit him.

"I could ask the same thing of you."

He was so frustrating. "Don't you have emotions? Do you ever get mad? Or sad? Are you really that insensitive that you can't understand anything that I'm going through?"

"The last time I was angry, I destroyed two cities." Uriel walked back into the room and sat on the couch, more stiffly this time. "While I understand your situation, what I cannot understand is why you must incessantly whine about it."

She didn't have anything to say to that. Two cities? She didn't know much about angels or the Bible.

"Sodom. Gomorrah."

Oh, those two cities. It was freaky having him in her head like that. She sighed and sat back down in the chair across from him.

"I don't mean to whine. I just… I just don't know what to do. I can't help but want my old life back. It was crappy sure, but it was mine."

A straight razor appeared at her feet.

She looked at him, unsure if he was fucking with her or not. She couldn't read him. His radiant face was impassive, carved from living stone. Reaching down, she picked up the razor and opened it. The blade was sharp, she discovered when it cut her finger.

"Your old life is over. You have two choices: accept your new one or end it. Choose."

He was serious. "What kind of angel are you? Where is the comfort? Where is the understanding? Isn't this a sin or something?"

"Choose."

Roberta dropped the razor when the tears flooded her eyes. It wasn't fair. She didn't want to die but didn't want to be a slave either. She had thought her life had more meaning than that.

"Most humans search all their lives for some fundamental truth, some deeper meaning while missing the point entirely. The fundamental truth is this: you can either flow with life or against it. Your life is entirely what you make of it. Your choice. Live or die—it makes no difference to me."

She cried harder.

"You wanted to see the City. Get dressed. I will take you."

Still crying, she managed to shake her head.

"Suit yourself," Uriel said and vanished.

The razor remained, still shiny in the moderately lit room. She kicked it into a corner, then drew her knees into the chair, and closed her swollen eyes. The chair was remarkably cozy. In fact, her rooms were very comfortable indeed, considering where they were. The living/sitting room was nicely furnished, the view out of the balcony intriguing. Her bed was inviting. There was electricity and running hot and cold water—everything designed to give her comfort physically.

But she was a prisoner. She was trapped. All cried out, Roberta sat in the chair wishing she had the courage to go to the corner and pick up the razor.

Fifteen

Kai watched Te dress from his comfortable burrow in the bed. Te's blood eased his hunger, but his heart still ached.

"You should go see your new property."

"I know. I've been avoiding her."

After Te had finished dressing—in a rather dapper, fuchsia suit with light yellow piping, complete with pork-pie hat and yellow bowtie—he sat on the bed. "With Luc gone you'll have a lot more time on your hands. While technically a slave, she could also be a companion."

Kai had propped himself on his elbow and now dropped back down with a sigh.

"I took the liberty of informing her of her new role as well as giving her some background on the City," Te said before filling Kai in on his encounters with Roberta.

"Parade her out during the Rendering. It would do your reputation a world of good," he advised, fiddling with his tie until it sat to his liking—in Kai's opinion, there was no difference from the way it looked before.

Kai buried himself under the covers. "Do me a favor and threaten to publicly castrate me the next time I do something stupid like rescue helpless humans."

Te's hearty laugh made his insides tingle. He felt the bed dip, and the covers were pulled back.

"Are you kidding me? This is highly entertaining," Te beamed, but then his face grew serious, and he stood, bringing the covers with him. "Now, go see that woman. She's not my problem anymore."

Kai playfully groaned and got up. Te was right. He'd delayed long enough.

* * *

Half an hour later, Kai was knocking on her door. The answering call to enter had been so low that, had he not had superior hearing, he'd never have heard it. He opened the door and stepped in, closing it behind him. Roberta was curled in an armchair. By the looks of it, she'd slept there. She looked miserable, and his heart broke a little.

Maybe he *had* grown soft or tame. Maybe he really was weak after all.

"I guess you expect me to bow or something," she said, her voice dull and resigned.

Kai didn't converse with humans often and wasn't sure how to proceed. Luc loved television, and thanks to him, he'd sat through hours and hours of reality TV. From what he could gather, humans responded to power and honesty—and sex and money, but those didn't apply here. He decided to go with honesty.

"This not being a formal situation, it's not necessary."

The lines around her mouth relaxed slightly. "Oh."

"What Lord Te has told you is the truth." Sadness filled her pretty face. "However," he added quickly, "I thought we should talk, understand each other."

Seeing her now, an idea began to form.

"So, I'm your property, but you want to get to know me."

Given the circumstances, it sounded ridiculous, but it was no less true.

"What I want is for us to reach an understanding." Her wary face told him she was skeptical. He sat down opposite her on the couch. "Accepted practice states that you would become my thrall—obedient and without a will of your own. I find that unacceptable."

"Thrall. Isn't that what got me here in the first place? What Uriel did to me?" Her posture was still closed, cautious.

"Much the same, different mechanism."

"You're an angel too?"

"Vampire."

Her eyes closed at that, and she brought her knees on to the chair and buried her face in them.

"I wish someone would tell me what I did to have my life go so wrong," she whispered. After a bit, she appeared to pull herself together and dropped her feet back down to the floor before hugging her body with her arms. "Uriel said I didn't have a choice and that I should get used to it."

"Uriel is… well, Uriel." He shrugged. "He has a point, but what I'd like you to understand is that, as your master, I'll be making adjustments as well."

"From the other end of the leash? My heart bleeds for you," she replied, obviously before her mouth gained permission to speak from her brain.

Kai watched, slightly amused, as she realized her candor and sarcasm might not be appreciated. The woman was brave—he liked that, and it made what he was about to propose more likely to work.

Ignoring the fact that she was bracing herself for violence, he spoke. "We have an opportunity to create something that could work for the both of us."

"Why? Why do you care how I feel? Uriel doesn't. The other guy—Lord Te? He doesn't care. What makes you so different?"

Roberta had noticed the absence of violence and rolled with it, using that momentum to chance speaking her mind. Of all the humans he could stumble across, he was feeling extremely lucky. She had wit but could temper her tendency to lash out with respect. He was feeling more confident that she would not only understand his reasoning but appreciate it. Time would tell.

"Most vampires are raised in blood and pain—power and brutality are accepted and respected. My master was different. He believed in honor and discipline, to only take what was needed and to leave the rest. That was what he taught me." After fifty or so years of insatiable bloodlust, Aram had taught him control. "He taught me to respect human life, for without you, I could not exist."

Kai paused a moment, looking away from her to the balcony. He didn't want to have to justify himself with the tale of his human upbringing as a slave—he didn't like thinking about it. It may have been almost a thousand years ago, but that didn't mean it hadn't left scars that ached when picked at.

"I was afraid that Uriel went too far. I brought you here to try and salvage what was left of your life because you didn't deserve to just waste away and die, and for all practical purposes, your life has been saved. You will soon be free of Uriel's thrall, and while still bound by your contract to Gregory, you no longer have to toil semi-mindlessly for him." He shrugged at the minor win. "Since all of Gregory's possessions have been transferred to Lord Te, you belong to him. He has chosen to give you to me. And as your new master, I'm proposing an alteration that could ease the situation for both of us."

"Which is?" she asked, eyes guarded but inquisitive.

"Your choice to cooperate. If you'd rather not comply, I won't beat you or force you. Tell me, and I will end your life quickly. You will feel no discomfort." He paused to make sure she understood. He was giving them both an out, and truth be told, felt a little cowardly for it. "You still have many years left. While your life may have been unremarkable, you are anything but human refuse. Should you choose to, you will live a life of comfort and see things that few others have."

"You're asking for my permission."

"I prefer to think of it as your consent. But that could be seen as quibbling over semantics." He smiled. "The main point I'm making is that you don't have to lose yourself.

You will have to make concessions, but you will still have the freedom of choice in most things. I don't know of any other of my kind that has done this, but I'm willing to try. Are you?"

While he spoke, her eyes rested on a shiny object that was partially obscured under a table in a corner of the room. At length she nodded, tears rolling steadily down her face. "I get to choose. I will try."

* * *

They were standing on the balcony looking out into the City. Kai had sent John to fetch him a spyglass from Te's office. John had returned quickly, and he handed the spyglass to Roberta, who took it, her oval face calm but serious. She held it, waiting for his permission to use it, unaware that she waited with submission and obedience. Gregory most likely honed what was a natural tendency. It would make things easier between them. He gave his permission with a gesture. The minute she looked through the eyehole she gasped.

"Lord Te told me he gave you some background on the City."

She nodded, the spyglass moving back and forth. "There's so many… uh…"

"Nonhumans?" he asked, amused at her attempt at tact.

"Yes, and oh my god—"

Roberta snatched the glass away from her eye and then almost immediately brought it back. She'd found the human slave pens. Fear, acrid and pungent, wafted from her suddenly too-still form. It was unfortunate to scare her, but he needed her to understand.

She had to clear her voice before she could talk, and even then it came out as a whisper. "I could be down there."

"True. But you're not and won't be." He guided her back around and pointed across the cavern. "Look there." She complied, raising the glass to her eye again. "That is the banner of my clan, Clan Air."

Each of the more powerful factions—vampires, werewolves, and Kazat—had specific districts in the city designated by banners or flags. The vampire clan banners were decorated with their clan colors and symbols: black with swirling clouds for Clan Air, blue with a waterfall for Clan Water, and green with mountains for Clan Earth.

The werewolf clans had the same, although the banners were golden. Each symbol was different because they had all started out as the same clan. Clans Orion, Zenith, Aurora, and Lumina had all sprung from the Celesta Clan. As far as Kai knew, the werewolves were the only wereanimals left—the last sighting of a weretiger had been over fifty years ago.

He pointed to a large section at the other end of the city. It had a red banner with a large claw on it—the Kazat section. Almost everyone in the City fell under the protection of a vampire or werewolf clan. The small percentage left took their chances alone. No one but the Kazat lived in their district.

"But what about Lord Te?"

"Lord Te oversees the City. He makes it so that the different races can cohabit peacefully—he is the ultimate mediator and authority here. Otherwise, each district has their own rules, and taxes in some cases. Some districts treat their citizens better than others, some worse.

"Incredible," she remarked.

Kai was pleased at her calm and adaptability. He was also glad that he was enjoying her company.

"The majority of the time, I will be with you. When we are out in the City, it is imperative that you keep your eyes down and be the obedient slave. If anyone addresses you in my presence—they shouldn't, but if they do—I will take care of it. You speak only to me, and then only when I specifically address you. 'My Lord' is the proper honorific at those times. If we are separated for any reason, John will be your escort. The Eineu are under Lord Te's protection, and you are under mine. No one should be stupid enough to bother you given those circumstances."

He paused, wondering if he should tell her about slave marks. His mark would identify her as his and therefore provide active protection. He decided to leave it for now, as there were other things for her to worry about. He'd have it done before the Rendering, but it could wait. She wasn't going anywhere alone now anyway.

"If you must talk to someone that is not Lord Te, myself, or John, you will address them as 'Master.' Te is always Lord Te, and in private, you may address me as Kai. Also in private, you have permission to speak freely. I know that is a lot to remember, so repeat it back to me."

She did, flawlessly. He was impressed and said so.

"Fifteen years working for executives, five years," she made a face, "working for the—Mr. Gregory. I've learned to follow instructions."

Telling her that she'd probably been conditioned without her knowledge would not be helpful, so he only nodded, led her back into the main room, and pointed to the couch. Next, he walked over and picked up the discarded garment and dropped it on the table, before lounging in one of the chairs.

"Lord Te tells me you have a problem with this."

She looked away, her face gone from interested to miserable in seconds. "Please, don't make me wear it."

"The humans you saw," he gestured to the spyglass still in her hands, "were they wearing clothes?"

She shook her head no.

"It's warm enough here that exposure to the elements isn't an issue, so there's no risk of losing a slave to the weather. Protective clothing is expensive; slaves are cheap—with the prices going down every day. There are billions of you. Even at capacity and high turnover, the slave trade in the City would never come close to making the slightest dent in your numbers. You do that yourselves." He continued despite the fact that she would not look at him. "I'm telling you the reality. This," he gestured to the heap of leather and metal chain with his foot, "means I value you, because I've taken the time to decorate you."

"Decorate me. Like an object."

"Like a beautiful, valued asset. Which, actually, is what you are." He smiled at her, and even though she blushed, she still wouldn't look at him.

"Does…" She had to clear her throat and begin again. "Does that mean… you intend to use me for sex?"

He got up and sat next to her on the couch. Kai touched her hair and gently turned her face so she was looking at him. "Use? I won't take what is not freely given."

Roberta shivered. A faint warm spice that signaled her arousal despite her discomfort tickled his nostrils.

"Do you not find me attractive?" he teased.

"Um, no. It's—it's not that." The faint scent grew stronger. She tried turning her head, but he hadn't let go, and she couldn't. She settled for keeping her eyes down.

Kai enjoyed making her blush. "Humans and sex. You make things so complicated when they aren't." He let her go. "Now, off to the shower with you. Once you've finished, call me and we'll get you into this. This is your first test. If you can obey me, then this will work. If not…" He would soon find out how committed she was.

She looked at him for a long moment, deciding. Then she got up and walked into the bedroom. He could hear the shower start shortly afterward.

* * *

Kai had no idea how long it typically took a human female to take a shower, but he suspected she was taking longer than usual. He stood on the balcony and watched the City from above.

He couldn't help but compare their circumstances, though he didn't like to think about his past before he'd met his master. Those were days designed to be endured rather than enjoyed. He was still quite young when his duties changed from cleaning and fetching water to more personal services. At that point, he had been expected to dress like the other girls and paint his face.

Never wanting to spend more time with the customers than he had to, he serviced them as quickly and as efficiently as he could get away with, which usually earned him a beating for not being enthusiastic enough. He hadn't been a good whore, and the proprietor of the establishment, Angelo, alternated between threats to have him castrated to make him more docile or to sell him off altogether. The man had been overjoyed when Aram had taken a liking to him.

Aram was rich, and Angelo strung him along with promises to sell the boy but needing to be sure so requiring outrageous sums to secure the man's intentions, saying that he couldn't let such a prize go so easily and cheaply. Angelo would have been surprised to know that Aram hadn't touched him—to Kai's delight and relief.

Instead, he took him out into the bustling city of Constantinople. They saw plays, museums, temples, and cathedrals. It had been his first taste of a world outside the brothel. He hadn't had a sexual encounter with Aram until long after he was purchased and given his freedom. Almost immediately after being bought Kai had begged to be allowed to please him, believing his life depended on it—he'd been expensive, after all.

But Aram rebuffed him, telling him he wasn't ready. His attempts continued until he finally realized that his master wanted him to come to him with something other than obligation.

Kai didn't need Roberta's love. What he wanted was her acceptance, which he believed he could gain by not over-whelming her with demands for her to perform for his pleasure. He would taste her, just not at that moment.

He'd been misguided and distracted when he'd made the decision to save her. In retrospect, he should have left her or killed her to spare her misery. He was beginning to acknowledge a tendency to suppress his own impulses in favor of Lucifer's wants and desires and wondered if he sometimes did things to compensate—things that in-evitably complicated his life, like behead younglings when a beating would have sufficed or attempt to rescue an in-nocent that he should have left to fend for themselves.

It was only odd luck that Luc disappeared, making this one thing easier. If this arrangement worked, it would be a huge boon to his reputation. If he was going to be here more now that Luc was away, it could use the lift.

* * *

Roberta had been given enough time in the shower, Kai de-cided as he left the balcony. Stopping briefly to retrieve her adornment, he walked to her room. Thankfully the door to her bedroom was not locked. She was still in the bathroom, and as a courtesy, he knocked. Receiving no answer, he opened the door—again, thankfully unlocked.

Humid air settled on his skin, bringing with it the scent of strong soap, freshly washed skin and hair, and something else—the salt of tears. He was pleased to see that she had obeyed him and taken a shower. But now she sat on the closed toilet lid, wrapped in a towel, crying.

"I don't think I can do this." She sniffled.

He thought a moment and then left the room. Going to the outer hall, he called for John to administer to her another dose of P2, which calmed her immediately.

"How do you feel?" he asked, taking her hand and leading her out of the bathroom and into the bedroom.

"Like a junkie," she scoffed.

"I would prefer you not remain so distressed."

She looked at him, her brown eyes as solemn as the P2 would allow. "I'm trying."

Kai held up the collection of straps and chains that passed for clothing, and she immediately averted her eyes. "No, look. I want you to look at this and tell me why it upsets you."

"What? You mean besides the whole slave thing?"

He smiled at her sarcasm. "Would treasured pet be better?" The look she gave him told him that no, it wouldn't. "Never mind. Continue."

She tried to smile, but it dissolved into a grimace. "Look at me. I don't even think I can fit into it. There's just too much of me. I'll stick out of it everywhere. How can you say that's attractive?" She was calmer, true, but misery seeped out of her pores, while tears leaked out of her eyes.

Kai looked at her and then at the garment. He had no idea if she would fit into it but had assumed since Te had given it to her that she would. Then it occurred to him that it really wasn't about being able to fit the garment but having to wear it and feel unappealing. Her race did have an obsession with appearances; both sexes fixated on what was considered attractive and what wasn't. Currently, that obsession circled around fat—too much or too little. They constantly chased a carefully cultivated ideal.

It would have been easier on him if her reluctance was due to the puritanical ideas about sex that prevailed in this age instead. On the one hand, he felt proud of himself for figuring that out; on the other, he wanted to call her stupid and tell her to get over it. Luckily for him, he had the sense and the restraint not to, although what he was about to do—he was sure—would have the same result. He threw the thing in the corner, the action causing her to jump and look at him warily.

"Stand up and remove the towel."

Roberta expected to be yelled at, he could tell, but according to her face, this was worse.

"Our arrangement is one of assent, agreed?"

"Agreed." She nodded, defeat in her eyes. She stood and, head bowed and eyes closed, let the towel fall to the floor.

"Yet she still lives." Kai murmured, letting the arousal he felt color his voice.

She was slightly taller than he, and while there was fat on her body, it didn't displease him. It made her breasts large and soft, just as he liked them. The size of her belly, hips, and thighs had probably garnered ridicule from the stick-thin women who fit the current human beauty ideal, but he felt himself hardening with the desire to take her there and then. Walking around her in a circle, he let his eyes roam freely while he talked.

"I grew up in a whore house." She inhaled sharply at the revelation. He was behind her now; her skin was smooth and lightly freckled. "Angelo, the proprietor, was notoriously cheap and made it a habit to underfeed the whores as an incentive to perform."

As a result, he was always half starved, getting even less as Angelo sought to starve him into happy compliance.

"The more clients came back, the more they got to eat. The more they got to eat, the plumper they became; the plumper they became, the more desirable they became, and more customers would ask for them. Of all the whores there, two were about your size—they were the most popular."

When he finished he stood in front of her once more.

Roberta peeked at him from under the hair that fell in front of her face. She was looking for something, most likely signs that he was lying. But she would find none, because there were none. He reached up with one hand and caressed her face and then brushed her hair back with the other.

"I am not displeased." His voice was low, seductive. She glanced up when he spoke, only to lower her eyes just as quickly. "I very much enjoy the sight of you."

Kai could feel small tremors in her body and smell the return of her arousal. Good. He let go of her and stepped back.

"In fact, this is how you will present yourself to me, until I say otherwise."

She froze, her mouth opened, and her eyes shot up.

"Did you misunderstand?"

"Uh, no," she replied in low voice.

He wanted to kiss the worry and confusion off of her plump lips while she rode his fingers, but he restrained himself. She would be a tasty morsel. He would wait and enjoy the view while he did.

"Good. Join me in the sitting room. Bring a pillow."

He turned to leave the room, when something on the dresser caught his eye. It was a gold necklace with a small ornate cross pendant.

"Oh."

At Roberta's utterance, Kai looked up at her in the mirror.

"I can see your reflection."

"Are you sure?"

His reflection had disappeared, even though he had not moved.

"What the…?" This time she sounded awed and little frightened.

Once again when her eyes flicked to his reflection. It was there, just like the first time.

"You're fucking with me." Roberta laughed suddenly, and he smiled back at her, happy she was distracted. He picked up the cross, brought it over, and fastened it around her neck. "This doesn't bother you either," she said.

"You sound disappointed."

"Well, are any of the stories true?"

"Come, and I'll tell you."

Kai led her into the next room, took the pillow from her, and placed it on the floor next to his chair.

"One thing you must get into the habit of doing is sitting on the floor. You will need a more decorative pillow for this purpose, but this will do for now. I will sit first, and then you will place your pillow on the floor to my right—whenever possible—and then seat yourself."

She didn't look happy, but she waited until he sat before settling herself onto the pillow.

"Good." He allowed himself to play in her hair. Still slightly damp from her shower, it was soft and thick, and from the contented look on her face, she was enjoying it. The cross hung low enough to rest right in the center of her breastbone. He decided to let her wear it not because of the symbolism but because putting gold or a pretty shiny thing on a slave meant two things: first, that he could afford to and second, that he valued her enough to waste resources.

He needed to start living with an eye toward his station. Luc would have hated it, of course. The thought of him brought with it a wave of melancholy that sucked Kai into its maw and wouldn't let go. A hole had opened in his life as sudden and huge as the one that had sucked Aram away from him, and like then, the idea of continuing on seemed tedious.

Roberta moved, drawing his attention and momentarily tearing him away from what could easily become a preoccupation. She fidgeted uncomfortably on the pillow, waiting for him to speak. His hand on her head had stopped moving and now lay nestled in the thick, wavy strands at the base of her neck. He set it in motion once more.

"Crosses and other holy talismans—of any religion, actually—have no effect on any of the three clans of my race. However, on mongrels—our bastard cousins—the effects are less than pleasant." Melting them with holy water was one of his favorite things to do.

"Mongrels?"

"Some members of the clans decided to mix their blood in a ritual to restore the glory of the long extinct Clan Fire. Not surprisingly, it went awry, creating the bastards we call mongrels. They have no allegiances, are unwelcome in the City, and are unequivocally killed on sight by members of the three clans. In fact, there are entire groups dedicated to their eradication."

She shivered under his hand. Mongrels always worked him up, and he had to admit that he sounded slightly unhinged just then talking about them. Kai soothed and petted her to calm her back down. He had to be careful not to let his more negative emotions get the better of him.

Having her afraid of him would not be conducive to their relationship.

Once calmer, she cleared her throat. "Why?"

He looked at her. "Why them and not us? Or why are we not bothered by holy items in general?"

The smile she gave him was both playful and genuinely interested. "Both?"

"In answer to the first, I have been told it had something to do with the magic used in the ritual." It was a partial truth. Lucifer and the dragon god Uru—which he now knew to be Te—had distilled Clan Fire into the existing three clans. No one but them could undo the separation, and that alone insured the results would be unstable and volatile.

"To answer the second question, from what I've gathered, the idea behind using them in the first place had something to do with the idea that we are dead and therefore unholy."

"I never thought about it, but that sounds about right."

"I am about as dead as you are."

"Stop messing with the folklore." Giggling, Roberta covered her ears with her hands.

He preferred seeing her happy and relaxed. "Lord Te told you about the origin of the beings here?"

"Yes, but he never said vampires weren't dead." She composed herself. "But what about not having a heartbeat and no body temperature?

Kai removed the hand from her hair and held it out for her. "Take my pulse."

Not looking at all convinced, she took his wrist and felt for a pulse. Apparently feeling nothing, she was giving him a triumphant look when she jumped, astonished.

"Slow but present. And as you can see, my temperature is no cooler than the room."

"But I don't understand."

He knew the smile he gave her was wicked, but he couldn't help himself. Pride will do that. "We are efficient predators. We can literally lie in wait for hours or days, still as the dead. Things that would kill a human cannot kill us, but we look like them. Humans appear to die when their bodies transition into ours. A tomb can be a quick and easy place to hide from the sun. It was an easy assumption to make." He shrugged.

"The coffin thing is probably not true then either."

"Would you willingly sleep in a coffin?"

She bunched up her nose in disgust then looked at him with dismay. "Do I have to sleep on the floor too?"

It took him a moment to catch up to what she was referring to, but when he did, he laughed. "No, beds all around."

"Thank god." Her face broke into a happy smile.

Kai let her take a break to stand, stretch her legs, and use the bathroom. In the meantime, he walked onto the terrace. He was beginning to feel restless; he'd have to find Te soon. When she returned to the room, they resumed their places.

"Each clan has certain talents that help to ensure our survival. Each has dominion over different things: Clan Air has the ability to alter perceptions, Clan Water has the ability to charm, and Clan Earth has the ability to control the body."

"So what you did with the mirror?"

"It's called a glamour. Anything your senses can detect, we can alter."

Roberta looked up at him, intensely interested and slightly skeptical. "Anything?"

He smiled, and her eyes lost focus, pupils blown wide, her mouth slightly parted.

"Right now, would you refuse me anything?"

"No." It came out as a whisper.

"Go into the bathroom and wash your face."

She got up and walked into the bathroom. The water turned on. He heard what could only be described as a squeak when she came back to herself. She returned to the room. "What did you do to me?"

He was chuckling at her from his chair. "I believe they're called pheromones."

Others of his clan, without the benefit of a know-it-all lover, simply called it the Seduction.

"That was both creepy and amazing." He gave her a little bow while she walked back to her place on the floor and sat down. "Thank you for not taking advantage."

Kai nodded. "We have agreed upon consent. You need to understand the world you have found yourself in."

He paused, letting himself enjoy the contours of her face and body for a moment, until she became too self-aware and started to fidget. He looked forward to the day when she could look back at him with confidence and maybe desire.

"We will talk more about the clans, and Other-kin in general, in the days ahead. Right now, the only other thing that is vital for you to know is about another vampire named Stephan. I have heard he's already been to see you once. He is afraid of me, which means he won't harm you outright. But he is curious and devious and will eventually manage to speak to you. He's a member of Clan Water, and as I've mentioned, they have the power to charm you. You must never, ever look him or any other of his clan, in the eyes. You can recognize them by their distinctive white blond hair and blue eyes."

Roberta nodded her understanding, but she looked afraid.

"Just be polite and remember what I taught you. You'll be fine."

She took a deep breath. "Okay."

But the look on her face told him she was still nervous, which was just as well. She'd need to be aware when Stephan finally cornered her, and Kai had no doubt that he eventually would.

Sixteen

"So, what happened back in the Ass—I mean, Mr. Gregory's office?"

"What were you going to call him?"

"The Asshole," Roberta replied, looking uncomfortable.

"The Asshole," Kai repeated, amused. "Why?"

"You saw him. He was always such an asshole." She scowled. "I think he enjoyed making my life hell."

"He was unpleasant. Do you make a habit of giving nicknames to those in your life?"

"Well, you were Tattooed Man for a while, and Uriel was Guy-Out-Of-A-Fairy-Tale." She gave him a cheeky look. He chuckled, liking her sense of humor.

"How old do you think Gregory is?"

Roberta shrugged. "Fiftyish?"

"Plus three and a half centuries, give or take. Gregory made a deal with Lord Te. He reneged. I came to collect," Kai replied and found her shocked expression endearing. Roberta's mouth opened in a small "o," and it took her a bit to collect herself.

"A deal? You mean a deal-with-the-devil kind of deal. Is... is Lord Te the Devil?" she asked, hushed and hesitant.

Yesterday Kai would have laughed at the question and playfully alluded to the inevitable circumstance of her actually meeting "The Devil." Today it only made him sad. He shook his head. "No."

She was silent, mulling it over. "I hate to say it, but it doesn't surprise me. He was such an awful person."

A knock on the door interrupted them. Kai responded with a command to enter. It was John with a tray.

"John brings food for Miss," the Eineu said, carrying the tray over to the table and setting it down. "John brings blood for Lord Kai."

Kai nodded his thanks, and the delicate creature hesitated for a moment, looking at Roberta. Having made a decision, it walked over to her and pulled a small glass jar from its tunic. Roberta shook her head and then John looked to him.

"Are you sure?" he asked her.

She took a deep breath and straightened. "Yes, I'm sure."

"That will be all, John." The Eineu then bowed and hustled out the door.

"If we were in public, it would be up to me to feed you. Either by hand or by giving you the bowl for you to feed yourself while still seated at my feet. In private, however," he stood and extended his hand, "I think eating at the table is acceptable."

He helped her up and led her over to the table. Once she was seated, he sat across from her. Kai knew John had meant well by bringing him blood, but he wished he hadn't. He never liked drinking it out of a glass. No matter what warming spell was used, it always looked cold and unappealing. While many felt this was more refined and civilized, Kai was never one to care about such things. He preferred blood directly from the source. Holding a warm body in his arms, the sensation of biting through the skin...

He sighed and looked at the glass filled nearly to the top with dark liquid. Feeding this way just didn't compare. Never one to waste food, however, he decided to snack on this now and then see Te later.

Roberta sat ignoring her steaming bowl of stew in favor of staring at his large glass.

"If you're not dead, why don't you eat food?"

"I can eat food," he replied, thinking of how many meals he'd eaten with Lucifer, who adored all food but hated to eat alone. "But it doesn't nourish me, at least not in manageable quantities. Blood is more efficient, I suppose."

He didn't mention the downside to eating. It hadn't bothered him as a human, but as a vampire, having to relieve himself was horrifying and disgusting. He didn't know why. When he refused to eat because of it, Lucifer placed a sigil on him that eliminated waste—he had no idea how—so he could eat with his mate.

Roberta seemed fascinated, eyes fixed on him then on the glass. He felt like a bug under a magnifying glass. "I will eat, as long as you do so as well."

She looked at her stew. "There's meat in this," she said, looking at him again and then back to her stew. "If we're underground..." She let the sentence trail off.

"It's not human." He hoped he wasn't lying. He made a note of asking John to make sure that whatever she was served wasn't made with human meat.

She didn't look like she believed him but eventually sighed and picked up her spoon. Kai relaxed, relieved he wouldn't have to play a guessing game as to what type of meat it actually was, and picked up his glass and raised it to his lips. He took a large mouthful of the warm liquid and let it slide down his throat. He'd been spoiled; after drinking angelic blood for centuries, human blood was flat and boring. Any of his brethren would have been smacking their lips with pleasure, but he remained unimpressed. It would keep him alive, but he craved more—that instant kick of power and effervescence, that *alive* feeling that human blood could not match.

The cramp hit him so suddenly and violently that he dropped the glass. Pushing back from the table, he stood. The feeling of heat and pressure came over him, and even as he felt disbelief, he raced into the bathroom, making it just in time to vomit the blood into the toilet.

Flashes of the night before flitted across his mind. This was not the first time this had happened. Kai's stomach continued to cramp, and he retched until, finally spent, he slumped next to the wall. Roberta had come in at some point and knelt by him with a damp cloth.

"Are you all right? What happened?" she asked as she cleaned around his mouth.

He shook his head. Feeling weak and ashamed to look at her, he looked past her into his reflection in the mirror on the wall opposite. His first thought was that he'd been poisoned, but that didn't make sense. The previous night came back to him in a rush—this wasn't the first time he'd thrown up after having human blood.

Kai looked at Roberta then, closed his eyes listening to her heartbeat. It was fast; she'd been alarmed. But what he should have been feeling—the thrill of the potential meal—was absent. The blood he'd drunk was warm and fresh. Being farm-produced, it had no impurities, yet before he'd taken a sip, he had no real desire for it. He looked back at the mirror, his vision narrowed, and he felt sick for a different reason.

He was wrong. He had to be.

Kai stood so quickly that he knocked Roberta over.

"Do not leave this room," he told her, apologizing with his eyes. Then, with one last look at himself in the mirror, he sprinted out of the suite, heading for Te's office.

Not finding him, he grabbed a passing Eineu who told him that both Lords Te and Uriel had gone to the Ashley House. He ran to the nearest portal, desperate for his suspicions to be false, but fearing he knew the truth.

* * *

In the beginning, Lucifer had applied the sigils one at a time, protection from various things. The first had been the practical sigil for immunity to the sun on his right wrist. Then came protection from fire, magic, and the one to remove waste. Increasingly, however, Lucifer had decorated him for his enjoyment, saying that Kai had such beautiful skin that he wanted to paint it and mark him as his own. Kai had stopped asking what the sigils meant.

Then one day Lucifer had tied him to the bed, which was nothing unusual as they often played bondage games filled with blood and sex. But this time had been different. This time, when Lucifer marked him, the experience had been filled with extreme pain—and power.

He could feel himself changing, while the intense pain made him delirious. It had lasted for days, Lucifer inscribing things on Kai's body whether Kai was conscious or not. He had whispered words of love and words Kai didn't understand—words in the language of angels, words that infused the sigils he'd drawn with power. Kai felt as though each line and curve was carved not only into his flesh but into his soul as well.

When he was lucid, which wasn't often, he'd ask Lucifer what he was doing.

"I'm protecting you, love," he'd reply. When he started in on his most sensitive and private of areas, in answer to Kai's question he'd whisper, "I'm loving you," and continue working.

When it was done, Kai was marked in a spiral starting at this right temple, down to his right cheek, over his chin to the left side of his neck, then down and curving around his back to his solar plexus from the right, down over his groin, back over his buttocks, and spiraling down his left leg to the sole of his foot. It had taken him days to recover, constantly in and out of consciousness, remembering less and less of the specifics, but basking in the loving care and reverence Lucifer had showered upon him afterwards.

Buffeted by memories, once at the portal, he was in so much of a hurry that he had to redo the spell twice because he was unable to focus. Not waiting for the vertigo-like effects to subside, he staggered through the house looking for Te and Uriel. Kai found them in the living room, chatting amiably, cats lounging at their feet, in their laps, and on the nearby furniture.

Te noticed him first. "Kai? What's wrong?" he asked, untangling himself from the felines surrounding him before rising.

Thus agitated, every cat in the room stood. Some hissed, others growled, but all readied themselves to attack. Kai tore at his clothes. He was in too much of a hurry to concern himself with buttons and fastenings, ripping and shredding his clothing until he was finally down to bare skin.

When he was naked he looked at both seraphs.

"What do they say?" he demanded, gesturing to the delicately intricate patterns and symbols that swirled about his body. Neither spoke, but Te looked particularly upset. "I know you can read them. What do they say?"

He was grasping at calm but knew he would start yelling again if he didn't get answers. Te didn't appear to want to give him any.

He pointed to the one on his neck. "Let's start with an easy one. This prevents beheading."

The responding silences were a confirmation. Betrayal twisted deep in his belly.

Skipping over the few he knew the meanings of, he chose another one at random. "What does this one do?" he asked, pointing to a large sigil on his left shoulder.

"That symbolizes strength," Uriel responded. He hadn't moved since Kai came in and, in contrast to Te, seemed unperturbed by Kai's frantic demands. "He's made you stronger."

"What about this one?"

"That symbolizes resilience," Te responded, still looking uncomfortable. "He's given you the ability to resist injury and augmented your natural healing ability."

Kai screamed in frustration. Most of the cats hissed and yowled back, echoing their own frustration. He knew they both could read his body. Why wouldn't they just tell him what it all meant? Why did he have to pull each meaning out one by one? It was tedious, and he knew he was missing something, but what? A few times he pointed, but the swirls and shapes were just decorative flourishes. Apparently, the word "love" was written in many ways in different places, but there was no power in it, just the sentiment. There had to be more here, but so far, the only thing he'd learned was that Lucifer was extremely paranoid and possessive—something he already knew.

Finally, he pointed to the one over his solar plexus. The look of dismay on Te's face told him he should have started there.

"That concerns your blood lust," Uriel said.

"Concerns my blood lust how?" Kai demanded.

Uriel made a dismissive gesture. "Your desire for human blood has been… muted."

"And if I have some?"

"I suspect you know the answer to that already." Uriel sat back in the chair and quietly challenged him to press further.

It was with a listless gesture that Kai pointed to the cluster of sigils that began at his groin, wrapped around his penis, flowed over his balls, and ended at his anus. The dread pressing on him told him all he needed to know, but he wanted confirmation.

"All of those revolve around sex," Te said, refusing to look at him.

Kai was losing control over the calm he thought he had. "How exactly?"

"Makes you more," the big angel shrugged, "receptive."

"Receptive or insatiable?" Kai asked, his throat so tight it hurt to talk.

"Your sex drive, your appetite and stamina, is… heightened." Te still wouldn't look at him.

"You knew." They had spent the day in bed. How could he have not known? "Did you want to be there, or were you just following orders?" Kai asked, tapping the sigil on his chest that matched Te's.

Te took a step toward him and finally looked him in the eye. "Both."

He would digest the implications later; he couldn't stop to do it now, caught up as he was in the momentum of finally getting answers. He picked out the sigil covering his breastbone. "This. What does this do?"

Te stared at it and said nothing. Kai looked around him to Uriel, who stared back obviously not inclined to answer him.

"Well, Te? What does it do?" he asked again.

"That symbolizes love," Te answered quietly, looking past him.

"Love," Kai repeated, feeling detached and glad for it. "What about love?"

Te walked away from him, head down. When he got to the mantle above the fireplace, he stopped. Taking a deep breath and crossing his arms, he turned. "Lucifer knew how you felt about Aram. I think he was fascinated that you could love someone so much that you were willing to die when they did." He paused, considering his teal shoes. "He wanted you to love him as you loved Aram."

"Oh." Was all he could manage as the weight of understanding settled over him. He truly was Lucifer's bitch. He wilted to the floor.

How long? Were all of his feelings for Lucifer manufactured? He knew Lucifer needed control, but like this? Kai had never, ever thought his mate capable of a treachery of this magnitude. Kai had never thought he was in an equal relationship; it had never bothered him because at least—he thought—he was respected.

He'd been a fool. He'd let himself be dressed up and fussed with—like he'd seen humans do with their pets. He laughed with Lucifer at their foolishness, and all along, he'd been exactly like those pampered pets.

Kai bent over and dropped his head in his hands. The sound that began in his belly was nothing like he'd ever heard himself make before. It grew into a wild thing that burst out of his mouth and sent most of the cats running. He felt them flee and rejoiced that something in the room feared him. He was Lucifer's bitch, leashed and tame. The best he was good for was scaring cats. One steadfast straggler stayed behind; it circled him and hissed. Snake-quick, Kai reached out and grabbed it. His entire body froze.

"Vampire, I suggest you reconsider your actions."

"The minute you let me go, Uriel, I'll kill it." The cat had gone limp out of fright or Uriel's influence. Kai didn't know which.

"You will do no such thing. As you are under protection here, they are as well." The calm superiority with which he spoke made Kai want to throttle him.

"I was putting up with these beasts out of love, which I now realize was manufactured. I want every one of them out of this house. Now." His voice was shaking with rage at still being constrained.

"You know the cats are part of the warding protection upon the house," Te said.

"Then change it."

"Emotion has left you unreasonable, vampire." He was released, and every cat, including the one he held, vanished from the room. "Nothing has changed. They have been instructed to stay away from you."

Kai didn't feel grateful, so he did not offer his thanks. Uriel got his way, like Lucifer had gotten his, like all the angels did in the end. He had no intention of thanking him for ignoring his wishes. He was struggling to hold on to his righteous anger, but he still felt the deep, all-encompassing love for Lucifer he'd felt for centuries. Knowing what the sigils meant made him angry, but it didn't change the fact that he loved him. He no longer trusted the feeling, and he wanted it to stop altogether. The pain of being betrayed was playing tug-of-war with his desire, and he wanted it all to just stop.

Kai got up, suddenly wanting to feel clean, even if it was an illusion. Te looked as if he intended to say more, but Kai ignored him, running past him, up the stairs to the bathroom, and into the shower. Turning on the water as hot as it would go, Kai just stood there and let it stream over him.

When he finally had the impetus to do more, he grabbed the soap and poured some in his hand. The sandalwood scent assailed his nostrils and brought him to his knees with a cry. He would grab the soap that Lucifer had picked out for him. Kai let it wash it away without using it and then searched for another—all the shampoos and soaps were scents that Lucifer liked and had chosen. It was too much.

Was there anything in the house at all that was his? He gave over so many of his choices to Lucifer that even the soap wasn't his. Kai thought he did it because he didn't care. Did he? A sob escaped when he realized that he didn't know. He sat there long enough for the water to run cold. Te poked his head in the bathroom door.

"Kai?"

"Get me some soap," Kai said in a tired voice. "Anything without a scent."

Thankfully, Te didn't bother asking why. He just produced a bar from somewhere and gave it to him. Kai ignored him as he lathered the soap and washed himself. He knew it would never remove the marks from his body, but he could dream.

"I want these gone," he said.

"I know."

Finished with his shower, Kai turned the water off. "Remove them. Please."

"I can't," Te said, a sorrowful look on his face. "Lucifer is much more powerful than I. Plus, he did things that I can't begin to understand how to replicate, much less undo."

Kai believed him; he didn't want to, but he did. He needed to ask one more question. Of all of the answers he'd gotten tonight, this was the one he'd dreaded the most. "His name is here too, isn't it? I have 'Property of Lucifer the Morningstar' written on my body somewhere, don't I?"

Te stiffened and pressed his lips together; his silver eyes flitted to Kai's right cheekbone.

Kai raised his fingers touching his face. "Damn."

Throughout the night's revelations, his eyes had managed to stay dry, but now they filled with embarrassing tears. He brushed by Te and headed into the bedroom he shared with Lucifer. Grabbing one of the knives that he always carried, he sliced away the skin on his cheek. Clan Air didn't regenerate, a scarred face was something he was willing to live with.

"That will do you no good, you know," Te said from the doorway. He came into the room and took the knife from him. "This sigil here," he caressed one covering Kai's left forearm, "negates Clan Air's non-regenerative nature. The sigil will reappear with the skin."

Even as he said it, Kai could feel the skin growing back. Looking into the mirror, he could see the skin pink and new, driving the tattoo into startling relief.

"Then I'll just cut it away again," he replied, reaching for the knife in Te's hand. Te snatched his hand away, moving faster than Kai could follow.

"No, I will not let you continue in this futile attempt to mutilate yourself."

"Then erase it, please." Kai hated begging, but he was desperate.

Te raised his hands in surrender and backed up until he sat on the bed. "You don't understand. Lucifer was my commander, my teacher. I am bound to him more tightly than you are. I can't."

Kai felt Te's plea for understanding as he knew Te felt his. He sat next to him on the bed. "How did he get so much power?"

"He was magnificent."

He could not disagree.

They shared a quiet moment; Kai thought Te was think-ing of Lucifer, just as he was. Then he got up, walked to the closet, and opened it to clothes that were picked for him.

What do I like?

He fingered the silks, linens, and soft cottons. They felt nice, even though Lucifer had chosen them. It was hard to think past his emotions and the possible influences of the sigils. He lingered for a while, stroking and thinking.

What do I like? I like leather. He shifted, moving to the section that held leather of all types, textures, and colors.

Do I like leather because I like it or because He likes it?

Kai fingered a soft-as-butter pair of black leather pants and sighed, honestly not sure. Choosing them anyway, he slipped them on. They fit him like a second skin. Maybe he did like them, regardless of how they came to be in his closet. Next Kai loitered among the shirts. The silks caressed his skin. He liked that... maybe.

He shook his head. *I can't do this.*

Next he was tearing into the shirts, ripping them into shreds and even breaking the hangers. Then he ripped off the pants and repeated the process with the rest of the leather in the closet. He stood panting at the closet door, still naked, with a pile of fabric up to his knees.

"You will never get dressed this way," Te said from be-hind him.

"It was all his," Kai replied, not turning around.

"Try this."

Te dressed him in black jeans, a black T-shirt, and black boots. Kai turned to look at himself in the mirror. It was

274

something Lucifer would never have chosen for him and therefore acceptable.

"This will do. Just don't get comfortable dressing me," he replied, unable to help the small smile that curved his lips.

Te smiled back. "Wouldn't dream of it."

* * *

Roberta was seriously freaked out. Not only had Kai thrown up, but he'd run out of her rooms like he was being chased. Like he was terrified. Seeing him like that was disturbing. She couldn't go back to eating her own food, no matter how delicious it smelled, because all she could see was him leaning over her toilet, retching.

Staring at the bowl, she picked up the spoon, fished out a chunk of meat, and examined it. Kai had said it wasn't human, but did he know for sure? They were underground after all; there were no cows here. She'd seen the beings that occupied the city. If they could callously use humans as slaves, she was sure they'd have no trouble using them as a convenient source of meat as well.

She dropped the spoon into the bowl and pushed it far away from her on the table. The glass Kai had dropped hadn't broken but lay on the floor, its former contents splattered over the table and floor where he'd been sitting. Great. Any appetite she had left fled and left her queasy and even more freaked than she had been.

Roberta got up, not knowing what to do with herself. What was she supposed to do? She paced the room. Uriel would know.

The thought of him soothed her until she pushed it away. As agitated as she was, thoughts of him would only lead her to another bout of hysteria and another dose of that wonderful, wonderful P2. She was not going to be an addict—she was not.

If only there was something to do—television, a radio, magazines, billboards—anything to take her mind off of the forbidden things it wanted to chew on, like what was wrong with Kai? Was he sickly? He didn't look it, but what did she know? Before this she hadn't known vampires actually existed.

A large stack of magazines appeared on the table by the couch in a ruffle of paper. Beside them were novels she'd meant to read but never got around to. Roberta stopped in her tracks, nonplussed, until a sheet of paper drifted down and landed on top of the pile. Fascinated, she walked over and picked it up. A note was written in perfect cursive, probably the most beautiful handwriting she'd ever seen.

Your master is indisposed but is otherwise in good health. These should keep you occupied until he returns.

P.S. Rest assured, the meat in your stew is not human.

She slumped on the couch in relief at the last line, grateful for one less thing to worry about. If Uriel said Kai was fine, she believed him, and while appreciative, she was surprised that he took the time to ease her mind. She fingered the magazines. It looked like every subject was represented—fashion, cars, crafts, literary—it was a smorgasbord of probably useless information, just the thing to distract her.

"Thank you, Uriel," she said, comfortably sure that he could hear her.

Pulling one off the top—a *Reader's Digest*—Roberta curled up on the couch and let her mind sink into the pages.

* * *

"Careful. Keep that up, and your reputation as a cold-hearted bastard will be ruined," Te said. Since it was now just the two of them, he'd been disinclined to separate from Uriel, and subsequently, he'd seen what he'd done for Roberta.

Uriel looked lazily at him. "It was merely a reward for not bothering me."

Te thought he looked miffed for being called out. "Uh huh." He'd been smiling but now turned serious. "I've never seen Kai so upset. Do you think I should go after him?"

"You bedded him. You knew what Lucifer had written, yet you said nothing. Why?"

"What is this sudden interest in my love life?"

"Must you be vulgar? If you want to rut like an animal, that is your business."

"But you're curious as to what all the fuss is about, aren't you?"

"Certainly not. I would never sully myself in that way."

Te laughed and surrendered the subject with a gesture. "Suit yourself."

"I have been watching Kai. He is well, even though still upset. I will go to him," Uriel said before vanishing.

Relieved, Te relaxed into a chair. He hadn't wanted to talk about it. Of course he'd seen what Lucifer had written on Kai; he'd just chosen to ignore it. He'd had Kai because he wanted to. It had been the first time he'd willfully disobeyed Lucifer, and he planned to do it again and again—as much as Kai would allow. The price of disobedience would be guilt, and the sigils on Kai's body would constantly remind him of his disloyalty. Maybe the sting would diminish with time. Maybe not. He would live with the consequences.

* * *

Kai hadn't gotten far. He'd made it to the park at the end of the boulevard and stopped among the darkness of the trees. It would be dawn soon, and the ache of loss in his body echoed another loss long ago. The only difference was that this time he had the burn of his lover's betrayal muting the feeling and leaving him tired and slightly numb. He sat on a bench and realized it was Lucifer's favorite spot. He sighed and slumped back on the bench. It seemed like he'd never escape him, even for a few moments to collect his feelings.

"Pull yourself together, vampire. Your behavior is unseemly for a warrior."

Uriel had called him a *warrior*. It was something.

He didn't bother looking up. "Go away, Uriel. I appreciate whatever it is you're trying to do, but I just…" He trailed off, not having the energy to finish.

"He could have done none of it without your consent."

Now Kai looked up. Uriel's black suit blended so well with the darkness that it looked like his disembodied head floated in midair. It was unsettling even to him. "My consent? Are you kidding me? He tied me down. He never asked." Kai's hands balled into fists so tight it made his knuckles crack.

Uriel's eyes blazed in copper fire out of his face. "Yes, vampire, your consent. My brother, despite all of his power, was possessive and leaned toward the paranoid when it came to losing things he cared about. You were aware of this. Tell me his actions truly surprise you."

"But—"

"No, vampire. You know as well as I that you were complicit. When you fought the Ronin, you wished that he had ignored your wishes. As it turns out, he had. You cannot have it both ways."

Kai moaned, wanting to deny it but knowing it was true. Tied to that bed, he had secretly reveled in the fact that Luc was marking him, possessing him—forever. He'd never thought about it because it had made him feel ashamed, but he'd been proud to wear the marks, proud to have been claimed. He dropped his head into his hands, and grabbing handfuls of hair, he pulled hard enough to hurt. When would he face the fact that he was weak?

"Lord Uriel, at last. It is time you joined your brothers. Hell awaits, as does Lord Lucifer within."

By the time Kai raised his head, Uriel had turned and fired flaming arrows at the voice, all of which were caught and neatly extinguished. Fear momentarily stunned him.

The only person he'd known who was able to extin-guish Uriel's holy fire had been Lucifer. Five women stood around them, dressed for battle. Their skin, like Uriel's suit, blended into the darkness. The only parts of them reflecting light were their silver eyes and hair.

"Your family is gone. It is time for you to join them and let this place sink into the darkness it so deserves." The one in the middle spoke.

Kai rose slowly from the bench, his instincts screaming at him to run and hide. Uriel had called him a warrior; the least he could do was die a warrior's death beside him. His movement drew their attention.

"Lord Lucifer's beloved." She looked him over. "His pro-tection has made you brave. You won't need those any longer."

She spoke a word Kai didn't recognize, and instantly his body was aflame. The flames weren't red but a bright blue—he had just enough time to register that he wasn't burning before the pain hit him. Each sigil and mark of decoration was ripped from his body. It was the reverse of what he'd felt when they'd been applied, although this time no care was taken. It felt like bits of his soul were torn away as well. Whatever Lucifer had done was being un-done, sloppily, carelessly—finesse ignored in favor of brute force. He didn't think he would survive and doubted he'd want to.

When it was over, and he lay on the ground bloodied, his skin torn and tattered, he looked up though blurry eyes and saw Uriel looking back at him, sorrow on his usually stoic face as he disappeared from view.

"Tell Lord Te, the Last of the Angels, that his punishment is not to die but to bear witness to the Darkness that comes to consume all." The women disappeared.

Kai lay unable to move. He had neither the strength nor the energy. He could see his bloodied wrist where the sigil that had protected him from the sun had been. The sun would be up soon, and as weak as he was, it would probably kill him.

Maybe that wouldn't be such a bad thing, he thought before closing his eyes.

Seventeen

Te was frantic. A blue light had covered the sigil connecting him to Kai and burned it away. About the same time, his connection to Uriel had been cut off.

Uriel was dead—did that mean Kai was dead too?

He had no idea and set out into the night to find him. Without the link between them, it was slow going. He stretched his awareness out and walked the streets, fearing the worst.

* * *

The young werewolf had been out enjoying the night. He rarely went this far down King, preferring to stay in his pack's territory on the Upper Peninsula, but tonight his girlfriend was being unreasonable, and he'd needed to get as far away from her as possible.

A powerful blood scent hit him, and he felt compelled to check it out. He'd never in his life smelled something like it—this was legendary, no *epic*—it was that intense. As he got closer, the scent got stronger. It was old—very old—and it was dying. He didn't know if that was good or bad.

When he entered the park, the hairs on the back of his neck prickled. The scent emanating from the figure on the ground brought tears to his eyes. He was torn between wanting to drink it, bathe in it, and howl in ecstasy at the joy of finding it. The only thing he was sure of was that it was his, and he would fight to the death anyone who challenged that fact.

When he was close enough, he nudged the body with his foot. No movement. Good. Scavengers would be here soon enough, and he'd have to fight them. He was glad he'd not have to fight the owner of the body to claim what he'd decided was his.

There was something familiar about the scent, something poking at the back of his mind, warring with his primal instincts. That was annoying. Couldn't he just enjoy this? He rolled the body on to its back with his foot and cursed aloud. He would be dead within days if he even tasted that sweet, tempting blood. Fuck.

He pulled out his cell phone, growling low to the inevitable scourge of vultures. He could hold them off long enough. He had to. The phone was answered on the second ring.

"Julian, it's Joseph. I need your help. This is bad."

He told his alpha his location and asked him to hurry. Then he took a protective stance over the body and waited for the first attack.

* * *

Te was not making any progress. There had to be a better, easier way to find Kai, but he couldn't think of it. He was at Calhoun and Meeting now. The city was just waking up, and soon the peninsula would be crowded with people. He had to find Kai before that happened.

It wasn't the first time that he'd wished he had the abilities of an archangel. If he did, he could be in multiple places at once. True, he could go nonphysical and cover more space, but he still couldn't split his consciousness—he'd still be a singular point looking for another singular point. Frustrated and scared for his friend, he headed up Meeting Street, scouring Hampton Park on his way past.

* * *

Even though Charleston had a pureblood master vampire in residence, it had a fairly large scavenger population. Joseph cursed this fact as he fought off yet another attacker. The young werewolf was well-trained, strong, and so far, holding his own quite well. The Orion Clan had done a good job in keeping the scavenger population low in their territory, but that just meant they went farther south.

These scavengers were a mix of mongrel vampires and unclaimed werewolves. Homeless, they squatted in sewers or abandoned buildings and ate whatever they could scrounge—pets, wildlife, each other. They rarely attacked humans, even though humans were the preferred meal. Weak both psychologically and physically—a pack of humans bent on revenge could easily take them down.

But these scavengers were emboldened by the powerful prize at the young werewolf's feet. He hadn't managed to kill any—armed with only his claws and refusing to give ground—but he'd drawn blood on all that came within reach. He'd known he was in for a long siege when they ignored the wounded around them and instead continued to attack him. Usually, they'd be on the wounded like a shark in bloody water but not now.

He breathed a sigh of relief when he heard the familiar purr of the Lincoln at the other end of the park. A glance in that direction reassured him even more as the van with more of his clan members parked behind it.

His attention snapped back to his current task. During his momentary lapse, one of the mongrels had snatched the body at his feet and was attempting to drag it away. Ducking a blow to his head, he lashed out at the one who'd just swung at him, his fist connecting satisfactorily with a face. He smiled when he felt bones crunch. Then Joseph leapt at the mongrel and broke its back, halting its progress.

"What the hell is—" Julian said running up to him, stopping short when he saw the body. "Oh sweet fuck, is that—"

"Yeah, I think it is."

The others behind Julian joined the fray and easily took out the rest of the scavengers.

He knelt with Joseph near Kai's body. "What could have done this?" He gently turned Kai over and audibly gasped.

Joseph had never seen Julian so freaked and afraid. It was actually reassuring, in a totally ass backwards way, that he wasn't alone in knowing that this situation was totally fucked up and warranted everyone involved being afraid.

"He's already been exposed to the sun. We have to get him out of here, but we can't take him home," Julian said, referring to the protections on the house that would have them all dead—except maybe Kai—before they reached the front door. It was a shame, since his house was right down the street. "We'll take him back to Risha. It's the best we can do," he said before reverently gathering Kai into his arms, standing, and then walking to the Lincoln to lay the unconscious vampire gently in the back seat.

"Joseph, you ride with me. Everyone else take care of those." He gestured with disgust at the dead and dying scavengers. "And then split up and find Lord Te. You will not tell anyone what you saw."

He paused and looked each directly in the eyes, cementing his point, until they looked away. They all knew it would not go well for them should they disobey.

* * *

Te had cut over to East Bay Street. He'd lost patience with the process around the time the sun was fully up. He wasn't going to find Kai now; there was no more time. Deciding against going home or to the City, he walked along the sidewalk staring at the cruise ship in the harbor, feeling helpless.

A car screeched to a halt and a young man—*werewolf*, he corrected himself—got out and ran toward him.

"Lord Te, it's urgent that you come with us," the were said after a quick bow. His chest heaved in quick pants.

Te frowned. "I really don't have time—"

The young wolf interrupted, his voice low. "It's about Lord Kai."

Te was in the car so fast he left the were looking bewilderedly around him. "Let's go," he commanded.

The were barely had time to jump back in the car before it sped away.

* * *

Risha directed Julian to place Kai in their bed. She had no other rooms suitable for one of his station. They lived above the club. The building was a solid metal structure with no windows, so he would be safe inside.

She and Julian were alone with Kai, and she honestly had no idea what to do. She wanted to clean his wounds, strip him of his bloody clothes and bathe him, but she hesitated. What if Lord Lucifer had done this because Kai had fallen into disfavor? Granted, that was highly improbable, but who else could have placed him in such a state? Was her relationship with Lord Lucifer stable enough to prevent him from retaliating against her if she intervened? It had never been tested before, and if she was wrong, her entire clan could be in jeopardy. It was a risk she was afraid to take.

Julian's phone rang, and before she could warn him to not even think of doing so, he answered. The conversation was short, and he held her eyes the entire time, pleading forgiveness.

"Lord Te is on his way. They found him on East Bay." His voice mirrored the relief she felt at the news.

"Thank the Mother. He'll know what to do."

* * *

Te burst in a short time later, his presence filling the room. Risha promptly sank in a deep curtsy, and Julian bowed. But Te ignored them and walked straight to the bed that held Kai. Even to her eyes, Kai looked small and fragile in that big bed. She hoped they had gotten to him in time.

Te stood over the bed, speaking in anguished tones in a language she didn't know. It wasn't the first time she'd wondered exactly what he was. He waved his hand, and the blood was gone—from Kai, from the bed, from Julian—everywhere it had been, it had vanished. She knew he had power, but that display shook her. He then sliced his wrist with a fingernail and placed it to Kai's mouth. The blood barely touched Kai's tongue before he was crying out and pushing him away. He still hadn't regained consciousness. Lord Te cursed and sat down by the bed.

"He'll need blood, Risha. Lots of it," he said, his eyes never leaving Kai.

She nodded to Julian, who left to fulfill the request. She knew he would go to the City; it was the only place they could get the quantity that was needed in so short a time.

* * *

Te sat next to his friend on the bed and felt weary with resignation. First Heaven, then Michael, Raphael, and Gabriel, then Lucifer, now Uriel—gone. Kai barely alive. Whoever had done this had not only stripped Kai of his

288

protections, but had torn into his very essence to do it. Lucifer had embedded his spells beyond Kai's flesh and into his being.

The assailants who removed them took no care in their removal. What they had done was casual and brutal, and he was afraid that Kai might not survive. If he did, he would be badly scarred. To complicate matters, he'd had enough exposure to the sun to poison him. Te had to trust that with enough blood Kai's body would heal on its own and his being along with it. There was nothing else he could do.

Te looked at Risha and did something he didn't do much of anymore. Having known her for centuries, he suspected that she could be trusted, but he had to know. She had risked so much in sheltering Kai; Te had to know how far she would go. He looked into her heart and sifted through all that she was until he was satisfied that she would not betray them.

"Thank you, Risha. I owe you a debt that I doubt I can ever repay."

"You can bring chocolate almonds to our next game," she said, trying for lighthearted but not quite making it. She was frightened.

Te wanted to reassure her but doubted he could.

Julian came back with a box containing bottles of fresh blood. Te took a bottle and, holding Kai's head, fed the blood to him. Kai was at the point where he would accept the blood even though unconscious—he was that close to death. For now, he would feed without struggle. The contents of bottle after bottle disappeared down Kai's throat, until finally he pushed away and turned his head.

Te sat back and sighed. He looked up at Kai's rescuers and then looked into Julian—the same way he'd done to Risha—and found a devoted and trusted mate who would support his matriarch and mate to his last breath. He didn't want to tell them, but he had to confide in someone. Kai was on the verge of death, and his brothers were gone. Plus, he didn't know how much time he had left. Kai needed caring for in his current state. There was no one else he could trust.

"What I'm about to tell you cannot leave this room," he said, placing a silencing ward around the room. At this, they both looked at him with curious eyes and possibly eyes that wished he'd say no more.

"Lucifer is dead, as are all the other angels."

Risha sank down to the floor, eyes wide with alarm. Julian immediately went to her aid, his expression one of shock and pain.

"I have no idea who did this to Kai or why. I know that what I'm about to ask goes against Other-kin culture, so I'm appealing to your honor, to your fondness for myself and for Lucifer. Kai requires looking after, and in case something happens to me, I'm asking you to do it."

"But why?"

Te held their eyes for a moment. "I am an angel—the last, actually. Someone or something has killed my brothers and will most likely come after me."

Both Risha and Julian looked horrified and awed—Te thought it odd that they could pull both emotions off at once—and instantly bowed low from their positions on the floor.

"My Lord," Risha breathed. "We are honored to keep your secrets and to extend our protection to Lord Kai."

Knowing she was deadly serious, Te relaxed somewhat.

"I'd like Kai to stay here for a while. If I... disappear," he couldn't bring himself to use the word "die," "even with an Eineu in the house, in the state he's in... he needs care. He won't be safe in the City."

"Understood. He is welcome to stay."

They would take care of Kai; Te felt that weight come off his shoulders. "I would stay and keep vigil, but I don't want my presence to put you in any danger. Here." He gave her a card with a symbol on it. "Use that to contact me when he wakes or if you have any trouble."

"Of course." She bowed again, taking the card.

Te vanished.

* * *

Kai slept the entire day. Risha stayed with him in shifts, trading off with Julian throughout. Now she sat in an easy chair next to the bed and contemplated everything she'd learned. The implications were staggering.

Lord Lucifer dead? The angels dead? Why? And the biggest revelation—that Lord Te was an angel. Like everyone else, she'd revered him as the one prophesied, and while she knew he was powerful, she'd never thought of him as something quite so magnificent. The angels existed to steward the humans. The fact that the Other-kin had an angel looking over them—and that ignorantly she had thought of him as a friend —was awe-inspiring. Even before his revelation, she would have helped Te, but the fact that he was an angel only made it all the more imperative that she devote herself—and her clan if necessary—to the task. She'd been placed in a position of honor, and she would not disrespect herself, her clan, Lord Te, Lord Lucifer, or Kai by betraying it.

There was movement from the bed and a pained moan.

"Lord Kai." She got up and moved so that he could see her. "You are safe and currently under the protection of the Orion Clan."

Bewildered black eyes looked at her. "Risha?" His voice was little more than a raspy whisper.

"Yes, I am here." She palmed the card Lord Te had given her. He appeared seconds later.

"Kai?" Lord Te spoke softly, as if the volume of his voice could wound Kai—and knowing what she now did, she supposed it could if he wanted it to.

"Te? Uriel... I saw... he's gone." Kai frowned. "They said to tell you..."

"They, Kai? Who are they?" Lord Te sounded frustrated, like he wanted to press but was afraid to.

"Last... bear witness... darkness."

Risha shared a look with Te to see if he understood what Kai meant—it appeared he didn't either.

She watched as Lord Te sat by the bed, stroking Kai's hair back from his face. He murmured more words she didn't understand that seemed to soothe Kai back into sleep. They sat like that, watching and waiting for Kai to wake and feed so the true healing could begin.

Eighteen

Roberta was roused from a pleasantly erotic dream involving Kai by the door opening. Thus startled, the *Reader's Digest* fell to the floor, still propped open at the article "The Most Heroic Dogs in America" that she'd dozed off reading. Thinking Kai had come back, she stretched and smiled, looking forward to seeing him again—especially after that dream.

To her surprise, a tall, blond man entered. Luckily for her she'd managed to remember to drop her eyes when he turned around. He had to be the person Kai had warned her about—Stephan. She hadn't thought he'd be so bold as to barge into her room like that. Her feelings on being a slave were irrelevant—she was Kai's property, and he would definitely be learning of this invasion of her privacy.

The way John followed him into the room gave her the impression that Stephan had barreled right past him. When she locked eyes with the creature, he gave her an apologetic smile, confirming her suspicions. Roberta gave him her best reassuring smile and turned her attention toward her guest.

Stephan stood tall and looked down at her. She had no idea what the protocol was—according to Kai, this sort of thing wasn't supposed to happen. She did remember that she wasn't supposed to speak unless spoken to, so she kept silent and hoped for the best. Remembering his warning, she kept her eyes fixed on Stephan's nose. From what she could tell, he was gorgeous—as in drop-dead, mouth-watering hot. He was dressed in a red and orange kimono-like robe. Gold bracelets adorned his wrists, and he wore a huge diamond on the ring finger of his left hand. She got the impression that he expected her to genuflect and was waiting for her to do so. He would be disappointed. Kai gave no indication that that would be required for anyone, and she was going on faith that he told her the truth.

Realizing that she wasn't going to do or say anything, he spoke. "Do you have a name?"

Such coldness. Even the Asshole hadn't made her feel so insignificant. Under Stephan's gaze, Roberta was acutely aware that she was naked, longed to grab a cushion—anything—to cover herself, and had to force herself to do no such thing. The contrast was startling. In Kai's presence, it wasn't that she forgot; it was that her awareness had been elsewhere. He had made her feel at ease, and therefore it was no longer an issue. She took a deep breath, realizing she'd taken way too long to answer, and that would only antagonize him.

"Roberta. My name is Roberta."

"What are you supposed to be?" he asked, striding further into the room and taking a seat in one of the chairs across from her.

She was struck by how different Kai and Stephan were from each other. Stephan glided about, oozing presumption, as if he owned the place, while Kai had walked in as if he owned her—a difference that oddly made her feel safe in his presence. Absently, she wondered if Stockholm Syndrome applied here.

"I belong to Lord Kai," she said, at the last minute remembering to add his title.

"Do you now? I don't see any mark of ownership. Look at me when I speak to you."

She didn't move her eyes higher than his nose. "Yes, I am his. Ask John; he'll confirm it."

Stephan's mouth twisted with disgust, and he looked at John. "Go away, John. Come back when I'm gone."

"Yes, Master," John said, looking like a kicked puppy and moving toward the door.

"Wait," Roberta said. The Eineu stopped and looked at her. "I want you to stay. Please."

John's smile brightened her heart. "Yes, Miss, John will stay." He sent a neutral look that leaned toward triumphant at Stephan.

"Do you know who I am? I have considerable pull and influence here. It would be in your best interest not to piss me off."

Roberta wanted to counter with *do you know who I've worked for?* She'd had years of working for despots and despot-wannabes and had heard variations on this particular speech from every one of them—although usually not directed at her.

"It was never my intention to piss you off... Master." She had to bite out that last word.

"Yet you continue to insult me by sitting on that couch and speaking to me as if we were equals."

And so it begins. Roberta stood and walked over to her pillow, which was, inconveniently enough, at the foot of the chair in which Stephan chose to sit.

"Much better. It appears Kai has given you some instruction," he said once she had settled herself on the pillow. "He's also told you not to look into my eyes, hasn't he?" Stephan sounded a little amused but more disappointed.

"Yes." She had no reason to lie.

"We could be friends, you and I." Roberta doubted it but kept her mouth shut. "After all, you don't want to be a slave, do you? You want to be free to go back to your life and forget all about us. Don't you?"

"Of course." Stephan obviously knew nothing of her situation and was most likely digging for information. She would not be the one to enlighten him.

"Well then, you help me, and I'll help you," he purred, his already deep voice dropping even lower, becoming seductive.

Roberta almost felt sorry for him. Over the years, she had met all kinds of sleazy corporate characters—people who could charm a glass of water from someone dying of thirst. She might not have been in a corporate office now, but she recognized the play. Only this time, and maybe for the first time ever, she had faith that her "boss" had her back. It gave her enough courage to speak her mind.

"I have no reason to trust you and every reason not to."

It was a while before he spoke again. "I see." It didn't seem possible, but his tone, even frostier than before, made her shiver. Suddenly afraid, she lowered her head as tears filled her eyes.

"All slaves in the City are marked by their owners."

This was news to her.

"I wonder why Kai didn't put his mark on you." He crossed his legs and tapped his ringed hand on the armrest. "I know why."

Although Stephan's voice had lowered to a confidential, friendly tone, it felt like he was dragging a knife up her back. It made her want to move as far away from him as possible and dismayed her more because she couldn't.

"It's because he doesn't plan to keep you. His lover is away, and he's bored. When his lover comes back—and make no mistake, he will come back—Kai will drain you dry. Why? Because there is no room for you; that's why. You were a plaything, and an ugly one at that. So he'll keep you here, away from prying eyes, until he's done playing, and back to his normal life he will go."

Roberta had burst into tears midway through Stephan's speech, unaware of this unconscious fear until he'd voiced it. She was openly slobbering on herself and questioning everything by the time he'd finished. Then he'd gone in for the kill.

"By the way, did he mention something called a Rendering?"

Having no idea what that was, she managed to shake her head in answer.

"I see." Those two words were starting to get on her nerves. "It is a gathering of every important Other-kin. A time when, if he planned to keep you, he would trot you out for all and sundry to see—show you off, in other words. If, that is, *if* you wore his mark and *if* he was proud to have you as a slave. Which apparently, he does not intend to do, because he does not intend to keep you around."

At this, she lost control.

"There, there," Stephan said, in a faux sympathetic tone. He stood, "Should you change your mind, send John. I'd be happy to help you, dear," he said before sweeping out of the room.

Every fear about her situation assaulted Roberta, leaving her terrified and hysterical.

"Miss, please. John help," John said, thrusting a dose of the P2 toward her. "Please."

Roberta didn't hesitate and felt better almost immediately upon taking it.

"John trust Lord Kai. John trust Lord Te."

Calmer, she managed to smile at John in gratitude. "I believe you, John. Thank you for taking care of me."

John smiled his wide, black-gummed smile. "Is John's duty to take care of Miss."

"I'm going to take a shower, and then I want you to take me to get Lord Kai's mark."

John's already wide eyes grew wider. "Miss must stay. Miss must have permission. John cannot do this."

She had wondered if that was going to be a problem. "So go find Lord Kai or Lord Te. I want to do this now."

John bowed before leaving. "Yes, Miss."

Wiping her face, Roberta walked into the bathroom and turned on the shower. The spray was forceful and the water hot—just like she liked it. Stepping into the stall, she let the water beat on her, enjoying the combined sensations within and without.

Stephan didn't know that her arrangement with Kai was based on consent, and she was glad of it—it wasn't a stretch to imagine all the ugly things he would have said had he known. In light of their arrangement, she was sure that Kai would have told her about the marks and waited for her consent.

Why he hadn't told her, she didn't know. Maybe he was waiting for her to change her mind. Maybe he thought it would freak her out even more. Maybe he was testing himself and hadn't decided to keep her. She shuddered as fear lanced through her at that unwelcome thought.

Well, she was getting one. She'd consented after all—in for a penny, in for a pound. If Kai did change his mind, she'd deal with that when, or if, she had to. Until then, if his mark solidified her position and kept Stephan away, she would wear it gladly.

After her shower, Roberta stood staring at the flimsy thing made of leather and chain that now hung in her closet. John must have come in when she was asleep and put it there. She'd noticed the spilled blood and glass had disappeared as well. Getting Kai's mark meant going into the City. Going into the City meant that she'd have to wear that damn thing—or go naked.

She took a deep breath. Neither of those options was appealing. In fact, they were pretty equal on the scale of Things She Found Terrifying. Luckily, the P2 helped her to detach emotionally and remember what both Kai and Lord Te had told her about slaves and their decoration. She could go naked, true, but her status as a slave would be higher, such as it was, if she wore the thing. If she was going through with getting Kai's mark, it stood to reason that she should accept the gift of his adornment as well.

Roberta heard John come back into the outer room. *I can do this.*

John looked miserable when she entered from the bedroom. "John not find Lord Te or Lord Kai," he said, clasping his hands in front of him.

Damn. Coming over to stand in front of him, she caught his eye. "John, I need to do this."

The Eineu shook his head. "Miss must stay. Is John's duty to care for Miss."

What she would say next made her feel lousy, but she was going to say it anyway. "It's your duty to care for me, John. Lord Kai told me that you could be my escort. You can care for me by taking me to get Lord Kai's mark. I will be safer with his mark, won't I? Maybe Stephan will leave me alone?"

She could tell he didn't like the idea, but at her mention of Stephan, John straightened and looked into her eyes with new resolve. "Lord Kai's mark protects Miss. John will help protect Miss."

Roberta released an audible sigh of relief and smiled. John smiled brightly at her in return. She then quizzed him about the marks—what they were exactly, where to get one, and if he knew the exact mark that Kai called his own. As it turned out, they ranged from simple, uniform geometric designs to individual creations. Since Kai had never owned a slave before, what exactly he would use as a mark was a mystery. Roberta was a little surprised at her feeling of urgency and desire to see this through. She'd become fixated on getting Kai's mark, and that's what she would do.

"The ones who make the marks, can they design something that's suitable for Lord Kai and my decorated status?"

"Yes, Miss. John know great artist make beautiful mark for Lord Kai and Miss."

"Okay, so let's get me into that thing in the closet."

John managed to help her into it, and to Roberta's great surprise, not only did it fit, but she found wearing it was not uncomfortable. Strips of chain led down from the wide leather choker-type collar, branching off to thin leather bands around her arms. The chains scalloped over her torso, attaching to another thin leather band under her breasts. More chain scalloped like webbing from it down to separate at slightly thicker leather bands that wrapped around her upper thighs. The chain was light and made a high tinkling sound when she walked.

She made a point of avoiding her reflection for two reasons: the first was that what she thought didn't matter, and the second was that the moment she saw herself, there was a good chance that she was never leaving that room—ever. Knowing her courage was a finite thing, she wasn't pushing her luck.

At the door to her suite, she took a deep breath and tried to calm her nerves. The possibility of taking another dose of P2 flitted though her mind, but she decided against it. Her life was out of her hands as it was. She didn't need to abdicate her emotions as well.

Nodding to John, who, in a surprising but not unwelcome move, took her hand and squeezed it before letting go, she stood out of the way while he opened the door and led her out. Roberta had gotten the impression that being under Kai's—and when she was with John, by extension, Lord Te's—protection meant something. At least she hoped it did, hoped as she stepped barefoot into the corridor that it was enough to keep her safe.

The walk through the curving corridors was uneventful. Roberta carried her pillow and kept her eyes down, thankful for her long hair that enabled her to break the rules and peek out from behind it now and again to take in her surroundings. They passed many openings along the main stone walkway. To her left, intermittent archways opened out to balconies overlooking the large cavern. The few to her right appeared to be rooms. Whether they were like hers or not, she couldn't tell.

They turned right onto a long, gently spiraling ramp. They followed it downward until it opened out into the space she'd seen from her room. It was huge and hot—being naked in that heat, she realized, wasn't such a bad thing. She longed to let her eyes roam, take in every detail and squirrel it away so she could examine it later—maybe discuss with Kai what she'd seen and ask questions.

Of course, she didn't dare, but she let her other senses take an accounting instead. The sounds of the different languages flowed around her—some harsh and guttural, others tinkling and musical. The smells reminded her of New York in the summer—the high, burnt, sweet notes of rotting garbage, the savory notes of cooking meat, the sharp funkiness of undeodorized bodies. At one point, they passed a group of chittering beings that smelled heavily of spices. Given the crowd, progress was slow which enabled her to take in what she could.

"Ooh, this looks tasty."

John had stopped moving. As close as she was, his abrupt movement almost had her bumping into him. He smelled faintly of oranges. Glancing out, Roberta could see four very large and terrifying beings standing in their way.

"Lord Te selling this one, John? Go on, we'll take it."

Roberta knew he was referring to her—being called "it" felt odd.

"Miss not for sale. Miss has master. Please excuse."

The four giant, green men moved in closer. An accompanying stench, worse than any she had smelled before, filled her nostrils. Roberta hugged her pillow higher, scrunched her head down further, and cursed everything that had led her to this point. One stepped into her space and loudly sniffed, making her whimper and shudder in response.

"This one's from the surface. Plump and juicy," he said.

"We give good price." She heard what could only be money jingling.

The one who'd sniffed her was now drooling on her. She closed her eyes tighter as she felt his fluids drip over her shoulders and down her back. She felt movement in front of her—opening her eyes, Roberta saw John closing the small distance, coming right up to her, and trying to shield her with his body.

"No sale."

She was grateful for the effort but knew it was a lost cause.

"John thinks he can get more on the block." They all laughed. "Leave the pouch. We take it now," the drooling one said.

So much for Lord Te's protection, she thought, knowing that at any minute the drooling one would get tired of waiting and take a chunk out of her. If she was lucky, he'd bite her neck and paralyze or kill her instantly. All things considered, it was pretty much the best she could hope for.

"No." John's voice had changed, becoming deep and resonant, startling her—apparently startling the mutants surrounding them as well. The drool had stopped, and the stench had lessened. Risking a peek, Roberta opened her eyes and raised her head slightly in order to see out of her curtain of hair. What she saw caught the breath in her throat and caused her to look up sharply, which no one noticed because the area immediately surrounding them had gone quiet in shock, all eyes on John.

The meek, lithe creature that she'd felt a strong affinity for was gone. In his place was something terrifying. The only way she knew for sure that it was John was the lavender fabric encircling his body.

The being that stood in a protective stance before her was now the same height as their aggressors. Thicker muscles covered this larger frame, and his formerly iridescent scaly skin, was now pitch black. A corona of red spikes fanned out from a triangular shaped head, and a set of nasty-looking red claws protruded from each finger. As she watched, a thick, black tail tipped with a huge, red stinger wrapped around her, the stinger darting around, poised to attack any who got too close.

John turned his head and looked down at her through vertical pupils and red irises. His expression might have been one of reassurance, but it felt like possession—a feeling that was confirmed when he looked at the crowd.

"I said this one is not for sale. This one belongs to Lord Kai and Lord Te." John's voice had transformed into a dark and deadly thing, matching his body.

Two more beings that looked exactly like John—tall, black-scaled, red-spiked and clawed—came racing toward them. Once they arrived, they took up flanking positions.

"It has been long since we have tasted living meat," said the one in yellow that had just joined them.

"Yes, and we hunger," said the one in red whose eyes flashed briefly as it moved to stand directly in front of one of the big, green men threatening her. It stood before it, licking bared red teeth.

Holy shit.

This could only end badly. Had this been a confrontation on the surface, maybe she would appeal for calm—maybe.

Here? If she actually believed that she could run to her rooms and hide, she'd do it in a heartbeat. As it was, Roberta doubted she could get free of John's tail and make it more than a few steps before something ate her. So she did the only thing she could do—hug her pillow and pray for a quick and painless death.

The vicinity had gone silent except for the slow swishing of tails, the low growling of John and his companions, and her heartbeat. The green giants weren't backing down, and neither were John and his friends.

"Hey, fellas, whatcha doin'?" a merry voice chimed in from the crowd.

Roberta tore her eyes away from the tense scene and toward the direction of the voice. It didn't sound like Lord Te, unfortunately—did they have police down here? Whatever the equivalent, she hoped the authorities had come to keep the peace. Once defused, maybe she could get John to forget this whole fiasco and take her back to her rooms.

A half-man, half-animal stepped into the hot zone and stood grinning at them with his hands on his hips. Long, curly brown hair flowed around curved horns and framed a ruddy, pleasant, human face. His torso and arms were human as well, GQ-quality in fact—muscular and finely chiseled. A green and red tartan kilt sat on his hips. Two brown-furred animal legs with hooves flowed out from under it, giving him a decidedly surreal appearance.

"Whoa, John, is that you? Holy shit, motherfucker, ain't you a scary sumbitch?" he said, laughing and admiring John before catching her eye.

Shit.

"And what do we have here? Well, hello, my chunky goddess." He moved closer, only to stop when John hissed at him. "Be cool, John; be cool. Let me guess, this sexy goodness is at the center of this mess, right? Not surprised. I am not surprised." He went on to make more appreciative noises.

Roberta was rarely on the receiving end of this kind of attention, but when she was, it always made her feel uncomfortable. That discomfort was exponentially worse now as she felt this creature's eyes roam over her exposed body. Falling through the floor would not have been a bad thing right now.

With a parting noise of regret, he looked back at the seven figures facing off against each other. "Okay, here's the skinny. As much as I'd like to see who'd win in a knock-down, drag-out between you—my money's on John and company, by the way—Lord Te would tear you guys a few new holes if you so much as scratched his boys. Know what I'm sayin'? Kazat, I'm talkin' ta you. After what your boy—" He cut off when one of the Kazat looked at him and drew a knife out of a sheath at his belt.

"Unborn," he said with a snarl.

The creature raised his hands, still smiling. "Hey, Unborn or not, you think Lord Te is gonna give a fuck?" He made a circle, making sure to address them all. "If you're gonna piss him off, it better be worth it, is all I'm sayin'." He turned toward Roberta once more. "I'm hoping I see you again." He licked his lips and pointed both cocked hands at her in shooting motions before backing past John to the edge of the crowd.

What he had said hit the right chord, because the Kazat gradually eased out of their fighting stances.

"We get fat slaves from the surface for free," the one with the knife said as he re-sheathed it.

"So many, fat and juicy."

"Slow and tasty." It sounded like an inside joke or part of a song. They broke out laughing as if nothing happened. Without another look at her or John, they lumbered off together, making plans.

A sharp pain in her shoulder had Roberta flinching and looking toward the source. John had punctured her with a claw and she was just in time to see his tongue come out to lick the bloodied digit. His two companions moved closer, hands outstretched, intent on repeating the action. John hissed at them; they hissed back. A short staring contest punctuated with vocalizations ensued, finally ending with his companions abruptly changing back into their more familiar serene forms.

"Miss safe now," the one in yellow said to her, a happy black-gummed smile gracing his face before he and his companion in red both turned around and left the area in the direction they'd come. Roberta and the crowd, still fascinated, stood silent witness for a few moments, digesting the scene.

"Yo, John," the half-man creature said, drawing near once more. "Let's jaw." He looked John up and down whistling. "That's some Superman shit you pulled." The creature shook his head. "Been holdin' out on us all this time. So does the Big Cheese know?"

"Go away, Rys." John's red eyes fixed on Rys. His tail still encircled Roberta, and it gently nudged her into moving again. The crowd mostly went back to what they were doing, but throughout their slow progress, eyes lingered on John as they passed.

Rys trotted up and continued speaking as if he hadn't heard. "Bet he doesn't, am I right? Brill, man, so fucking brill! Anyway, all I want is a favor, dig? Half hour tops with the dish." He glanced back at Roberta, running a hand over the bulge in his kilt she hadn't noticed before.

John stopped and turned toward Rys. "Leave me, or I'll gut you where you stand."

Rys raised his hands in surrender. "A'ight, you da boss. I'm makin' like a tree." With a parting glance at Roberta, he melted back into the crowd.

As much as she wanted to go back to her rooms, she wanted to talk to John even less. He still hadn't changed back, and his tail still caged her in, trapping her. She had to call on the last of the reserves of her courage just to keep moving. Thankfully, the rest of the trip was uneventful.

She'd seen the auction block through the looking glass, and from a distance it was nothing like it was up close. Surrounding the central platforms where slaves were displayed and sold, stood vendors. There were stalls with cages for sale, stalls selling "decorative" wear, and stalls selling things she couldn't name and didn't want to think about. There were also stalls for medical care that she couldn't get past quickly enough. Those would give her nightmares for sure.

What chilled her to the core was the air of casual disregard for her species. The word "it" was commonplace in referring to humans—as in, "Use this ointment on it twice a day," or, "You should get a good five or six years use out of it before it wears out." Nothing Lord Te or Kai had said had adequately prepared her for the reality of what she was seeing.

In an area past most of the vendors, where John was leading her, were what looked like holding areas. The humans were separated in cages by sex—all were naked and filthy. The entire area stunk of unwashed bodies and waste. Not only were none dressed as she was, none of them looked at her with anything resembling recognition of their shared fate. But then, she didn't share their fate, did she? It was this contrast that made her feel ashamed for the fuss she'd put up. Even naked, she didn't share their fate. As a result, her protests felt prideful and selfish.

They moved into a section where slaves were lined up at various tents getting marked. Instantly, she understood why Kai hadn't mentioned them to her and cursed Stephan and his meddling. But she was gullible enough to fall for it, wasn't she? The first line of slaves getting their marks received an "X" branded onto their faces.

Tears filled her eyes, and she had to hold her breath and clutch the pillow to keep from breaking down. Holding her breath wasn't a good idea, she remembered, because she'd probably end up panicking and hyperventilating, which would call attention to her, and like earlier, that had the potential of ending badly.

She relaxed somewhat when John led her past the branding booths to an area with artists doing actual tattooing with pointed instruments dipped in ink and tapped along the skin. Some artists she could tell were better than others. Or maybe it was that some symbols were more attractive than others. There was no backing out, but even so, she dreaded ending up with some ugly, crude symbol gouged into her skin. But then, it would be Kai's mark—that was the whole point, right? It wasn't supposed to be about what she wanted but about pleasing him. A dose of P2 right now would turn off her brain nicely, but she was afraid that this version of John wouldn't be so solicitous.

"Sit," John said, gesturing to an area and unwinding his tail. Following his instructions, Roberta placed her pillow on the ground and sat.

* * *

"Sta… Starr?"

She'd been sitting awhile, trying to calm her nerves, when she heard the familiar voice. Turning her head in the direction it came from confirmed her suspicions. The Asshole stared back at her from the bars of his cage. He was sitting on the floor on his right side, a bandage covering his left buttock. There was also a splint on his left arm. Dirty and bruised, he still looked every bit the Asshole she remembered.

"What are you supposed to be? Halloween come early this year?"

The man is in a cage, naked, and still feels the need to be insulting. Unbelievable.

She just looked at him. For the first time in her life, she didn't feel the need to respond, even to be polite. It felt good.

"Sorry, old habits. Anyway, you're not in a cage so you must be doing good, huh? You and I, we go back. Made a good team. Maybe we can help each other."

"Why?" Her brain was shutting down at the absurdity of the suggestion.

"I gave you a good job. Paid you well, seems you owe me."

"I owe you." She had to feel how that felt in her mouth when she said it. It felt as ridiculous as it sounded. "Do you know why I'm here? I'm here because I was your slave. Yours. For five years. When Lord Te called you in, I became his slave. I owe you nothing."

"You belong to Lord Te? Well, that's perfect. You can talk to him, see? Tell him it was all a mistake. I don't deserve this."

In typical fashion, the Asshole didn't hear a word she said.

"Hello, beautiful," a man said, smiling at her. He was sitting in a corner of the cage opposite the Asshole. "Did I hear that right? You're a slave because of him?" When Roberta nodded, the man reached over, hauled off, and socked the Asshole in the jaw. "William, you have always been, and will always be, an asshole."

Roberta felt the same sense of satisfaction she'd felt when Kai had done the same thing. In her life, she could count on one hand the number of people—men especially—that had ever defended her. How many times had she longed to do just that? Watching someone else act on her behalf as a response to an affront to her was so very satisfying. She liked this man; she liked him very much. There was something about him that looked familiar.

Gregory ducked, wary of another blow. "What was that for? I don't know you."

"Aw, Willie, it breaks my heart that you don't recognize your own brother. It truly does." The man put his hand over his heart in a sorrowful gesture that turned sour when he gave the Asshole the finger. Roberta suppressed a laugh.

"Edward? You can't be. Edward is… he is…"

"Is what? Dead?" The man chuckled.

"Edward died over four hundred years ago."

"How convenient. If it were only true."

Roberta looked at the two brothers and found it hard to believe—they were so different. Where the Asshole was dark, the other man was fair. Dirty, matted blond hair fell over his blue eyes and brushed past his shoulders. A full, untamed beard covered the lower half of his gaunt but still handsome face. The Asshole, on the other hand, had a harsh, thin face—which, she considered, could be due more to her hatred of him than a true reflection of what he actually looked like.

"You don't look anything alike," she said.

"Well, mother fancied the liveryman, didn't she? Father suspected, which was why he ignored me, even if I was the eldest."

The Asshole's mouth dropped open in shock. Edward ignored him and looked at Roberta instead.

"After Willie and the others made their deals, I snuck in and made my own. Figured, what the hell, you know? Used to sneak out to the theatre, thought nothing could be better than performing for the crowds. But even though my father hated me, I was still considered noble, and performing was frowned upon by the upper class. My deal was my way out. Everyone thought I'd died, but I was free."

"How did you end up here?" Roberta asked, too caught up in his tale to notice that the question was probably rude.

Edward sighed and rolled his head on his neck, stretching. "I think it was inevitable, really. Humans aren't cut out for immortality." He gestured, indicating the City. "These guys? It's in their DNA; living hundreds, even thousands of years doesn't faze them. But us, we live too fast, too hard." He paused, looking inward. "I got lazy, stupid. Pick one. Did a bunch of action flicks in the '90's, blockbuster stuff."

Roberta's eyes lit up, "Oh my god, you're..." His name was on the tip of her tongue.

He laughed, suddenly self-conscious. "Marc Michaels."

Gregory stared at him in disbelief. "I saw one or two of those. Shitty acting."

Edward ignored him. "As I was saying, I think I wanted out. Real fame—the kind I wanted, the immortal kind—took so long to achieve. But as usual, I couldn't keep it, could I? I had twenty years tops before I'd have to disappear again. Willie here was lucky in a way—big-business types have a longer shelf life, especially when they don't make the papers. I got tired of all the running. Missed the run of silent movies because I was running. I was at the height of my fame, thinking, this was it. Even twenty years from now, I can never do another movie. It was depressing."

"You're still a whiner, Edward. Four hundred years and you haven't learned a thing," the Asshole said.

316

"I'll get to you in a minute," Edward said and then promptly ignored his brother again.

"I did what everybody does eventually. You know, Lord Te made six contracts that night. We were the first. Of those six, Willie here was the last to be brought in." He looked at Gregory. "None of us could handle immortality. Everyone gave up."

"I don't know what you're talking about. I didn't give up."

"Then what are you doing here? You go broke all of a sudden?"

"It's all a mistake. You'll see."

Edward's laugh was bitter, mocking. "That tattoo on your face says otherwise."

The Asshole covered his face with his hand and tried to scoot away from Edward, but the cage was too small; there was no place for him to go. Edward saw that and laughed even harder.

Gregory's humiliation was uncomfortable, even for Roberta, who had to look away. When she did, she noticed John talking to her artist—well, threatening, actually. "This one is Lord Kai's first and most treasured," he said, pointing at her. "Make him proud, and I won't come back and eat your eyes."

A low whistle sounded from the cage. "Well, doesn't he mean business? I'm impressed. What is it? I've never seen one like him before."

"That's John." Roberta related the earlier events.

"No shit? That's new. You were lucky he could do that. Saved you a whole lot of grief. See, as far as I can tell, those Kazat like two things: hunting humans and eating humans." He looked at Gregory. "You thinking about running, you think again. Kazat chase runaways for sport. I've heard where they'll catch you and let you go just to catch you again. They also like to take trophies: fingers, toes, noses..." He was visibly delighted by the horrified look on Gregory's face. When he'd had enough, he addressed her again.

"Lord Kai is an enigma around here. He was there with Lucifer the night we made our contracts." He gestured between himself and Gregory. "Never thought I'd see him again, but lo and behold, he came to retrieve me. Of course, I fought him—I was an action star, right? I knew some moves. Maybe I would have stood a chance too—if he wasn't a centuries old vampire warrior. Kicked my ass seven ways from Sunday." He laughed. "You know what he did afterward?" Edward's eyes sparkled as he looked at her. "He *thanked* me. Not for the challenge, mind you, but for *trying*. Said I showed him respect by my willingness to fight him for my life." Edward was shaking his head, a bemused smile on his lips at the memory.

Roberta noticed Gregory's embarrassed look. He caught her looking and blanched. She'd seen him begging. Another time, she may have thrown that out for Edward to mock, just for the satisfaction of contributing to the Asshole's embarrassment. But right now, she was stuck on one word: Lucifer.

"So Kai has his first slave." Edward looked at her, speculation alight in his eyes. "Lucifer must be loosening his grip."

Roberta's thought processes had stalled at the name *Lucifer*. She had asked Kai if Lord Te was the Devil, and he'd said no, conveniently omitting the fact that he was apparently chummy with the actual Devil.

"Lucifer?" She whispered, looking at Edward with helpless, frightened eyes.

"You didn't know. Well, that's interesting." He leaned forward, "Lucifer is his lover; they've been together for centuries."

Now it was Roberta's turn to look horrified. Stephan's words drifted back to her. She was just a diversion. This entire trip had been a waste after all. She couldn't help the feeling of helplessness as her eyes filled with tears.

John was instantly at her side thrusting a cloth in front of her face. When she'd wiped the tears that wouldn't stop, and blew her nose, he gave her some P2 which she gratefully took without complaint.

"You," he addressed Edward. "I will have one of your arms for upsetting my charge." He took a step toward the cage; Edward ducked his head and raised his hands in surrender. Before John could take another step, Roberta grabbed his arm causing him to stop and turn to her.

"It's okay, John. Please don't hurt him."

"It is my duty to see that you are unharmed."

"I'm fine, really. It's been a stressful day."

He studied her. Once he was satisfied, he gave Edward a warning look before walking back to the artist.

Edward looked at her with obvious relief. "Thank you. Who knew such a timid creature could turn into something so damn scary." He watched John for a moment before turning his attention back to her.

"P2—that stuff is amazing, and I've done heroin." After a pause, Edward said, "You really didn't know."

She shook her head.

"Look, I wouldn't worry about it. Kai's given you clothes—such as they are. You're getting his mark. That means something."

"How do you know so much?" Roberta asked, thankful the P2 was muting her initial reaction to Kai's association with Lucifer and desperate to move the subject away from another thing she couldn't control.

"Live and learn." Edward seemed happy and eager to continue answering her questions.

Roberta assumed he didn't get much opportunity for conversation.

"Take that fella Rys you mentioned. He's a satyr. The satyrs run the brothels down here. He's seen my movies—big fan. When Lord Te gave me to his brothel, he took a special interest, if you know what I mean."

"I always knew you were a fag," Gregory spat, recovered from his earlier embarrassment.

Edward sighed and rolled his eyes. "I'm not gay, you idiot. But here, it doesn't matter. Nobody gives a shit."

Gregory's eyes grew wide at the implications.

"To them, it's all just sex. Besides, the satyrs are walking sex machines—they secrete something that makes you beg for it. Oh, to be a fly on the wall the first time that happens to you," Edward said, with an expression that made Roberta shiver despite the P2. As much as she hated Gregory, she could get no pleasure from the idea of his violation. Edward, on the other hand, reveled in it.

"Lord Te gave you to Rys's brothel?"

"Yeah. See, our lot," he gestured to himself and Gregory, "is different than the slaves that were born here or your random captures. We're special. We ultimately belong to Lord Te. You know how money drives everything on the surface—the more you have, the higher your social standing? Well, down here it's different. Here they thrive on status—if you get the chance, take a look at what passes for money. It's everything from actual coinage to glass beads and trinkets. Why? Because it has no value; it's all a matter of personal preference. So us? Call us rentals." He cracked a smile at Gregory's look of dismay. "Yes, Willie-boy, that's our punishment—to spend eternity as party favors."

"If status is like money, how do they get it?" Roberta asked, intrigued—there was so much to learn.

"Depends." Edward shrugged. "Take Atal over there," he said, gesturing to her artist, scribbling and erasing under John's close scrutiny and direction. "He's the best artist here, so he got his status through skill. Your friends, the Kazat, got theirs through brute force."

"What about Lord Te?" She couldn't imagine what he had to do to be in a position to run this place.

"Now, that's a good story." He changed position to face her fully, eyes sparkling with anticipation. He was enjoying his audience. Maybe it wasn't just the opportunity for conversation; maybe it was her. She liked the idea. "So this place used to be overseen by this huge dragon, a god named Uru—"

Gregory snorted, interrupting him. "Nonsense. There's no such thing as dragons."

"Says the guy who sold his soul to a demon. As I was saying," Edward turned his full attention back to her, "you see those lighted pillars embedded in the walls that run to the ceiling?" He pointed up. "Nobody can get near those—too bright, too hot. So before he dies, Uru extinguishes one. Like, poof! And says that the one who reignites it will take his place."

"Fairy tale nonsense," Gregory muttered, but Roberta ignored him, more interested in Edward's tale.

"So Lord Te reignited it?"

"Oh yeah, but in the meantime, it was real Sword-in-the-Stone shit. Everybody tried. From high ritual magic to power words—you name it, they tried it. And one day Te walks in, waits patiently in line until it's his turn. When it is, he walks up, places his hand on the pillar. Everybody's laughing at him, 'cause, you know, who does that? Like that shit hadn't been tried before. So he places his hand on it, and within seconds, and without so much as a word uttered—the pillar is blazing. That's some serious power." He held her eyes then, cementing the implications. "Lord Kai is his best pal."

So Lord Te was a demon; that explained his association with Lucifer. But then why had he taken it upon himself to not only educate her but to be fairly solicitous in the process? He was the one that gave her the P2 to combat Uriel's thrall. Uriel had been here in the City—weren't angels and demons supposed to be enemies? This whole situation was making less and less sense. Gratefully, she let her confusion drift away on a P2-tinted cloud.

"Just how long have you been here?" Gregory asked him.

"What year is it?"

Roberta told him, and he whistled again. "Wow. Just before the turn of the century. Tell me, did Y2K ever happen?"

"No, we all got scared for nothing."

Edward seemed to get a kick out of that.

"What about the rest of the slaves; what are they used for?" She asked, any fear of the knowledge conveniently absent in her drugged state. In light of the circumstances, maybe being an addict wasn't such a bad thing. She embraced her desire to stop feeling.

"Well, you got different classes. The ones born down here are mostly bred for food—magic is used to speed up growth. Birth to table in about a year. Those ones you probably saw getting branded?" Roberta nodded. "Yeah, all food—blood for vampires, etc."

"They were so docile."

"Yeah, and dumb as posts. They don't get a chance to develop like normal, so they don't know any better." He shrugged. "I've been told it's part of the magic."

"I had no idea magic was real." She looked at Gregory, who stared back, unapologetic.

"Oh, you have no idea. On the surface, we got technology; down here, it's all magic. Some of the stuff I've seen." Edward whistled. "Pretty amazing. Anyway, the smarter ones not used for food mainly end up as personal servants and pets. The ones from the surface, if they survive the training, are used to replenish the breeding stock or in mining, tunneling, chos farming, mushroom farming, or as whores."

"Survive the training?" Gregory and Roberta asked simultaneously. "Chos farming?"

Once again, Edward gave Gregory a chilling look. "Yeah, Willie, you're gonna learn how to be a good slave. Each job has different requirements, see? Usually they lose a bunch 'cause most folks from the surface can't handle this reality, but us? As Lord Te's property, we're protected from the luxury of insanity."

Edward held up his left hand. The middle finger was missing at the second joint. "We're also protected from other things. Chos took the whole finger a while ago. Vicious rat-cat-looking things. Hairless, ugly as fuck, and will eat you if given half a chance." He pointed to a missing pinky toe. "These are growing back. Lord Te ensures we will always be able to work." He looked at Gregory again. "Welcome to Hell, Willie. Couldn't have happened to a nicer guy."

Roberta had watched Gregory's face during Edward's orientation. It had run the gamut, now settling on terrified. She guessed he finally understood the reality of his current situation.

"Given the choice, I'd go back to the brothel and Rys any day. It was the only time I could be clean, get a shave, and sleep on a real bed on a regular basis. Plus, he's a big movie fan—if it's out on film, VHS, DVD or Blu-ray, he's got it. That and an endless supply of P2. It's the best life I can hope for now."

Roberta wondered if she was headed for the same fate, only with a different master. Kai had made a good case, but everything she'd learned today cast doubt on its validity. Stoned as she was, her mind presented this truth to her from behind the comforting wall of P2. If Stephan was right, Kai would discard her when Lucifer came back. But why should he be right?

Her brief time with Kai had begun to build her trust. She'd hung on to it in the face of Stephan's derision, so why couldn't she hang on to it now? Because Kai had lied. Not only did he have a lover—and maybe that shouldn't bother her, but it did—but that lover was *Lucifer* of all people. Everything Kai had told her was now tainted. He had been clever, though. By presenting things to her the right way, her compliance and cooperation had been assured. He probably found it all very amusing—how easily she'd fallen into the trap, especially since it sounded so reasonable, and since she really had no choice, given the alternative. She couldn't trust him. She couldn't trust any of them.

The sketch the artist made finally met with John's approval, and Roberta was called over.

"It was really nice meeting you, Edward. I hope to see you again," she said with a smile, even as doubt of the possibility clouded her mind.

Edward smiled back, his face light and handsome, despite his years living in such harsh conditions. "Thanks. Me too."

Gregory grumbled something, which she ignored.

The artist was big, Andre-the-Giant big. He had her lie down on her right side, left cheek up. The last thing she wanted was a tattoo on her face, but the time to change her mind was long past. She closed her eyes and accepted her fate.

Since leaving the surface, marking the passage of time proved impossible. Hence, Roberta had no idea how long she lay there before the tattoo was finished. She'd been surprised that, for such a large man, the artist had a gentle touch and did nothing to overtly hurt her. Even so, the tattoo hurt like a bitch. P2 was not designed for pain relief.

A loose bandage was placed over her cheek, and the artist gave the aftercare instructions to John, who looked offended to be told something he obviously knew. The entire day had been exhausting, and all she wanted to do was go back to her room and sleep.

With a parting wave to Edward, she followed John back to her rooms. The return trip was much less exciting. Even John's new appearance garnered less attention on the way back. When she was safely back in her room, John helped her out of her "decoration."

"So, is this how you're going to look from now on?"

He stopped and looked at her, taking a few moments to reply. "I am as I'm supposed to be," he said.

She had no idea what that meant, and after the day she'd had, had no mental energy to figure it out.

"I should bring food."

"Could it wait? I just want to lie down."

"As you wish. You did well today." He smiled at her. In his current from, his smile was horrifying. The blazing red eyes and red teeth did not lend themselves well to cheerfulness sans torture.

John took up a position near the bedroom door as Roberta entered it and closed the door behind her. Her feet were filthy, and she still had the remains of stinking, dried, and flaking Kazat drool stuck to her. A shower would have been nice, but her nerves were taxed and overstrained, her body wanting nothing more than to shut down for a while. Once stretched out on the bed, she was asleep within minutes.

Nineteen

Kai's rise to consciousness was slow but inevitable. As awareness returned, the pain became more acute, and soon his body was screaming with it. The scent of ozone and cedar nearby told him that Te was in the room.

"You know, decency dictates that you put me out of my misery," he said, concentrating on not opening his eyes.

Te chuckled. "You should know by now that I'm far from decent. How are you feeling, my friend?"

Kai groaned. "Like I've been dragged along the pavement for few miles."

His voice was weak, a true reflection of his debility. He was also simultaneously ravenous and nauseated, two things that were the hardest to reconcile. It had been a long time since he'd had sun poisoning, but the symptoms were hard to forget.

"I'd be lying if I said you didn't look it."

Te's words plus the pain that would come from opening his eyes shored up Kai's resolve to keep them shut for the time being.

"I know what happened. Julian found you and brought you to Risha. After they called me, you were rambling, and I needed to see what did this. So I looked into your mind."

Good. At least Te knew what happened. At the moment, his memory of the events past the agony was fuzzy. They would talk about it and the true state of things later.

"I had wondered about the stench of were. Here I thought the sun poisoning was bad enough."

A hearty, masculine laugh filled the room. "Given your current circumstances, I can hardly take offense."

Kai opened his eyes a crack, but searing pain had him shutting them again immediately. "Julian, I am honored by your hospitality."

Ordinarily, Kai would have felt embarrassment at not only having the weres see him like this but at having to come to them for protection in the first place. While he still felt some discomfort at the situation, it was tempered by the assumption that Te must have revealed more about himself to Risha than was comfortable.

"It is my mate, my clan, and I who are honored. You are welcome to stay as long as you need to. The Orion Clan extends its full protection."

"I can't stay." While Kai was grateful, he didn't want to owe them anymore than he currently did.

It sounded like Julian was about to protest when Te beat him to it. "Don't be ridiculous. You can't even open your eyes, much less stand. You will stay until you can do at least those two things."

Kai wanted to argue but had no good arguments to make. "How bad?" He couldn't keep the anxiety out of his voice.

The silence that followed only amplified his fears.

"The sun exposure was minimal, but it will complicate the healing process of your other injuries."

His entire being felt like an open wound. He hadn't expected to live through both the removal of the sigils and exposure to the sun. Sun sickness, like radiation sickness in humans, was measured by degree. He was old and so recovering from minimal exposure to the sun was possible—if painful. He needed to feed, but the idea nauseated him—it was that dichotomy that would hinder his recovery the most.

Te cleared his throat. "I've postponed the Rendering."

Kai was relieved to hear it—getting out of bed right now under his own power was impossible.

"The reason?"

"My desire that everything be perfect." Te laughed. "What good is having power if you don't make unreasonable demands once in a while?"

Kai's smile felt wan and lopsided. "Postponed until?"

"Until I'm satisfied."

Kai relaxed. "You're as bad as Luc."

Te's warm laugh soothed him. "I'll take that as a compliment."

"Roberta—"

"I will check in on her. Right now, I'd like you to feed."

Kai's stomach turned at the idea, but he knew Te was right.

"Leave it; I'll get to it." Te's silence said he was dubious. "Promise."

"Lord Te, if you need to go, I'll make sure he feeds," Julian said.

Any other time Kai would have challenged Julian's ability to do so. If he tried it now, he knew it would be all bluster and nothing more than a feeble show of defiance that would only embarrass him. He settled on sulking instead.

"I know you don't want to, but you need to feed. I cannot heal you, Kai. Your body is too weak. You can't even tolerate my blood anymore."

"Maybe I can build up a tolerance. Try it, please."

Te sighed, but before Kai had to convince him further, Te's wrist was at his mouth. At the first taste, he was pushing Te's arm away and turning his head. It was too much. Te was right; Kai wouldn't survive if he tried using his power to heal him. Disappointment welled but was forestalled by the blood's unexpected soporific side effect. The pain eased as he gratefully slid into sleep.

* * *

Te watched with concern as Kai drifted off to sleep. Something happened in the City that tripped the wards he'd placed to alert him to trouble. Almost as soon as Kai woke, the wards called him to the City, but he needed to make sure Kai would be all right before he left. He stood from his seat at Kai's beside and addressed Julian.

"I'm needed in the City. You have my card; call if you need me."

Julian stood as well and bowed. He looked tired. He'd sent Risha off to bed, taking it upon himself to watch over their honored guest. "I will, my Lord."

Knowing he could trust Julian didn't make it any easier for Te to leave. Julian seemed to sense this.

"On my life, my Lord."

Te hoped it wouldn't come to that. With a last look at Kai, he disappeared.

Never as skilled with wards as Lucifer, Te had always meant to talk to him about making them better and more precise, but he'd never gotten around to it. As such, he had no idea what he'd find as he entered the City and was more than a little relieved to find things as they should be. His task now was to find out what had set the wards off in the first place. As if on cue, Rys jogged up to him.

The thing that had made it easier for Te to be lax about the wards was the fact that there was no shortage of Other-kin who made it their business to keep him informed—usually for a price. If he was willing to pay it, there was very little he didn't know about his chosen domain.

"Hey, Big Man. Whoa, who died?"

Rys stopped and looked him up and down. Te never wore black, choosing instead to wear every color in celebration of their existence. Now, with his family dead or missing and his close friend on the verge of death, those cheery colors only mocked him.

"Anyway, we almost had a rumble of epic awesome-ness," Rys said, once he'd recovered.

"You want to tell me about it?"

"You know, Daddy-O, I would, but I ain't no snitch, feel me?" Te had been humoring him, but he was in no mood, and the look he gave Rys said so. "Okay, maybe you could do me a solid? Saw Lord Kai's new plaything. Maybe you put in a word and he lets me take her for a spin?"

"Up until now, I have forestalled direct action in response to the Lisatu complaints of shortages in Corolon spirits. Maybe that could change."

Rys stared at him for a moment, pretending to think. But once he opened his mouth, the story flowed in its entirety.

"We cool?" Rys asked.

"We are, although I'd advise caution. If things continue as they are, I will eventually have to intervene. You may find the results less than satisfactory."

"I hear ya, Boss. I hear ya," Rys said before moving off into the crowd.

Even knowing what happened, Te still found it hard to believe and so was shocked when he entered Roberta's room to find John in the form Rys had described. Closing the door behind him, he stood staring at John, who stood tall and stared back—every line of his body tense, challenging.

"Are we going to have a problem, John?"

"No," John replied, still not lowering his red eyes or reducing his posture in any way.

Te had a feeling that dealing with the "new" John would be tiresome. Walking into the room, he sat on the couch, made himself comfortable, and studied the creature before him. The change in John was remarkable—the height, the musculature, the demeanor. This was not the same being, yet there were eyewitnesses to the transformation.

"I've heard the story. You want to tell me what's going on? Who are you?"

John stared at him and then slowly relaxed—he retracted his claws, the barb in his tail, and the spikes around his head. His bearing subtly shifted as well—no longer ready to fight, he faced Te as a respected peer as he stood by the door to Roberta's bedroom.

"How much do you remember from Before?" John asked.

Te was momentarily taken aback by two things: the articulate question and the revelation that John somehow knew he was more than he said he was. "Enough," he replied, wanting to know just how much John knew.

John smiled at the answer, apparently knowing he had hedged. There was, however, no warmth in that smile. It was a "smile" in the same way humans thought a dog who was showing his teeth was smiling—it wasn't so much a smile as it was a warning or show of aggression.

"There were three dominant species on this world: my race, the Jh'tishal, the Banari, and the Kazat. We were in constant conflict. By the time you and yours came, we had all but eradicated the Kazat and set out to do the same to the Banari. But you did that for us." Again, that smile.

334

"Then you know."

"Know what you are? Yes. In case you're interested, the Black Stone know, the Lisatu suspect, and the Kazat have chosen to forget as payment for saving them from extinction."

Te had wondered how many of the old species knew. Since word had not spread, it seemed that they didn't care enough to share the knowledge.

"Why are you here?"

"Ah, but you mean to ask three questions. Why are the Eineu here, and why and how did I come to be here? Because you see, I cannot answer the last without first answering the first."

Te was right—tiresome. In this case, repeating the question would show weakness. What Te wanted to do was throw John around the room until all the answers spilled out, but instead he took a deep breath and waited. He didn't have to wait long.

"You came, and suddenly we were all dying. Uncivilized and civilized alike—it didn't matter; we were all approaching oblivion. But then there was sanctuary. Even the Kazat were welcomed. Tell me, do you regret that?"

"Occasionally." Te shrugged.

"We needed sanctuary."

"You never asked."

"Would you have granted it?" John's eyes flashed when Te didn't answer. "Ideas and suggestions as to our survival were exchanged. The one most accepted was to put a select number in hibernation until such a time when we would wake and reclaim our world. Eventually that idea evolved into hibernating in plain sight. As the most magically gifted race, we knew we could accomplish this—all we needed was a powerful catalyst. We waited until one of your number was wounded, and blood was… stolen."

At this, Te stood, as he could no longer sit casually and listen. He walked over and stood towering over John, adding inches as necessary. "The blood of my brothers was used? To what end?"

"To transform, to create a disguise. To create the Eineu." John smirked, that expression looking more at home on his face. "Tian welcomed the Eineu."

"Tian fell."

John inclined his head, acknowledging the point. "It did. We had miscalculated. Our true nature was close to the surface, and that nature does not lend us to flourishing in close quarters."

It was Te's turn to smirk. "You don't play well with others? Surprising."

For the first time since Te had walked into the room, John dropped his eyes and moved away, creating distance between them.

"Yes, well. It was then that the Eineu took it upon themselves to retreat to the trees. We had not expected them to take the initiative to willingly separate from us as a race unto themselves. It was suspected that the blood of your brethren tainted them in some way."

Although the use of angel blood in the Jh'tishal's blood magic still stuck in his craw, Te relaxed his posture and moved to sit down again. At least the Eineu were as harmless as they seemed. The question was, would they remain that way?

"Them? You speak of them as if they are not you."

"They are essentially another species. As an Eineu, my memories of being a Jh'tishal are distant and dream-like. Likewise, my Eineu memories are alien to me now, as if they belong to another. I speak of Eineu as them, because they are not me."

John frowned, looked at his hands, and flexed them, providing further proof that he found the whole situation as unnerving as Te did.

"And now? Why are you back now?"

"I have puzzled over that since my charge went to bed." When John looked at him, Te could see the confusion in his posture more than in his face.

"Eineu received from the Jh'tishal a highly developed sense of duty—to each other, to our race. When Roberta was placed in John's care, he bonded with her and accepted her as his *matah*. The best translation is 'sacred charge.' His duty was to care for her, protect her. I believe the Kazat triggered my return. As Eineu, John had no way of protecting his matah, and thus his need to fulfill his duty called me—the Kazat's ancient enemy—out of hibernation. John compelled me to satisfy the ancient ritual requirement, and she is now my matah. I am surprised he was able to influence me. I believe he was close to the surface then. He has since gone into hibernation."

"So Roberta woke you up. What about the other two?"

John smiled that creepy smile. "My sisters."

Te couldn't hide his shock. "You mean John-red and John-yellow are female?"

"Yes."

"As Eineu, they look alike. From the account I heard, even as Jh'tishal you look alike."

John didn't seem offended. "You would think so. The females have shorter tails as well as an identifying scent." He breathed deeply; his expression turned lecherous. "Even now they call to me." He seemed to lose focus.

"You were telling me what woke your sisters." Te had to assess whether or not the remaining Eineu were a threat.

John snapped his attention back to Te. "I did. It was out of my control. Our racial hatred for the Kazat is strong. I called them to feast."

"They reverted, but you didn't."

"I released them, just as I had called them. At first, it was my matah's blood that kept me anchored; now it is my will."

Te stood again and walked over to stand in front of John.

"Are we going to have a problem?"

In each other's eyes, they shared the knowledge of what that problem could be and the inevitable solution.

"No."

"Do you have a name you'd prefer to go by?"

"John is as good as any. I will not reveal my true name to you," John said.

For a species as magically adept as the Jh'tishal, Te wasn't surprised and took no offense. Names had power.

"What about Roberta? What does being your matah mean for her?"

"She is my charge, and I will protect her."

"She belongs to Kai."

"If Kai had done a proper job of protecting her, I would not be here."

Te had to concede that point.

"I will not interfere between them. I will also not allow her to be hurt," John said.

Te stepped back and walked toward Roberta's room. "Let's take a look at this mark, shall we?"

* * *

Roberta woke but couldn't be bothered. There were voices in the outer room, but she couldn't tell whose. Probably Kai and the "new" John. She burrowed down into the covers, wishing that they'd go away so she could sleep some more. But she couldn't sleep because her face hurt, and she was hungry. She'd been hungry a lot since arriving and really didn't like that aspect of living here. That aspect—who was she kidding? There was more than one, and she had no control over any of them.

Suddenly hot, she pushed the covers away and groaned. Her face felt tight under the bandage.

Great. I've got an infection.

She had purposely not thought about the hygiene of the slave market, especially after passing the medical stalls. Now it was all she could think about. MRSA on her face would be bad. Did they have antibiotics down here? Or was she doomed to live the rest of her life with half a face?

That is, if she lived. Once again, her eyes filled and over-flowed onto her now-dirty pillow. Her head throbbed in time with her heartbeat, and she lay there afraid to move.

The door opened.

A big man was silhouetted in the door way. Fuck, it was Lord Te. She was going to have to get up and act slave-like. Too bad her body wasn't cooperating. When the lights came on, it took a few blinks before she could see him clearly. He was wearing a black suit much like the one Uriel had been wearing. It was weird seeing him in black. She'd had the impression that he didn't feel at home in black in the same way that she couldn't imagine Kai in anything else. He approached the bed, and she cried harder.

"Shh, what's this about? I know you're not afraid of me." He sat on the edge of the bed. "I've heard the tale of your mark. Let's see it."

He gently turned her face toward him and reached for the bandage and pulled it off. He frowned. "I'll bet you don't feel well."

John had come in behind him. "Atal will die for this."

"That may be an overreaction."

"I warned him," John said with a growl.

"I need a doctor, don't I? Maybe some antibiotics? I don't want to die." Roberta said, sniffling.

"It is infected, but you'll be fine," Te said before touching the hot, swollen skin.

Within seconds she felt better. The tightness in her face subsided and with it, the headache and fever.

"That was magic, wasn't it?" she asked him.

He smiled a beautiful, perfect smile. "You could say that." His face took on an admiring quality as he examined her mark. "Beautiful. I think Kai will be quite pleased."

"Then I will not kill Atal. I will eat only one of his eyes instead," said John.

Te looked at him. "How did you come about that reasoning?"

"I told Atal I would eat his eyes if he did not make Lord Kai proud. You say he will be pleased, but his slovenly ways proved injurious to my matah. I will eat one eye."

"If that is indeed what you said, you included nothing about preventing infection. Punishing Atal so severely because you weren't specific will be seen as unjust."

"This cannot stand." John's lips pulled back over his teeth in a snarl.

"Break a few fingers if you must as a warning to be more careful. Anything more than that is unwarranted and may gain enemies for not only you but your matah as well." Te shrugged. "It's up to you."

All at once, it was just too much. Roberta had thought she was adjusting, but as she lay there, naked, with those two arguing over John's threat to eat someone's eye, her capacity to adapt had reached its limit. Crying with any vigor, as it turned out, took way too much energy, so she lay and let the tears fall, needing everything to just stop for a moment.

John had moved around to the other side of the bed and removed the jar of P2.

Roberta shook her head. "No. I won't become an addict. I must be over the thrall; I don't think of Uriel. I don't want it." It was a lie—now that she was sober again, she did want it, especially the peace and detachment it provided. The part about not wanting to be an addict was true though. It was only when stoned that she didn't care if she became addicted.

Te was looking at her again, but she was unable to read his face. "When was the last time you thought of Uriel?"

"I don't know." She had to think back. "Probably after he sent me the stuff to read."

"Hmm. Okay." He looked at John and waved him off. "John will still have it, so it's available if you need it."

"Thank you."

"I know I told you—and I'm assuming Kai told you as well—to stay in this room. So tell me, why did you disobey?" he asked her, after producing a box of tissues and handing one to her.

Shit. Shit. Shit. She'd forgotten she'd been *ordered* not to leave the room. Focusing on his big hands, she said, "Stephan came by. He said Lord Kai didn't mark me because I was disposable. I was afraid he was right. But I was afraid of him more and hoped that if I had Kai's mark, he wouldn't bother me anymore. I asked John to go and find Lord Kai or you, but he couldn't. So I pleaded with him to take me himself."

There was more, and it was intent on bubbling out of her regardless.

"Why are you being so nice to me?" What had been a steady trickle of tears became a stream as the fear the P2 locked away yesterday burst into her consciousness. "In the City, I learned a few things. I know you're a demon. I know you and Kai are friends with Lucifer—well Kai is more than friends. I know that Kai is just playing with me until Lucifer gets back. I'm not a religious person, but I know what the Devil is, and if you have him for a friend and lover you have to be evil. I don't understand what part Uriel is playing, but it can't be good. He wanted me to kill myself. Is this how you get your kicks?" She took a big hiccupping breath. "Do you think it's funny? Psychologically torturing the helpless human? God damn every single one of you." Great big sobs escaped after the last word and she scooted backwards on the bed, creating as much distance between them as possible.

A familiar growling started up, and she opened blurry eyes to see John, tense and coiled, preparing to attack. Te was still sitting at her bedside, ignoring him. She couldn't look at his face; she didn't want to see what would only be a nasty gleam in his eye now that the jig was up.

"Roberta, look at me," he said.

The tone of command in his voice was something she could not disobey. She looked up. His eyes held the same compassion she'd seen before.

"Stop it. Why are you doing this?" she cried harder.

"Shh, calm down." He reached out and gently caressed her head.

Instantly she felt comforted, her emotions calmed.

343

"Remember how I told you that the myths behind the so-called magical creatures were inaccurate?"

She nodded, accepting another tissue.

"That holds true for other things as well. The devil you've heard of does not exist."

"But—"

"No. If the humans on the surface knew of us, they would classify every one of us as demons. It's merely a classification used to distinguish between what they believe to be good and evil. It has no bearing other than that."

She blew her nose and studied him.

"You felt Uriel's thrall. Did Kai demonstrate his thrall to you?"

She nodded.

"In each case, you felt your will consumed by theirs, correct?"

She nodded again.

"What you're feeling now is not a thrall, but the essence of who and what I am. Your will is still intact. I mean you no harm. Kai means you no harm. Do you believe me?"

"But—"

"No. Do you believe me?"

She nodded, because it was true. She felt safe.

"The residents of the City love to gossip. You will hear things. Some true, some not. Once you've lived with us awhile, you will be able to distinguish between the two. Until then, trust that you can rely upon us to tell the difference."

She wanted to let it go, but something nagged at her. She moved her eyes to the wet tissue in her hands, uncomfortable looking at him while she spoke.

"Kai told me why Gregory was taken. He sold his soul; how can that not be evil?"

Te chuckled. "If I told a random human that I could extend their life indefinitely and help them to gain everything they ever wanted for half the profits, do you know what they'd say?

"What's the catch?" She couldn't help the wry tone in her voice.

"Exactly. Every one would demand to know my angle, even though I told them up front. It's too easy." He shrugged. "Since the mythology behind the devil was already in place, I simply used it. Interestingly enough, those I make deals with are happier thinking that they're getting away with something.

"And people like Gregory?"

Te sighed. "The downside to thinking they're getting away with something is that they'll always try, even with me. Given what they're supposed to represent, the contracts are worded rather harshly—'do this or you'll be sorry.' If any of them, even Gregory, had come to me and said, 'This has been fun, but I'm tired and would like to stop,' I would let them. Why? Because this," he gestured between them, "is all about choice."

"You said I had no choice." She reminded him.

He smiled at her. "Some choices come with better consequences than others. Besides, I was trying to make a point.

Anyway, people like Gregory end up punished because they expect it."

She mulled that over. It was all so reasonable.

Taking a deep breath, she asked, "What about Lucifer? What happens to me when he returns?"

"Once Kai and I explain the situation, he will accept you. He'll have to; Kai has no intention of disposing of you."

The situation still worried her. It probably showed on her face, because Te frowned.

"That's not something you have to worry about. Let us deal with it."

She looked over at John, who seemed calmer but hadn't moved.

"Is John okay?"

"He's fine. He reacted to your distress." He shrugged, "And to the fact that I won't let him attack me. He'll calm down, once you have."

Now it was her turn to frown. "I don't understand."

"He feels your emotions and reacts violently to perceived threats to you. You may belong to Kai, but John will always protect you from harm."

Sudden movement from John caught her attention. She looked over to see a shiver go through his body and watched as he relaxed, spines retracting.

"Do we have a problem, John?" Te asked, still looking at her.

John shivered again and blinked. "No."

"Good. Roberta?"

"I'm okay." She couldn't explain it, but she was. At her core, she knew he was telling the truth.

"Okay. You've gone through a lot. Take a shower. You smell like a Kazat. Eat and rest. Kai will be indisposed for a few days."

Even though she wondered what Kai was doing to keep him away, she was grateful for the reprieve—for just a little time to relax and absorb.

Te stood. "John, get new sheets for the bed and bring her some food. When Kai is ready, I'll come and collect you." He disappeared.

Roberta wiped her face again and got up to take her shower.

Stopping in front of the mirror, she kept her eyes down. Taking a deep breath and steeling her nerves, she slowly raised her eyes, unable to help the quick intake of breath her reflection caused. It *was* beautiful. In shades of black and grey, the tattoo was intricate and delicate. She recognized the symbol for Kai's clan circled by other symbols—ones she assumed represented Kai. Staring at the mark of Kai's ownership, she realized she could live with it. While she'd rather not have it on her face, it was comforting to see that it wasn't hideous. Given the overall rise in popularity of tattoos, it was actually rather hip. She smirked at the idea that she could in any way be considered trendy.

It was with relief that Roberta stepped into the hot shower, letting the water further relax her stressed body. Te had healed the tattoo and her infection with a touch, and while he didn't come right out and say it during their conversation, she suspected that he was so much more than he was telling her.

Since she'd been here, she'd learned more about the world than she'd ever wanted to know, and she knew there was more to come. But it could wait. By the time Te came to collect her in a few days, she'd be recharged and ready to start her new life. In the meantime, all she wanted was to finish her shower, have a meal, and read *Cosmo*. She didn't know if they had access to chocolate down here, but maybe John could find her something sweet and indulgent; that would be really nice too.

* * *

Te sat at Kai's bedside, watching him sleep. He'd sent an exhausted Julian to bed on his return. It had been a surprise to find that Roberta was free of Uriel's thrall. He supposed that was a win, if he measured such things. He was also surprised to find that he was actually grateful for John's current incarnation, even though he'd had to restrain him to prevent an attack. John would take care of Roberta like Kai would—possibly even better, since Kai was in no position to do it himself. Another win.

Ordinarily, he'd expect Kai to punish Roberta for disobeying them, but given her breakdown, he'd suggest leniency. Her adventure in the marketplace, plus the fears compounded by the gossip she'd heard was punishment enough. Te was surprised by how much he felt for her. He was reminded of his brothers who stayed true to their purpose—was this how they felt about humans? Having

348

spent so much time with the Other-kin and with Lucifer's mocking treatment of them, his overall view of humanity was less than complementary. Roberta was changing that.

He hadn't meant to reveal as much as he had, but he'd felt compelled to comfort. He was pretty sure she'd guessed his true nature, and that revealed another problem. Given her inclusion in Kai's life, she would be privy to secrets, and since Kai refused to secure her silence with his blood, they needed to ensure that their secrets remained among them. To that end, he'd suggest a binding. As long as she was vulnerable, they would all be as well.

She had been right, though; with Kai's mark, even a whiff of impropriety on Stephan's part meant that Kai could retaliate. If the mood Kai had been in lately was any indication, Stephan might lose a body part—or worse. Vampires Stephan's age usually had a master to keep them in line. Te was going to have to step into that role. The residents of the City gave Stephan leeway because of his status; Kai had no such respect for his title. If Stephan was going to survive, Te needed to impress upon him the necessity of keeping out of Kai's business.

Right now, his most pressing issue was Kai's complete recovery, which was directly in Kai's hands. If Te had his way, he'd pour as much blood into Kai as he would stand, desperate as he was for him to get better.

The idea that he was entirely alone scared him. He had been saddened and bewildered by what he'd seen in Kai's mind. Who were those women? He marveled at the extent of their power—their ability to extinguish Uriel's holy fire, to strip Kai of Lucifer's protections, and to send Uriel to Hell, where he supposedly joined Lucifer. His brothers may not be dead, but they might as well be.

In the beginning, he and his brothers had fought Darkness, beat it back—did they mean it was returning? If so, how? There were protections in place to prevent that from happening. No wonder they had let him stay. One angel, while still powerful, was no match for the returning Darkness.

Kai stirred, and Te was grateful to be dragged out of his thoughts.

"Good, you're awake. Let's get some blood into you." He may have sounded overly cheery, and if Kai thought it was on his behalf, that was fine.

"Let's get this over with," Kai said with eyes still closed.

Te laughed, not worrying that the merriment didn't reach his eyes. "That's the spirit. You'll be up and around in no time," he said, as he carefully propped Kai up and helped him drink.

Kai managed two mouthfuls before he pushed the bottle away. "That's rancid."

"There's nothing wrong with the blood; it's just the poisoning talking."

"Well then, you drink it," Kai groused before attempting to drink again.

"What, and rob you of the opportunity? Never."

Kai managed to drink a quarter of the bottle before putting a stop to it. Te helped him settle back down.

"It looks bad, doesn't it?" Kai asked, his voice low.

"I'm told that chicks dig scars."

The laugh was unexpected. Kai reached for his hand. "Thanks, Te."

"Get some rest, my friend."

Te kept vigil as Kai once again slipped into sleep.

Twenty

The first thing Lucifer noticed when he woke was pain. Intense. Debilitating. He passed into unconsciousness.

When he next woke, he took note that he lay in broken glass, fine bits of which scoured his corneas when he opened his eyes. Squinting through tears, he had the urge to reach up and scribble 'wash me' in the grimy, cloudless sky. This sky would never rain, nor would it ever be clean. He didn't know how he knew it, but as he lay there taking census in his body, it felt true.

The air was flat and stale—breezes never blew here either. It appeared to be twilight, but there was no light source that he could see. His body ached, every nerve raw and screaming. He felt heavy, the clothes he wore even heavier. The glass ground into his joints and poked into the soft tissue. Even his soul felt ragged and beaten.

He had to sit up, stand up. The idea of moving in his current state was not appealing, but the thought of just lying there was even less so. His effort to sit up was aborted when the motion caused every hurt in his body to ratchet in intensity. His stomach roiled, and his body felt wrong as he experienced its sudden desire to turn itself inside out. The feeling—nausea?—was new and something he instantly disliked.

All he could do was lie still until it passed. Most if not all of his body was broken; the idea that he could hurt that much and still be intact seemed impossible. He loosed his power, checking his wounds. Pain flared; already taxed senses whelmed, he passed out again.

Rising to consciousness again was unavoidable. The pain was a living, feeding thing. With his eyes closed, he waited, riding the pain-beast until it grew tired and content to graze.

Once it was no more than white noise in the background of his senses, he slowly and carefully sat up. That managed with little distress, he continued the motion until he was standing. On his feet at last, he looked at his surroundings. He was standing at the bottom of a crater, at least a mile wide. Slamming into the ground at terminal velocity might explain why he felt so wretched. But there was more to it, wasn't there?

The ground was not made up of broken glass, he discovered, but of a dull, pale brown powdery dust, the same color as the sky. It clung to him everywhere—in his hair, down his shirt, in his pants and shoes—abrading his too-sensitive flesh as well as his fastidious nature.

When he got back home, the first thing he would do was take a bath. And maybe if he complained loudly enough, Kai would indulge him and wash his hair and give him a massage. Once he got on a roll and embellished a detail or two—not that it was really necessary—he was sure that

Te would even crack the seal on some Ambrosia. Then, cleaned and refreshed, he'd find his brothers and plan what to do about the Nammu.

With home firmly in mind, he transported…

…and crashed back onto the ground in a cloud of dust and enough pain to send him into unconsciousness once more.

Lucifer viciously cursed the Nammu when he regained consciousness for the fourth time. He'd face-planted in the dust when he fell, and carefully rolling on to his back, he wiped his face of the cloying powder as best he could and lay at the bottom of the crater gazing up at the twilit sky.

He was trapped. Without warning, the washed-out brown sky and matching dirt closed in. Unable to fight the fear and the pain at the same time, he let the fear come—it bore down on him with suffocating intensity. Only when the aches in his body subsided could he concentrate enough to stop the overwhelming emotion. Since he got in, he could get out—it was possible, just not easy. Emotions under control, he slowly stood when he was able.

Next on the agenda was finding out what was possible. He tried cleaning himself up and was relieved to find that he was able to remove the dirt covering him without so much as a twinge of pain. He wasn't completely powerless. That was something. The next test was transporting to the lip of the crater.

He reappeared only a few feet away, barely conscious and on his knees. The rising heat of rage was a welcome change.

It seemed his only choice was to pick a direction and walk. Trying to scramble up the side of the crater in what he was currently wearing proved impossible, though. The fine dust afforded no traction, and it billowed at every step. If he was coated in dust from the fall, now he was cloaked in it—the sensation of it on his skin made him feel filthy, tainted. It was also cold—not bitter cold, but cool enough to be uncomfortable—another thing added to the shopping list of "Things Lucifer Wasn't Used To." Of course, there would be more, much more. Cursing the Nammu again, he stopped to change clothes.

With little effort, he changed into leather pants tucked into sturdy boots. He chose a calf-length, leather coat, buttoned up from its high neck to his waist. Leather gloves covered his hands and the ends of his sleeves. He wrapped a scarf over his face and head so that only his eyes were visible. He may have been in hell and dressed like a biker, but that didn't mean he'd stoop to wearing anything other than white—he also made sure the powdery dirt didn't cling.

Pleased with the outfit, he set off up the hill again. The going was easier this time, and he was able to dig in with both his glove-covered hands and boots. Progress was slow, but he made it to the top. Looking out over the barrenness of the land around him, he felt the substantial weight of everything he'd gone through. His anger drained away, and desolation settled around him while he took in his surroundings.

Welcome to Hell.

With fear threatening to once again consume him, he laid out everything he knew about the situation. *One, I'm in Hell. Alone. Well, that's not exactly true—supposedly some Fallen came here willingly. I'll believe that should I see it.*

Two, the Old Man is supposedly here. Somewhere—see number one.

Three, I am powerless. Well, less powerful. How much less remains to be seen.

Four, Kai—

He stopped. Why was he thinking of Kai now? Because he might never see him again, and their parting had been so mundane. His chest felt hollow, and he rubbed it, trying to dismiss the feeling. Funny how he'd been outrageously vigilant in his protection of Kai, making sure that he would live through the most outrageous of circumstances. But in the end, Kai didn't die; for all intents and purposes, Lucifer did. He might never see his fussy, strong-willed but honorable mate again.

When did he start thinking of Kai as his mate?

Fool, only now that you have lost him can you acknowledge it. That voice sounded suspiciously like Michael's, a fact that made it no less true.

When Kai had proclaimed them mated centuries ago, he'd derided him. "I am Lucifer. I am mate to no one," he'd said.

Only now did he feel ashamed. Kai had merely looked at him, his black eyes knowing, and never said another word about it. Now he had the urge to apologize and scream, "Yes, I am your mate!" until the earth vibrated with the sound. Tears made his vision swim, and he closed his eyes, accepting the lie that it was because of the dust.

Now is not the time for sentiment. Pull yourself together. Michael's voice again. Even in hell, he would get no reprieve from his brother's nagging.

Suddenly very tired, Lucifer let his legs crumple him to the ground in a puff of brown dust. What did he think he was going to do, really? Literally in the middle of Hell, with nothing around him that he could see—what was he going to do? There was no point to it. He was stuck, trapped in Hell, and the Nammu would fill the earth with Darkness.

It felt good to know that Kai would live through it, but if the earth returned to its pre-Purge state, he may not want to. Even if he had managed to save Michael, Raphael, and Gabriel, they would be hunted, eventually killed. The same fate awaited Uriel and Te unless they fled, and he doubted that would happen. It hurt to think about, but he needed to face reality.

Speaking of facing reality, maybe the Nammu weren't lying and the Old Man had been sent here. If He was imprisoned here... well, that meant that escape was impossible, didn't it? If they sent all their prisoners here, what hope could Lucifer possibly have of escaping? If he found the Old Man, what would he say?

Lucifer was pretty sure He would be happy to never see him again—which would only be fair. He'd been disrespectful, boasting, arrogant, disobedient. The list of things he had been—and continued to be—was incredibly long.

And really, would it have been so difficult to do what He wanted? Would it have been such a hardship? Why did he have to be different and difficult? What was fundamentally wrong with him that he couldn't have been a better son? He could have learned to love the humans, couldn't he? They did make the most fabulous things to eat and were clever with gadgets—it wouldn't have been impossible, but he hadn't even tried.

Lucifer looked back down the crater, debating whether it would be better to go back down or stay where he was. Moving seemed like it would take more energy than he was capable of producing. Just the act of thinking about moving was more than he wanted to do.

Stop this right now, Michael's voice snapped at him.

"Oh, will you shut up?" Lucifer said aloud, noticing how flat and wilted his voice sounded. He dropped his head in his hands.

I will not. This is Hell. Do you not feel it? The very nature of this place wants you to give up. You will not give up. You will fight. Even when he was imaginary, Michael was a pain in the ass. *If, brother, I am to be a "pain in your ass" to remind you of your nature, then so be it. Now, get up.*

The thought of sitting there being berated by Michael's voice was worse than the thought of moving. Lucifer got to his feet once more. The pain was mostly gone from his body, replaced by a heavy fatigue. With effort, he focused and looked around once more.

As far as the eye could see in three directions, the landscape was a flat, bleak, brown nothingness. In the fourth direction, far off into the horizon, a mountain broke the landscape. He dreaded walking off into the desolate scene—at least fire, brimstone, and demons with pitchforks would have been interesting.

It's better to rule in Hell, my ass. Only a stupid human could come up with something so… stupid. His heart wasn't even in human bashing, something that always made him feel better. Maybe the atmosphere here did cause despair and depression.

To survive, you must guard your mood. Raphael's voice that time.

He pushed the fact that he was hearing voices aside—it wasn't as though he didn't have enough to deal with. But the voice was right again. Not only was he cut off from everything and everyone that could help him, he was losing his mind. *Perfect.*

Vigilance is required. Gabriel's voice. It was all he had. Shoring up against the despair that constantly threatened him, he turned in the direction of the mountain and began to walk.

Dear reader,

We hope you enjoyed reading *Coming Darkness*. Please take a moment to leave a review, even if it's a short one. Your opinion is important to us.

Discover more books by Susan-Alia Terry at https://www.nextchapter.pub/authors/susan-alia-terry-paranormal-fantasy-author

Want to know when one of our books is free or discounted? Join the newsletter at http://eepurl.com/bqqB3H

Best regards,
Susan-Alia Terry and the Next Chapter Team

Biography

As a child, Susan was a voracious reader of all things not sanctioned by the educational system. Comics, along with tales of ghosts, vampires, witches, and monsters, fascinated and delighted - even as they fueled her need to sleep with the light on.

As the years passed, while still content to read what was offered, she noticed a growing desire to read something a little...different. The desire continued to grow until it became apparent that the easiest way to read what she wanted was to write it first.

And so, Coming Darkness was born.

Blog: http://www.susanaliaterry.com/
Twitter: @susan_alia

Lightning Source UK Ltd.
Milton Keynes UK
UKHW041909090421
381754UK00001B/89